A Reconstructed Life

A.M. Overett

A Reconstructed Life

A Reconstructed Life

This book is a work of fiction. Named locations are used fictitiously, and characters and incidents are the product of the author's imagination. Any resemblance to actual events or places or persons, living or dead, is entirely coincidental.

Published by
Lighthouse Christian Publishing
SAN 257-4330
5531 Dufferin Drive
Savage, Minnesota, 55378
United States of America

www.lighthousechristianpublishing.com

Table of Contents

CHAPTER 1
An Old Conflict Ends and New Journey Begins.

April 9th, 1865

It was the final day of the conflict. A conflict that had torn a nation apart. A Confederate soldier who had been separated from his unit at the Battle of Cumberland Church was trying to find his men in a wood just outside of Cumberland. He was hungry and tired and was not aware his fellow rebels were soon to bow out of the war. Grant and his northern hoards were now in Appomattox and had defeated the last remnants of Lee's army. Lee and his generals had agreed to surrender the army and shortly the war would be over.

Lawrence Ambrose was desperate to fight on. For the past two days, he sat in an abandoned shack just north of the town of Cumberland. The battle of Cumberland Church, a decisive and brutal attack by one of the Union divisions, had sent Ambrose's regiment into confusion and retreat. The young, fanatical Confederate lost track of his brigade after a brief exchange of fire with northern troops, and headed north away from the action, assuming the rest of his comrades would rejoin him in Cumberland. He found shelter in an abandoned rickety old shed on the north side of town and kept a lookout for stray Confederates whom he could shelter. None seem to come. He waited hours and soon days. In the meantime, he met one of the few families who had not fled the town. The Wilson family were die-hard rebels such as himself. They provided him cold provisions, blankets, and a warm overcoat. He refused their offer to put him up in one of their rooms for fear that the Union might bring harm to the family.

Lawrence sympathized with the family. They were good, sons and daughters of Dixie. God-fearing and strong. He especially liked the look of their oldest daughter Amelia, but he had no time for romance. He would do everything he could to defeat the Yankees and prolong the war for as long as possible. While his family was not wealthy enough to own slaves, he understood what the significance was if the southern way of life was destroyed. The wealth and well-being of the South depended on slave labor and he was not going to let it go by the way-side. Besides, nowadays slaves were treated like family, or so he liked to believe. The bottom line was that no northerner was going to tell his people what they could and couldn't do. He would give his life for what he believed and many of his colleagues had done just that including his cousin Jesse. He would not let the death of his dear cousin be in vain.

After waiting for two days, Lawrence rose early on the 9th, grabbed his pack, and headed West where he knew the front was. As he began to walk he felt somewhat at peace. A peace he hadn't felt for years. Having gone through the battle of Atlanta and the siege of Savannah, he had seen a lot of pain, blood, and death. Now walking through the rolling hills just outside Cumberland, he felt a serenity. There were what looked like miles of dogwood trees. There was a grayish purple mist that seemed to sparkle at times as the rising sun's rays began to penetrate. He chewed on a piece of dried meat and took a long swig from his canteen. His rifle was strung across his shoulder and he began to feel its weight as he carried on further. He felt for the first time like a solitary figure, completely alone. He missed the comradery of the men from the 12th Battalion, Georgia Light Artillery.

After walking several miles he could see a clearing through the trees. He slowed down to make sure he wasn't walking into the enemy camp. He could make out a road and walked as fast as he could toward it. He walked through a steep gulley that was partially filled with water and quickly ran up the other side placing him right into the side of the road. It was the road to Lynchburg. He looked north and could not make out anything. Looking southward toward Appomattox, he could see activity and people. He cautiously walked south. As he neared Appomattox he could see what looked like several Union troops. He quickly darted into the woods and ran behind a large berm. His heart began to pound as he could hear the voices of Union soldiers calling out. He pulled himself up toward the top of the berm and peered over. Through the woods, he could see several rebels running as fast as they could. One with a pistol who turned and shot at the pursuing mob.

Lawrence slid back down the berm and began to prepare his rifle. He loaded shot and gun powder. Before he could raise his rife he turned to find the barrel of a Union soldier trained right on his face.

"Hold it right there my friend," came the raised voice of a negro soldier. "Put down your rifle and throw it over there," the negro soldier motioned his head toward Lawrence's left side. Lawrence slowly complied and threw his rifle to the ground.

"Get up and put your hands up." Lawrence again complied. As he stood up he could see what looked like the members of a negro unit walking through the forest scouring for Confederate soldiers. The soldier motioned for Lawrence to walk toward the road. Lawrence was marched about a quarter of a mile to what looked like a large mansion. As he entered through the gate of the property there was a large contingent of Union soldiers. In the back of the property was a make-shift prison for captured rebels. Emaciated and pathetic-looking men milled around like they were waiting for death. Once inside the backyard, the negro soldier pushed him inside through a makeshift gate. Lawrence stumbled and fell and the soldier began to holler with laughter as he shut the gate behind him. "Don't know how to walk reb?" the soldier continued to mock him. Lawrence looked up at the soldier and could see his taunting expression. It was a look he would not soon forget. It was the ultimate humiliation being ridiculed by a negro of all people.

The entire perimeter of the yard had been enclosed with a hastily constructed barb-wire fence. Although not tall, the twines were spaced close apart so that any attempt to escape would be very difficult without considerable injury.

"Hey Lawrence," a solitary figure yelled from the back of the yard. Lawrence walked closer and could see it was Billy "Sully" Sullivan. He nodded and began to walk toward him. Billy was one of Lawrence's original buddies from the 12th Battalion of the Georgia Light Infantry. They had fought together in the Battle of Atlanta and retreated together getting separated in the Siege of Savannah. Both were Atlanta natives, born and raised. They had grown up in the same neighborhood and had gone to school together. They both signed up for the army on the same day in hopes of protecting "the homeland."

"Hey Sully, you look like death warmed-over."

"You don't look so good yourself."

"I thought you got captured in Savannah?"

"No, I headed north like you. I was told by Duffy he had seen you a day earlier so you probably had a day's head start heading up to Virginia."

"Yeah, that was a hike. Didn't think I would make it."

"And now here we are," Sully's voice drifted off as he viewed his surroundings wondering how they would ever get out of their predicament.

"I'm guessing we only have a few more days to hold out?"

"No, it's done. Lee's signing the formal surrender as we speak. Down the road at the Appomattox Court House."

"Wow, so this is it?"

"'Fraid so."

"What do we do now?"

"Not sure. Rot in prison I guess. I hear things are bad in Andersonville and I'm guessing we'll get the same treatment."

"What happened at Andersonville?"

"Pretty bad from what I heard. Union soldiers were not fed, not treated for medical issues. Pretty much hell on earth from what I hear tell."

"I guess we'll get the same. Well, I don't mind. At least I know I gave everything for the South."

Sully smirked and shook his head thinking Lawrence's youthful exuberance for his beliefs would soon fade.

Later that day, news began to circulate through the prison that those incarcerated would be pardoned and set free once the signing of the surrender terms was completed. While the men pondered their fate they assembled at a table where a not very appetizing bowl of gruel was being served. For Lawrence, it meant something for his stomach and he was glad of it.

The following day it was announced that the Confederate prisoners would be set free. After a breakfast of semi-warm porridge, everyone was processed and then set free. They were given no provisions, no implements or weapons to help them hunt or forage for food.

After walking out of the prison camp, Sully and Lawrence began to walk toward the Appomattox Court House. There were civilians milling about, looking and snooping at things a little more intently now that the fighting had ended. There were Union troops stationed throughout the village and several horse-drawn cannon were now parked by the courthouse.

As for Lawrence and his ilk, they were like ghosts walking silently past the conquerors. The younger rebels were enthusiastic to get home, to see their loved ones, and have a home-cooked meal. The older Confederates were almost soulless as if they no longer had a homeland, no longer had anything to live for. Lawrence was somewhere in-between.

Sully and Lawrence continued to walk through town when they came by a nicer home near the courthouse. Outside, toward the back of the house, Lawrence could see a solitary figure smoking a cigar. Lawrence patted Sully on his shoulder to get his attention and pointed to the man. They couldn't believe who it was or that he was by himself. They quickly walked around the side of the house and stood in awe of the man; General Robert E. Lee.

"General, is the war really over?" Lawrence begged to know the answer. As they looked over the general they could see he had aged considerably since the beginning of the war. He was almost ghost-like in appearance.

"Gentlemen, I'm afraid so."

"What about the government, President Davis?"

"Oh, he's on the run now. He has some troops with him but we can no longer sustain a long fight. While we lose men every day for one reason or another, the North just grows stronger. I don't want to throw any more lives into a battle we cannot win."

And there it was, the straight factual answer they were dreading. They both saluted the general who returned a half-hearted reply. He turned and began to look out over the countryside puffing on his cigar. The boys, especially Lawrence were stung by the general's words. If it had been anyone else they would have had hope that the war could continue. But this was General Robert E. Lee, an engineer by trade, a top graduate of West Point, and brilliant tactician in the field. Even he, the greatest general of the South had given up hope. The boys turned and continued down the main road in much despair and uneasiness as to what they should do next.

As they neared the end of the town, Lawrence could hear a commotion coming from a house at the end of the street. It looked like a restaurant. The front door was open and he could see Union soldiers and officers relaxing around tables, playing cards, and smoking cigars. Women seemed to be running around frantically serving them hot food. The slaveholders had become slaves, or so thought Lawrence. His mind filled with rage. Would this be happening to his kin next?

Lawrence thought about going back to the Wilson home but didn't want to disturb them. Especially now when they themselves might be in need. Plus it was further north and he wanted to head south as soon as possible. There had been talk that the Union would provide rail transportation to the defeated southern troops, but the Union rampage down south had left much of the railway tracks destroyed or unusable. As far as he could tell, Lawrence would have to walk or hitch a ride all the way back to Atlanta.

CHAPTER 2
Ominous News from the Heart of Dixie.

April 11th, 1865

On their first night of freedom, Lawrence and Sully made it to the town of Concord. There was a group of former rebels gathered around a covered wagon. A family from the neighborhood had set up on the outskirts of town and were giving out soup to the defeated troops. Like the Wilson family before, Lawrence had lucked out. The South, for the most part, was in shambles. The lifeblood of the southern economy, which was cotton, had been made unsellable with the Union naval blockades of southern ports. Like many families, they were just trying to survive but still found the resources to help stranded soldiers.

The scene around the covered wagon was a welcome one. Many of the prisoners from Appomattox were there. Sully and Lawrence walked up to the wagon and were given a bowl of soup and a piece of bread. There were two young women who were ladling out the soup and an older woman who was carving up some bread. There appeared to be the older woman's husband running back and forth from a nearby house with supplies.

"This is mighty generous of you ma'am," said Sully.

"Yes, you're a godsend," Lawrence smiled as he took a large bowl of soup. Sully and Lawrence walked to a gully by the side of the road that was filled with hay. There were several other men there as well. They began to discuss where they would lay their heads for the night.

"There's a barn over there," the man from the wagon motioned. "It's part of our property but we don't use it anymore. Y'all welcome to it."

Sully and Lawrence thanked the man and along with the six other men nearby, grabbed their belongings and headed over to the barn. The barn was a bit ram shackled but it would keep the men warm for the night. The kindly host showed the men a pile of firewood and invited them to build a fire from which they did.

After their meal, the men sat around the fire. One man had a harmonica and began to play while another sang and hummed along. The rest of the men, including Sully and Lawrence, were in no mood for anything resembling entertainment. Their minds turned to the future. What future did they have now that the South had been defeated? What kind of work would they find? Lawrence was supposed to follow in the footsteps of his father who was a Baptist preacher. Lawrence was all for that plan had he been living in a victorious South. He would sing the Lord's praises but now he was questioning God. Questioning how He could have allowed such a catastrophe? How could He have allowed the destruction of the only way of life he had ever known? It wasn't about slavery directly as his family-owned no slaves, but now, those people who would fill the coffers of the church would be unable to.

He had been planning to go to college and then seminary after the war had finished, but now, how would he afford it? Lawrence's mind was on more urgent issues at the moment like how he was going to make it home alive. He had probably two to three weeks journey ahead of him.

As the men talked around the fire, they found that all of them had been flung far and wide because of the conflict. One man operated a general store near Meridian, Mississippi. Another man named "Dane" was a yeoman farmer from Charlotte, North Carolina. Two brothers were farmhands from just outside Galveston, Texas. There was an older bearded man who ran barges up the Mississippi near Memphis and a tall, scraggly looking character named "Clem" who hailed from Dothan, Alabama. Clem went on about how good he was on the banjo and wished he had it with him. "I'd blow the sails off this here place," he yelled.

Each man volunteered their thoughts on the future of the South. The common denominator was that their old way of life was over and they would need to live differently. Lawrence outwardly agreed but still was fuming over how the war had played out. He could never imagine aligning himself with the Yankees. At least the old tyrant Abe Lincoln was dead. Felled by a fellow son of the South. While each man commended the death of Lincoln, they had no illusions that things would be any different. The war was lost and the slaying of their adversary's leader mattered very little now. It was time to rebuild, and they would all be shocked at what lay ahead of them as they returned to their homes.

The conversation turned to an even darker subject; how many had each man killed during the war? For most of them, it had been multiple killings. Lawrence was aware of three men he had killed not knowing if some of his other fire had gone astray or hit its target.

"Any of yah killed a man face-to-face?" the banjo player from Alabama asked. As Lawrence looked at his face, it seemed to contort behind the flames of the fire. He looked sinister and seemed to ask the question with a perverse delight.

"Yeah, it was in self-defense so I don't have any qualms about it," said one of the brothers from Texas. "We were in hand-to-hand fighting at the Battle of Bull Run. I was behind a tree. I could hear the Union charging on our position. I took a shot and then had to load my gun again. I peered around the tree and as bright as day there was a Yank. He was too close to shoot so he tried to poke me with his bayonet. He missed and then I swung my rifle at him, nicking him on the forehead. Before I could swing again he had dropped his gun and lunged at me. We were rolling around in the mud when I finally freed my hand and punched him hard several times in the face. I was able to get up and pulled my knife out and then lunged at him. He rolled away just in time as I missed. He jumped on my back while I was on the ground and slugged me in the head a couple of times. He then grabbed my wrist. The one which held the knife and he tried to force it out of my hand. I was able to strike him in the face with my elbow, knocking him off of me. He was covered with blood as I dove again for him. We were soaking wet and he was able to grab my arm as I was forcing the knife down. I was able to put my full weight down on him and the knife slowly lowered to his chest. I looked him right in the eyes and he had a look of terror I had never seen before. We both knew however that one of us had to die or the other would get killed. I just kept applying my weight until the knife plunged deep into his chest. It was like his entire life-force, breath, spirit, whatever you want to call just blew out of him. He was then a cold corpse…lifeless. His eyes just stared up to heaven. There was chaos and shooting all around me but I didn't care at that point. I just rolled over and hid behind a fallen log. I think I was there an hour, just staring at him. He was like some kind of store mannequin. He didn't seem real. I couldn't imagine that he had ever been alive. Ever had a family. Ever had a girl. Ever had children. He was...just gone." The group sat quietly pondering the life and death situations that many men had faced during the war.

"Anyone else?" The banjo player asked. The other men were too sullen after that story. All of them had killed, but not in that way.

The next day, Sully and Lawrence grabbed their packs and headed out as early as they could. They were greeted by the Cummings family again with biscuits and coffee. The men were much obliged to the family's hospitality and pledged some sort of repayment, if not in this world then in the world to come.

After gulping down their food, Sully and Lawrence high-tailed it down the road. They wanted to see if they could find any trains in service. They were headed on the road to Charlotte where it was a major railway hub for the South. They assured themselves there would be some trains available eventually, or so they hoped.

The pair arrived in Lynchburg in the late afternoon and walked into the train station. It was deserted. A few years earlier it had been a bustling whistle-stop with people coming and going, but now it was dead. The tracks looked like they were fine but somewhere down the line they probably had been twisted and the piers destroyed by the Union Army. The town itself also looked dead and as they walked through the main road into town they would see only a few people here and there. As they were about to depart an elderly man came up to them on a horse-drawn cart.

"You fellas looking for the train?"

"Yes sir. Are they running any?"

"It won't be for a while. You can get as far as the Tennessee border but the rest of the tracks to Chattanooga and Atlanta have been destroyed."

"How 'bout the other direction? Are there any trains running to Richmond?"

"They say there will be in a couple of days but it won't get you any further south. I'm assumin' you gentlemen are headin' home down south somewhere?"

"Yessir, we're from Atlanta."

"Oh boy. That'll probably take you at least a couple of weeks if not more if you can't find a horse."

"Ain't got money for a horse."

"Yep, weez all broke now. Anyway, your best bet is to hike down to Danville, near the North Carolina border. The track there is supposed to be good."

"How far is Danville?"

"'bout seventy miles as the crow flies. There's not a whole lot between here n'there cept some farms and few small towns. You'll want to make sure you have plenty of provisions."

"Thank ya sir," Sully said, tipping his hat.

As the man slowly rode out of sight, the boys spotted an abandoned home and decided to make camp there for the night. They both consumed biscuits and honey that had been given to them by the Cummings.

The house was modest and it looked like whoever had lived there abandoned it in haste, most likely fleeing the Union Army. They made their way into the kitchen looking for any signs of food. In the pantry, there were boxes of flour, but there was nothing that had already been baked. There was an icebox but it was empty. They did find some dried meat in a shed in the backyard but it had a foul smell to it and they chose to avoid it. They did find some whiskey in a cupboard to which Sully gladly drank but Lawrence abstained. They then headed upstairs and each took a vacant room. All the windows had been closed and there was a musty odor with dust beginning to accumulate on various pieces of furniture. Lawrence, completely exhausted, didn't care and just lay down on the bed. He quickly fell asleep. He had not slept well in weeks and the soft bed was just what he needed.

Later that night, Lawrence had a feeling of extreme heat penetrating his face. He looked toward the window and it seemed as if a great fire had started outside. He opened the window and was immediately hit with a powerful hot wind on his face. He could feel soot in his mouth and sand blow on his face. He shook his head seeing a very blurred vision of some sort. He could see a vast desert with sand being blown everywhere. It was a bright orange and yellow scene. He could see waves in the sand that had been created by the intense wind. On a large sand dune, he could see many people walking in a straight line. They appeared to be negro slaves with metal collars on their necks. They were connected to each other with chains. A white man was pushing them across the dune, whipping them to move quicker. The men, women, and children were crying out in pain and they were suffering from the abuse and the harsh conditions. He then could see a little girl's face, cringing with agony. She could not have been much older than five years old and she was in extreme pain. She began to scream for help.

Lawrence woke up in a sweat, his heart pounding from the nightmare. He looked over at the window. It was dark and peaceful. Had Sully spiked his water with whiskey? He wasn't sure what could have caused such a realistic dream. Was it God? Was God speaking to him about slavery? It was something he was trying to reconcile now that it was clear slavery would be abolished. Or would it? Would southern men really allow a way of life that had been going on for hundreds of years just vanish?

The next morning Lawrence and Sully found a small roadside stand that was selling biscuits and gravy. They could see several women running frantically between a house and the stand. Several men were milling about. Some of them were broke and were asking for a hand-out. Lawrence was down to his last few confederate dollars which now had no value. He did have some pre-war coins that he hoped would cover it. Sully likewise had a similar sum and they were able to buy a couple of biscuits each with a few drops of precious gravy poured on top. From there to Danville they knew it would be mostly rural going and would have to live off the land. Both of them now only had a pack that had a canteen for water, a blanket, a pair of socks, and a hunting knife. Besides a couple of pouches of dried meat and two small bags filled with oats and nuts, they would be living off God's good graces for the trip home.

They decided to walk and eat at the same time, believing they needed to get as far as they could toward Danville. There was one good dirt road that was ferrying

Union troops and beleaguered Confederate refugees back and forth. On several occasions, they would pass a house that had elderly people sitting on the porch. They would wave with sad looks. Lawrence and Sully assumed younger occupants were working somewhere in the house or in the fields or had been lost to the war.

Lawrence began to study the men from the South who were also walking on the trail. Most men were walking southbound but there were also quite a few heading north. Many of those from the south had been cut-off in operations by the Union in the Carolinas and were now returning home. All of them seemed to have the same disheveled look. A look of weariness, a look of confusion, a look of defeat. Many had given their all. For some, who were still alive, they had given their minds and souls to the endeavor. They had a strong conviction that what they were fighting for was right. Lawrence was struggling with all of it. What was all the bloodshed for if it hadn't led to something good, something greater?

After walking all day and getting twenty miles nearer their destination, the two decided to leave the road and camp under a large oak tree in an open field. There was a farmhouse in the distance but it didn't look like they were disturbing anyone or anything. Lawrence threw his pack at the base of the tree and pulled out his blanket. He gathered a few twigs and branches, dug a pit, and threw them in. Sully gathered some tall grass and dried up weeds and threw it in for kindling. Lawrence searched around in his pack and found his flint. He took a sharp rock, stuck the flint once and a large spark immediately lit the dried twigs. Sully quickly blew a stream of air from his lungs into the makeshift fire pit and smoke was soon drifting up into the air. Within a minute or two a fire was in its infancy. The pair then walked around gathering rocks for the outside of the pit and bigger branches that they could throw on later.

As they gazed at the fire, they could feel their bellies growling. They felt too tired to hunt for any game at that point and just rested on the base of the old oak.

"I wonder how long this tree has been here?"

"A coupla hundred years, I reckin'." Lawrence peered up, looking through its great branches. Lawrence pulled a bandana from his pack and began to dab his forehead with it. He took some water from his canteen and poured some onto his bandana and then began to wipe his hair and forehead. It would be the closest thing to a bath he would have for the next couple of days.

As the sunset, an older man, probably in his late thirties walked over to the encampment.

"Mind if I join you, boys?"

Lawrence nodded his head in silence. His expression revealed a question in his mind which was why the man would want to join them? They had little food, but it was the neighborly thing to do he surmised. Sully also nodded his head.

"I gather you boys are not 'round from 'ere?"

"We're both from Atlanta," Lawrence offered.

"My my Atlanta. I hear good things about Atlanta. I had a friend from near there. Castleberry Hill, you familiar with it?"

The two men looked at each other with a knowing glance. Castleberry Hill had had a bad reputation prior to the war as a place for gambling, prostitution, and cock-fighting. It had improved prior to the war as many companies had built factories there but it was still not what one would call wholesome.

"We're from Five Points, where the original city began."

"Yeah, not much there now. Old Willy T Sherman did a number on that town."

"What do you mean?"

"Well, they pretty well burned down the place. They didn't want anything left for us Confederates to use so they burned all of it."

Lawrence and Sully sat there stunned. They had been a part of the initial battle but their unit had fled toward Savannah early on, hoping to regroup with another army that had been waging war in the North Georgia mountains.

"You boys look sick. You must'ave known?"

Lawrence slowly shook his head. "We heard some things but I didn't know the entire town was destroyed. What happened to the people?"

"Sherman ordered the city evacuated. I think a lot of them went north to Irbyville, that area."

Lawrence began to think about his family. His mother, father, and sister. Where would they live? For Sully, he feared for his mother. His father had died from a heart attack several years earlier and his mother was now all alone. She had relatives in Macon but had refused to move. What had happened to her? Terrible thoughts began to race through his mind.

"Where are you from?" Lawrence asked, trying to erase images from his mind.

"Richmond. The heart of Dixie…or what was the heart of Dixie."

"Are you infantry?"

"No, engineer. I actually went to West Point."

Both Lawrence and Sully were trying to drink it in. This even more disheveled personage compared to the average rebel was a graduate of West Point, where the beloved General Lee had studied? Both men nodded simultaneously in admiration.

"What brought you down here?"

"My corps was blowing up bridges just north of here. Trying to prevent the Yanks from getting to Appomattox."

"Wow, that must have been interesting work?" A rather sullen Lawrence asked.

"Yeah, I studied munitions at the Point."

"Were there many Confederates graduating from West Point?"

"Yeah, there were quite a few of us. I graduated back in 1855. Two of my buddies in the engineers graduated the same year. We were part of the Corp of Engineers based in Richmond. We built bridges, roads, wells, you name it we did it!" He said with great pride. "We had a great, great ole time! Until the war started. I lost my best friend right at the start of the war," the man began to look far away into the horizon and started shaking his head. His eyes seemed to glow. A glow of horror at watching a world burn.

"Toward the end, we saw all our hard work be destroyed. We were down in Tennessee and Georgia when the Union came. They had stores of munitions the world has never seen. Blowing up or burning everything in sight. We tried to keep the rail lines together but when they came into Georgia…it was like trying to stop a tidal wave. Anyway, I've got some bread 'ere if you want."

The man opened a satchel and produced a large loaf of bread that had been wrapped tight in some paper.

He ripped off two large chunks for each man and they began to devour them like they were wolves set on a deer.

"What'll you do now?" asked Sully.

"No idea. I was dreaming about one day running a mill or factory for someone, but it will probably be ten years before the economy recovers."

"Won't the Yanks help us out?"

"That's what they're sayin' but who knows."

The rest of the night the three men sat in silence, staring at the fire and contemplating their futures. They eventually passed out with fatigue and slept peacefully that evening.

CHAPTER 3
Journey to find "Home."

April 13th, 1865

The next morning, the boys awoke to a bright fresh day. It was clear with some light dew on the ground. Birds were chirping and the cool moist air was pleasant to smell. In a field off in the distance, a farmer was burning some leaves which added to the aroma. Sully and Lawrence were anxious to get moving, knowing they still had far to go. The boys said goodbye to their temporary companion and wished him well on his journeys. He had filled their minds with much to think about the previous night. The destruction of the South was complete and the boys were worried as to what they would find when they arrived home. Right now their thoughts were on getting to Danville and hopefully getting onto a train, assuming the tracks hadn't been destroyed.

When they arrived in Brookneal they were able to hitch a ride on a man's hay wagon. He was heading to his farm near Halifax and they would be there by late afternoon. The ride along the bumpy dirt road was a good respite for Lawrence and he began to ponder his future and occupation. Assuming his father was still alive, he would be pushing Lawrence to become a preacher and eventually take over their church, assuming the church was still standing. His faith over the past several weeks had been severely tested and he wondered if God was really on his side. Did God hear his prayers? Did God believe Lawrence had been on the right side of the conflict?

For the past several months, Lawrence had been living a life of survival, now that the world had stilled, he could again contemplate things much bigger than this earthly realm. Was there in fact another world, a spiritual one? As a child and a young man he had never doubted God's existence, but after so much bloodshed and death, he began to wonder. There were those moments when he spotted a group of deer near the forest, or a flock of yellow-billed cuckoos and would smile at God's presence. The clear gentle stream of a nearby brook would also call to mind something more ethereal. While it might take ten years to rebuild the South, would it take ten years to rebuild his faith? He would do everything possible to try and grasp the faith he once had, but he knew now it would be difficult.

Part of Lawrence's difficulties were not only spiritual but moral. He had been raised to believe that the negro was less than a white man. He has been created to help the white man with labor. After all, didn't the Bible in a way support slavery? Didn't Jesus himself say that servants should obey their masters? Wasn't it the true order of things? How would the South rebuild without negro labor? How would things get back to normal if slavery was not a part of the plan? At that point, Lawrence began to think of the slaves in his life. Was "slave" an appropriate term for those that took care of his family?

There was Mami Bledsoe that had taken care of him since he was a child. She was a wonderful and caring person. Was it wrong that she should want to be free? And her son Isaac. He was the same age as Lawrence and they had played together like brothers. Was there any reason why that relationship couldn't continue but in a different environment? Lawrence began to dread his arrival in Atlanta, not only for the physical destruction that would be present but all the other changes as well. Would the Bledsoe's and other ex-slaves seek some sort of retribution; physical or monetary?

Whatever changes awaited him, he knew it would be a long time before he changed his beliefs on the subject. There had been an order to the southern way of life and no Yankee was going to change that. But now he and his family might be reliant on the North. It would have to be the North and the Union Army that would rebuild the South. There was no other way around it. They would be dependent upon the very people they had hated, they had despised for years. His heart began to pound with rage. How could God have allowed this catastrophe?!!!

As they continued toward Halifax, they began to notice more and more negro families walking in the other direction – heading north. Some were in makeshift wagons, a few were on horse or mule back, while a few were on foot. The assumption was that these were freed slaves who were heading toward the promised land. "Thirty acres and a mule" was the promise. Many of these poor souls had been following the Union Army as it made its way up from Savannah and the Carolinas. Many of them could not keep up and were now separated, hopeful they would find a relative or a helpful hand as they made their way toward the Mason-Dixon line. Many were headed toward Baltimore where there was a large black population. It was also the home of Frederick Douglass.

Lawrence shook his head feeling they were all fools for leaving their homes in the South. They were well-fed, given rooms, and most anything a slave could ever dream of. For Sully, he was not such a die-hard rebel. His family did not own any slaves and he had spent a good deal of the war wondering why he had fought on the side of the Confederates. It was something to do he guessed. An adventure, a journey of some kind. But after what he had seen he could not classify it as an adventure. It was more of a nightmare. And luckily the nightmare was over. He just wanted to get home to his mother and try and find a way to support both of them.

As they pulled up to the farm, Lawrence and Sully jumped off and waved their hats to the man. He waved back and then headed up the road toward the farm. As they began to walk down the road toward Halifax they could feel a slight chill in the air. It was mid-April and the temperatures would drop from time to time. The sun was slowly setting and the scene was picturesque. Brilliant green pine trees on rolling farm hills. The outskirts of the town could be seen in the distance. There was a misty haze that sparkled bluish-purple. The thing they enjoyed most was the silence. They could hear their boots on the road, scuffling along. They could hear the distant chirping of birds. It was a nice change from the cacophony of sounds they were hearing only a week earlier. The sound of cannons would ring in their ears for the rest of their lives. It was a sound that they could never get used to.

As they walked into town they were happy to see some semblance of normal life. People were walking down the streets, engaged with each other in conversation. Children were playing in a nearby park, chasing each other like they hadn't a care in the world. For the first time in a long, long time, the two men felt as if the world was back to normal. But was it? Lawrence continued to wrestle with the idea that the South and everything he had believed in, all of his ideals had been defeated at Appomattox. When he spotted a negro he looked at them with contempt. What he wrestled with the most was his faith. How could God have cursed the South's holy crusade against tyranny? It just didn't make sense. The South was the agricultural backbone of America. How could it continue without the labor of slaves?

They walked toward a home that had been advertised as a boarding house and was welcomed by a lady who appeared to be in her mid-forties. She explained to the men that her husband had been killed in one of the last battles of the war and it was clear by the look on her face the war had worn on her. The men paid her a nickel and she showed them to their rooms. She invited them to join the rest of the tenants for dinner in thirty minutes. The men threw their packs onto nearby beds and peered out of the bedroom window to get the lay of the land.

Bannister Town, in Halifax, was a small village, maybe housing a hundred souls. All of them seemed to be either oblivious to the war or doing a good job of hiding their emotions. Lawrence began to realize that people were accepting the outcome of the war and were resigned to their fate. But was he?

Sully and Lawrence joined "Miss Amanda," for dinner along with two other gentlemen. Franklin Stearns, a Confederate soldier on his way back home to South Carolina, and James Hollis, a lawyer from Richmond.

"What brings you to Bannister Town, Mr. Hollis?" an inquisitive Sully asked him.

"I needed to check on some investments."

"What type of investments, may I ask?"

"I work with a family…just trying to make sure they are well-supported."

"That's mighty nice of you," Amanda smiled as she started to pass a plate of yams and potatoes. The lawyer smiled quietly and kept to himself for the rest of the evening.

"Where do you gentlemen hail?" asked the fellow Confederate from the Palmetto State.

"We're both from Atlanta. We're both returning from the front…heading back home."

"I hear it's a mess down south. The Richmond-Danville Railroad is pretty much torn up."

"Yeah, that's what we hear. May have to hoof it all the way home."

The men were then regaled by Nathan "Nate" Gale about his exploits in the Carolinas. He was attached to a regiment that had spent their entire stint in and around the border between North and South Carolina, fighting various battles. By the end of the war, he and only five others remained in his unit. He explained that there had been a lot of fighting between Charlotte and the coast as they tried to protect Confederate naval tools and parts that were produced in Charlotte and then shipped to the ports. The Union blockade eventually caused a reduction in value for these parts as it prevented the South from exporting their cotton and tobacco to Europe.

After a healthy meal of fried chicken, fried potatoes and yams, collard greens, and biscuits, the group, save Mr. Hollis, assembled on the porch. Miss Amanda handed the men drinking glasses. She returned with a picture of lemonade.

"Do ya happen to have anything a little stronger ma'am?" inquired Nate. Amanda smiled and nodded and headed back into the house. She returned with a bottle of whiskey.

"Made from a friend's still down the street. It ain't bad." Both Sully and Nate raised their glass to receive the golden nectar.

"How'bout you Mr. Ambrose?"

"No, none for me ma'am. I'll just have the lemonade."

"I apologize for Lawrence here, he's a bit of a teetotaler."

"Not a drinker then Mr. Ambrose?"

"No ma'am."

"Don't you need to unwind a bit?" an incredulous Nate asked.

"Not really. I rely on the Lord to unwind. I don't think alcohol's necessary. It's important to keep the mind and the body in shape. After all, it houses the soul."

"Hmmm…are you a Christian?"

"Yes, aren't you Mr. Gale?"

"I was before the war, but now…now I don't know."

"I understand what you mean. Every day I wake up though and stare at this incredible world and realize…we didn't get here by accident. There is someone behind it all and that someone is God."

"But after seeing all the death and evil around…doesn't it make you wonder?"

"Sometimes it does, but it more confirms that mankind is a sinner. We have fallen short of the grace of God and we have given ourselves over to the devil. We have to resist Satan and temptation."

"Boy, I wish life was as black and white for me," Amanda said, astonished at the young man's faith.

"How 'bout your companion here, are you Christian?"

"Irish Catholic and I never pass up a chance at some good Irish whiskey."

"Well, this is not from Ireland but it is from Mr. O'Boyle so it's kind of from Ireland." The group broke out into laughter, only stopping as Mr. Hollis walked through the front door and bounded down the stairs leading from the porch to the street."

"Will you be joining us for breakfast, Mr. Hollis?"

"Ah, sure. I'll be down at six a.m.," he said cricking his neck to look back toward Amanda. He then immediately returned to his quick step down the street.

"Where's he going in such a hurry?"

"Checking on his 'investments' I suppose?"

"Yeah, rumor is he's invested in the tobacco plantation owned by the Lawton family. They're all in a tizzy now that the negroes are free. They won't have any free labor anymore to help with the crops."

Lawrence shook his head. He didn't know what he was more angry at; the loss of slaves or knowing how people like Mr. Hollis profited from others' misfortunes. But he knew everyone was going to be hard up for money over the coming years. Hollis probably had a family and had to figure out a way to feed them like everyone else. The rumors continued that it would probably be ten years before the southern economy would fully recover from the war, and who knew if maybe longer now there was no free source of labor to help with the crops. It was clear that as Europe found new sources of cotton and tobacco, the South would have to figure out alternatives like industrialization. But it would be a hard row to hoe.

The next morning, after breakfast, Lawrence and Sully bid Miss Amanda goodbye. Lawrence looked at his backpack and frowned as he played with a bundle of worthless Confederate bills. What was the point of holding on to it? Lawrence pulled the wad of money out and handed it to Miss Amanda.

"I know this probably has no value, but I wanted you to have it for your hospitality toward us. From what we hear the coins still hold their value as silver pieces, but I'm guessing all this paper doesn't. Anyway, at least you can use it for kindling if you need it."

Miss Amanda smiled and gave Lawrence a peck on the cheek.

"You keep it. You boys might find need of it on some deserted field and you need to start a fire."

Lawrence smiled and tipped his hat. He then patted Sully on the back and the two were out the door and walking down the street.

When the boys came to the edge of town they spotted a large plantation. As they walked down the road they came to an iron gate that was the entrance to the large estate. LAWTON FARMS, the rod iron metalwork screamed out from its arched frame. Beyond the gate were massive fields of cotton and tobacco. From a distance, Lawrence and Sully could see negroes working in the fields. They could also see a negro family loading up a cart with their belongings from a nearby cabin which was the servant quarters. Clearly, they intended to leave shortly. They also noticed Mr. Hollis on the porch of the main house talking with what appeared to be one of the

Lawton's. The boys shook their heads and just continued to walk down the dusty road.

As the long winter shadows gave way to the mid-April warmth, the boys could feel the wind blow up the dust from the road. They began to encounter more and more people on the main road. Confederate soldiers on carts heading south, an occasional Union Calvary detachment heading north, sometimes south, and more and more negro families heading north. The one thing that Lawrence noticed was that while there were many happy negroes, there were many who had a look of trepidation. These appeared to be older negroes, probably those who had worked all their lives on southern plantations and farms and had no idea what they were headed to. While in utter servitude, they still had shelter and food. Would the promises of the North bring them the same? Would the great North bring them employment? Would the northern states really provide them a new way of life where they could be completely independent and self-sufficient? Lawrence typically shook his head in disgust every time he saw a family or individual negro pass by. He believed the promises of the North were worthless and that the average negro would not prosper there. They had a purpose and it was to serve the economy of the South.

The boys pushed themselves that day and they arrived in Danville late in the evening. They decided to sleep under the frame of a barn that looked like it had been set aflame, by the Yankees no doubt. The night air was cool but not oppressive as they set their blankets out. They found some kindling and Lawrence used the last of his Confederate script to start the fire. They could see the skyline of the town set against a bluish-purple sky. They tried their best to pick out various constellations. As they began to fall asleep, they were awoken by the sound of horse hooves clicking on the road nearby. They looked up and could see a large contingent of Union troops. They were close enough that they could see the faces of the young men. An officer on horseback left the road and headed toward the men. The boys thought for a moment to extinguish their fire but it was useless now.

"Where you boys headed?" the bearded officer asked.

"Atlanta."

The officer stared down at them, occasionally looking back at the columns of men that were heading north.

"Nice town," he said, seeming to be searching for something to say. The boys studied his face intently. They had never spoken to a Union officer before. They had fought with regular soldiers and on a rare occasion, each had engaged in hand-to-hand combat but had never really known or cared to know their enemy. The officer sat there like some inanimate statue. The boys wondered what his intention was. He would occasionally turn and look at them and then back at the column, this was interspersed with his spitting chewing tobacco onto the road.

"Well you boys stay safe," the officer said, nodded his head, and was soon back in formation with the long column of troops.

"What was that all about?" Lawrence asked as the officer rode out of sight.

"Hell if I know."

The boys quickly fell asleep and were awakened the next morning to raindrops splashing them on their faces. They moved to a part of the barn that still had some of the roof intact. They sat covered in their blankets watching as the storm slowly passed. The road was now muddy but the commerce had returned and the highway was busy again. As they got on the road they were greeted with another column of Union troops heading in the opposite direction. The reason for such a great presence of northern troops was soon apparent. Being a large railroad hub for the South, Danville had been a strategic target for the Union. As they walked through the now muddy town, they quickly saw the desolation that had been wrought by the Union. Railroad tracks had been destroyed. The remains of a large engine room and round table were still smoldering. Nearby buildings had also borne the brunt of the Union's fury. The scene made Lawrence physically ill. It was like a nightmare with twisted metal and piles of splintered wood lying everywhere. The war had been over for almost two weeks but it seemed like Danville had just been struck.

There was a flurry of activity as Union troops had cartloads of ammunition and machinery they were pulling out of the remaining buildings. Clearly, these were the spoils of war and Lawrence was seething. Sully just looked on with a look of weariness.

"You men, get out of here!" yelled one of the Union officers as the boys apparently got too close to the scene. They probably thought they were confused Confederates who didn't know that the war had ended.

For many in the South, the war was not over. As the boys walked through town they could still see Confederate flags hanging out of windows or stuck into some crevasse as a sign of defiance. Many of the banners had been ripped to shreds by bullets or cannon fire, or by a passing Yank. It was clear though that not only the physical land needed rehabilitating but the people as well.

The boys walked through town in a haze, somewhat sick from the noxious smell of burning fuel and metal. There were long horse-drawn carts that were pulling large parcels of the twisted rail lines to salvage yards. The metal would be melted down and then remolded back to the shape it had been previously. Toward the horizon, they could see large piles of wood being stacked and then burned. Most of it looked like the old rail pylons and ties that had been torn apart. It looked like a scene from hell and the boys could feel the heat from yards away. And the noise was horrendous. They had known peace for the past two weeks but now they were wide awake from the constant pounding of metal and hammering of machinery. They began to think that Danville had been damned and that they would need to get out of town as soon as possible. It was clear there were no trains going anywhere any time soon.

As they got through the center of town they began to walk down a narrow street where it looked like the dregs of society had congregated. Brothels and saloons were busy with activity and many a Union soldier was trying to relieve themselves of the past years of misery. A few grubby women with dirt on their faces beckoned to the boys but neither was interested in these ladies of the evening. For Lawrence, this was a sign of what was soon going to be pervasive in the South. Not only the physical but now the moral decay would set in. As they passed by another brothel, several Union soldiers began to heckle them. It was the ultimate humiliation. The conquerors had their women and now their manhood. For the first time in two weeks, Lawrence wished he had his rifle back. Not a violent man, but the scene of debauchery was all too much for him to take at that moment.

Even if the railroad had been operable in Danville, the main lines went to the coastline anyway and the trip might take just as long. Given the various parts of the rail system were torn apart, they probably would have made it to the East Coast and then could go no farther, taking them even farther away from the direction they needed to go.

The men decided that they would just keep heading south, hoping that somewhere along the way they might find parts of the rail system intact and still operable. They had been through so much with the war, that the lack of transportation did not faze them at that point. It was just another obstacle in the hundreds more they expected to encounter.

As they made their way out of town they bartered with a traveling salesman, trading a small buck knife for a compass. While unsure of their orienteering skills, they thought it a good trade. By nightfall, they made it to Pelham, North Carolina, and stayed at a small inn on the outskirts of town. They both felt a sigh of relief knowing that they were back in rebel territory. Virginia had been swarmed over by Union troops and now in Pelham, they felt somewhat out of eyeshot of the victors. Pelham was named for artillery officer John Pelham who had fallen at the Battle of Kelly's Ford two years earlier. His innovative use of cavalry and artillery had caused the Union much aggravation in the early part of the war. Now, although a hero, there was little to celebrate, and like other towns they had walked through, this one was also an abhorrent image of a ghost town. Occasionally townsfolk would shuffle here and there, but there was little enterprise being put forth.

The boys settled into their rooms and then headed downstairs for dinner. Kindly old Mama Bell was the innkeeper. Her son had fought for the Confederates in the Battle of Bull Run and had had his head torn off by shrapnel. Another southern woman who had lost her son to the carnage of the previous four years. Mama Bell quietly dished out some ham roast, collard greens, and mashed potatoes. It was another feast, and although thankful, they were not quite sure they deserved it. There were no others boarding in the house that night and Mama Bell was grateful the men were there. She asked them if they could fix a fence that had broken down in several places and the men were only too happy to oblige her. They were able to rustle up a couple of hammers, nails and a saw from a neighbor just down the road. They worked by lamplight but were able to quickly fix the missing and broken boards. Mama Bell had chickens and a couple of goats in the back yard and the carpets she had thrown over the broken boards were not going to prevent their departure too much longer.

Once the boys finished they were offered some dessert of apple pie with two large glasses of buttermilk. They had not tasted milk in a long time and it was a welcome sight. As they ate their dessert they began to wonder how long Mama Bell's supplies of food would last. Would she be able to make enough money to keep the inn going? Would she be able to provide such sumptuous meals? The rumors were flying that food supplies were low and inflation was going to make most essentials difficult to obtain. Yet, it was clear she had a quiet strength. She was a religious woman and had many pictures and images of Christ throughout the house. Lawrence smiled when he saw that. If soon lacking in material wealth at least she would have spiritual wealth. But would that be enough? Could the spiritual feed the physical? Lawrence began to wonder. It seemed yet again another example of the Lord abandoning the South. But maybe they deserved it. He would go to bed that night pondering the Bible. Your ways are not my ways, saith the Lord.

Down the street, in a building that had been a warehouse for grain, twenty-seven of the men of the town were meeting. They were scheming, plotting, and venting their frustrations from the results of the war. A man named Phillip B. Barnaby was the apparent leader of this rag-tag group. He had been a Confederate soldier during the war. Many of the men assembled had also been soldiers. What started as a quiet assembly, soon ignited into something more.

"Gentlemen, we are meeting to discuss where we go from here. Our leaders have abandoned us to the immoral North. Even with Lincoln dead, we are subject to those bastards. It is here tonight that we sow the seeds to get our revenge on the North. We are planting now what we shall reap for our race in the future. It may take many, many years, but we will overcome. We will throw off this oppression and see the South rise again. The southern people are a strong people..." men began to shout in agreement. "...southern people are resourceful people..." again shouts came from the crowd. "...southern people are proud, we are good and we are god-fearing!!! God will see us regain what is rightfully ours...that is, our way of life."

Barnaby began to pace back and forth. He walked on a makeshift platform of palettes that creaked as he continued to walk.

"Make it known that we as southern men will not stand for this injustice! We will take back what is ours and make us a new country. We will not let our proud southern women bow to the yoke of the Union. We will not endure this humiliation. We will begin anew and we will fight!!!"

Many men stood and cheered for Barnaby and applauded for several minutes. One of the older men in the crowd got up from his seat and walked toward the front where Barnaby was.

"Phillip, what are you proposing?"

"Jed, I am proposing we rise up against the North."

"Rise up?" the man said incredulously.

"Yes, Jed. Rise up and take back our freedom."

"Are you talking about organizing an army?"

"Maybe. It may take a while but why not?"

"I lost my son in this war. Are we all really ready to take on a new fight?"

Barnaby walked over to Jed Bishop and put his arm around his shoulder. Jed was the local barber and was known for dispensing his brand of southern wisdom to anyone who would listen.

"Right now we are just meeting like old friends Jed, nothing more. We're just shooting the breeze. Nothing more than a social club. But, if we should talk about other things well, who can stop us? If we develop plans…ideas…well, it's just between us right?"

Jed nodded his head but his expression betrayed his confidence that the meeting was the beginnings of terrorist intentions.

"Anyway, Mary brought us some food and drink. Gentlemen, enjoy!"

After breakfast early the next morning, Lawrence and Sully grabbed their packs, gave Mama Bell a hug, and headed down the road. They were greeted by Phillip B. Barnaby who was walking in the opposite direction toward the main part of town.

"Don't worry boys, we'll get our revenge. Just be patient!" Barnaby said as he passed, raising his hat as a salute. Both Sully and Lawrence stopped, turned back, and looked at Barnaby continue on, practically skipping with joy. They wondered how anyone could be happy at that point.

Having obtained a map from Mama Bell that covered North Carolina, they decided to avoid the roads and get a better view of the countryside and so headed into the fields and orchards of the Piedmont state. They thought that they might be able to head in a more southwesterly direction as opposed to keeping to the main roads. They hoped their compass worked.

North Carolina, and especially the northern parts of the state, were the home to many tobacco farmers. Trying to protect their trade, they often went to war. Everywhere they went, they seemed to see men lighting up cigars, as they baled and packed the local produce, getting it ready for sale. After speaking with one farmer, Sully and Lawrence were told that they were barely making enough money to make ends meet. With the blockades of the ports toward the end of the war, North

Carolinian farmers were unable to sell their product overseas. European traders found other places to get their tobacco and cotton. It would be a dire time for southern agriculture.

As the boys made their way through the fields, they heard a shot ring out from behind a group of trees on the horizon. The bullet barely missed Lawrence's head as it splintered a nearby branch dangling from an old oak tree. The boys immediately jumped into a small gulley and rolled over to one side. As they peered over the top of the berm another shot rang out.

"Get the hell off my property!!!" yelled a man who stepped from behind a tree. He began to walk toward the boys. They quickly grabbed their packs and began to run as fast as they could through a nearby forest. They ran and ran for five minutes, continually looking behind them to make sure the man wasn't still in pursuit. While not paying particular attention they stumbled down a hill hitting brush and thickets as they rolled down. They soon rolled onto the top of the banks of a river and plunged twenty feet into the icy water below. They luckily hit a deeper part of the river and were soon surfacing and bobbing along on the current downstream. Several minutes later they landed on a sandbank and were able to pull themselves to safety. In the torrents of the river, Lawrence lost his pack along with his blankets and food rations.

After resting from their encounter with the river, Lawrence and Sully decided to take their clothes off save their skivvies and hang them from nearby branches to help them dry. They gathered some kindling and Sully grabbed a rock and used it with his flint to start a small fire. They were hoping they were now far enough away from the shooter and would not draw his attention. Lawrence played with his compass and determined that they were still heading southwest. Once the fire was in full flame, they rigged several large sticks in such a way as to hang their clothes over the fire. It was starting to get into the late afternoon and the air was cooling. They hoped their clothes would dry soon. Once their pants dried they switch to putting their skivvies over the fire and wearing their pants only. Their boots were taking a while to dry and while they waited they tucked into Sully's food rations which by now were starting to get low. They would be gone soon now that Lawrence was relying on them too.

As Sully handed Lawrence a stick of dried beef, they both noticed something move on the sandbar about 50 yards away. Emerging from a group of bushes were several gray wolves. The wolves stopped once they spotted Sully and Lawrence and lifted their heads in keen observation. Sully and Lawrence slowly looked around for weapons. Sully grabbed his pack and took out his buck knife. The three wolves began to walk toward the men and as they neared began to growl. Lawrence reached over and grabbed one of the large sticks they had used to dry the clothes and got ready to retaliate. The wolves were hungry and sensed that the men had food or potentially were food. The men stood erect and still and hoped that by some miracle the wolves would go away. Lawrence began to pray. Finally, the wolves struck and one jumped at Lawrence. Before he could land, Lawrence struck the wolf as hard as he could hitting him on the snout. The wolf whimpered but returned to the attack grabbing the stick in his jaws. While Lawrence was defending himself, another of the wolves began to attack

Sully. Sully's arm was caught in the wolf's jaws but Sully was able to stab the wolf in the chest with his free hand, causing instant death. The weight of the dead wolf fell onto Sully causing him to lose his buck knife. The last wolf then attacked Sully. Sully managed to push the dead wolf off him and then grabbed a nearby rock and smashed it on top of the head of the attacking wolf. Lawrence struck his assailant again and it was enough to send the wolf in retreat. He then ran over to Sully and clubbed the wolf that was again regaining the advantage. With a mighty wallop, the wolf was sent on his way.

The men sat on the ground, panting and trying to regain their breath.

"Do wolves normally attack humans?" Sully questioned. Lawrence was too exhausted to form a response.

"With all the destruction 'round here maybe they're lacking food," Lawrence eventually replied.

"They looked demonic," Sully said. "It was like they had fire in their eyes."

It was now night and the two settled on the sandbank, gathering branches and sticks to create a makeshift shelter. Not knowing where their next meal would come from they decided to use the wolf carcass for food and the pelt as a covering.

The two men slept little that evening. The rushing sound of the river and the howling of nearby wolves meant they could not easily rest. When Lawrence did finally manage to fall asleep his mind became filled with alarming images. He sat up from his makeshift bed and could see a large hut in front of him. Rushing from both sides of the river were white men. He deduced they were slavers as they began to round up negro men, women, and children from the hut. A large negro man was talking with another white man who appeared to be the slaver's leader. Many of the negro men had been sleeping by a fire in front of the large hut. There were bottles lying everywhere and they apparently had been made intoxicated by alcohol. This made them unable to resist and they were soon slapped in chains. Lawrence began to tremble, especially when he saw how terribly the women and children were being treated. Like the dream he had a week earlier, a little negro girl began wailing as chains were being placed on her wrists. How could people treat other people like this? Lawrence began to ask himself.

"Hey wake up Lawrence! It's time to get going!" Sully yelled as he pushed Lawrence. Lawrence sat up like he had seen a ghost and began to struggle for breath.

"My God, what's wrong with you?!!!" Lawrence slowly regained his breath and the look of terror faded from his face as he realized where he was.

"Let's get some rations and head out." Lawrence nodded and they began to finish the last of the dried beef. Lawrence grabbed his shirt that had been drying overnight and put it on. It was still a little damp but would dry in the sun as they moved along.

The boys began to pick up their pace as they walked through the various fields on their new path. The going became slow as they trekked through valleys and ravines and occasionally through creeks. They wondered if it had been a good idea to go off the beaten path.

The boys spent the entire day not having seen a soul and decided to take refuge in a cave at the base of a mountain. They would have to scale the mountain the next day. It would take several hours to do so and so they decided to camp out at its base that evening. They began to curse the Yankees for having taken their rifles. Guns would be handy at that point to shoot a rabbit or other game. There were a few pieces of dried beef but that would not satisfy them for very long. It was clear that Sully was beginning to resent Lawrence for having lost his knapsack and having to use up his rations. His demeanor had significantly changed as the supplies began to dwindle.

"Look, I'm sorry I lost my pack."

"Well, sorry's not gonna feed us. We need to figure out where we're gonna get some food."

"On the other side of this mountain is a river. We'll see if we can get some catfish or trout tomorrow." Sully sighed and nodded.

"You know that the devil is tempting us right now and it is important that we stay strong."

"Whatever you say, preacher man. I suppose we have to get used to it anyway. Sounds like supplies are running low throughout the South, especially near Atlanta where those bastards destroyed everything. Not only the city but the crops!"

"God will take care of us!"

"Do you really believe in God? I'm beginning to think you're stupid if you think there's some sort of higher power. Why does God allow all of this death? What was the point of the last four years?" Lawrence could tell Sully was getting agitated as he began hitting his flint against a stone to get a fire going.

"God didn't cause this war. God doesn't cause death. Man created this mess. Man created death by his own pride and sin." Sully shook his head and continued to hit the rock with the flint until the kindling began to smolder and then ignited. He breathed into the small embers and soon it was in full flame.

"I guess I understand the theory but why does he wait so long to come back. I mean it's been almost two thousand years now…hasn't He learned by now that man cannot govern himself? Why doesn't He just end all the pain and suffering?"

Lawrence studied Sully's face and could tell he was sincere. He could see that he was being pushed to his limit and it was important that Lawrence give him good answers. Lawrence had tried proselytizing southern troops in the past and had had some success. Many, like him, had believed that the war had been a holy one, a crusade to kick out a wicked invader. But there had been others who didn't believe. Others who did not share his vision. Some were criminals and some were evil, just looking for an excuse to kill. The war had opened Lawrence's eyes in many ways. He had seen suffering but he had also witnessed man's capacity to do evil. For some, killing was not in their soul and had only done so as a last resort, out of necessity to protect their homeland. For others…they had seemed to take real delight in the death of others. For Lawrence, whenever he had killed anyone, he immediately had sent up a prayer asking that God would forgive him and that He would forgive the soul of the man he had just killed. He began to think about the first man he had killed. It had been at the Battle of Chickamauga. His commander had led a charge up a hill to capture an artillery position. On the way up the hill, he had tripped and landed in a gulley. The Union troops, still a mystery to him to this day, led a counterattack. They had every advantage where they were as they had the high ground, but for whatever reason, there had been a charge led by the Union commander. As the Union troops headed down the hill they were picked off one by one. One man, running from the chaos tripped and fell into the same gulley Lawrence was in. Only thirty feet apart, both men looked at each other in the eye, drew their rifles, and fired. Lawrence's shot was fatal, having hit the soldier in the chest. Luckily for Lawrence, the shot from the now-dead Union soldier only grazed his ear. From that day forward, Lawrence had seen that encounter as God's providence. God had spared the devout Christian over the godless enemy. Or so he hoped was the case. It had seemed to be an especially righteous act as the invader was attacking his home state of Georgia. He began to think of all the other men he had killed since. Were these killings all really acts of God smiting evil men? Was Lawrence really on the side of good and what was right?

"You and I have been through a lot over the past few years Sully. I don't think it was in vain. God has a purpose in everything. I think He wants every man to repent and change their ways and He is willing to give us as much time as He thinks necessary to make it happen. You've learned, especially because of this war how evil man is…"

"Then why does He put up with it? Why doesn't he just wipe us all out and get it over with?!!! It just doesn't make any sense!"

"Because there is also good in man. There is love and kindness and God wants every man to come to that realization and to love God. If we all truly followed God and loved God then there wouldn't be all this fighting and bloodshed. We would be able to reason with each other. That is our goal, to follow God."

"You make it sound simple."

"I think it can be if we really want it to be. If we seek God, seek to do good. Obey his commandments and love each other, then the world wouldn't be the way it is."

Sully shook his head and began to look up at the stars that were now visible in the blackish purple sky. The night air was fresh and warm. Both men studied the stars.

"You know that one star there. It's called Sirius. It is so far away that the light traveling from it takes over nine years to reach us. Just think, we were thirteen years old when the light we're looking at left that star." Both men marveled at the thought of how large the galaxy was.

"Doesn't the vastness of space make you believe in God?" Lawrence asked.

"Makes me think we are all insignificant. Why would God care about us we are just peons?"

"I think quite the contrary. I mean look at us. Look at the way we are made," Lawrence held up his hand and began to wave it, then began pointing at each individual finger. "Look how we are made. Look at our bodies and how complex it is. Look at our minds…they are like galaxies that are inside our heads. With our minds, we can imagine anything. That didn't just happen by random chance."

"I hear that guy in England came up with a theory where everything just evolves. Many scientists think it's true."

"Maybe, but maybe that's the way God made things. He created something and it evolves into something else."

Sully nodded. He had a slight smile on his face. "I can see you're a die-hard believer aren't you?"

"Yes. And it's not just because I grew up the son of a preacher. It just makes sense. I don't think we just came into being out of nothing without something willing us to life."

"I wish I had your faith."

"You can. Read the Bible. That's God's message of love directly aimed at you." Again Sully nodded and smiled. Lawrence couldn't tell if he was taking his words seriously.

"It's important that you seek God Sully. If you do you will find him. And if the words don't hit you at first, they eventually will. But you also must pray. You must pray to God for help." Lawrence could tell Sully wasn't completely convinced.

"When we get back home I want you to come visit me. You'll come over for church in the morning and then have dinner with my family in the afternoon. Once you've heard one of my father's sermons you will be inspired!" Lawrence had a large smile on his face remembering Sundays with his family. They were so pleasant and sometimes downright fun. He then became sad remembering those days but then thinking about the destruction that awaited him when he got to Atlanta.

"I'll have to take you up on that."

The two men lay back on the blankets, both courtesy of Sully, and they were soon sound asleep.

CHAPTER 4
A Presidential Encounter

April 20th, 1865

The next morning the men set off at dawn. They spoke little to each other. Sully had begun to resent Lawrence for having lost his backpack but there was little he could do or wanted to do about it. After they hiked to the top of the nearby mountain they decided to head in a more easterly direction, hoping they would get back to civilization. They were hoping they would be in Greensboro by nightfall.

When they had reached the summit of the mountain, they caught their breath and took a quick break. They finished off the last of the dried beef and hoped they would find provisions before that evening. On the ridge of the mountain, there were plentiful pine trees and thankfully there were clear and dry paths to walk in and around the forest. They found the going steady and continued their journey south with nary a word between them. The two men were enjoying the scenery greatly. The Piedmont area had been largely untouched by the war and they felt a relief knowing that any such conflict would not soon befall them. They even began exchanging small talk, pointing to the various rock formations, animals as well as the varied flora and fauna.

"I think we are making good time."

"We still tracking southeast?" Sully asked.

"I believe so. On the map, it shows this ravine to our right as going in a southeasterly direction. I've also been keeping an eye on the compass and looking back at landmarks to see if we are going in the right direction." Lawrence was relieved he could provide some sort of value given he had been relying on Sully's provisions for the past couple of days.

"In about five miles we should hit Lake Hunt. I'm sure we'll find a general store around there and we can get some food."

"I hope you're right."

The two men continued on a determined march. They wanted to be in Greensboro as quickly as possible. When they finally arrived at Lake Hunt, they could see several houses by the lake's edge. They saw multiple horses tied up near a stable. As they approached one house, a gentleman in a Confederate uniform walked out of the front door.

"Can I help you, gentlemen?"

"We're just headed on our way to Greensboro. We left Appomattox almost two weeks ago after the surrender. We're soldiers in the Confederate Army, or used to be."

"Gentlemen. An honor. Please join us inside."

Lawrence and Sully slowly walked inside the house, cautious that something was amiss.

"Gentlemen, please join us." An older man resembling Jefferson Davis waved for the two men to come forward. The man was sitting around a table that was stacked with papers and maps. As the two men walked nearer, the light revealed that it was in fact Jefferson Davis, the President of the Confederacy.

"Gentlemen, where do you hail from?"

"We're both from Atlanta but most recently we come from Appomattox."

Davis was silent and nodding his head. His deep, translucent eyes looked troubled. At the table were two other men. One was the North Carolina Governor Zebulon Vance and the other was General P.G.T. Beauregard.

"Isn't the war over Mr. President?" Sully asked.

"Yes, yes it is. We've just moved out of Greensboro and are deciding what to do next. I have been communicating with some of our contacts on the coast about escaping out of the country...Cuba, South America, possibly Europe. We have a lot of contacts in Europe and could set up the Confederate government in abstention there. We also have some contacts in Cuba and we could possibly set-up shop there." The President looked beaten and his hand was trembling as he began to go through some papers on the table. His words sounded like that of a desperate man with little belief that he would be able to escape.

"Isn't Sherman on the way here Mr. President?"

"Yes, he will be here in a day or two."

"Mr. President, we need to start heading out. My coach is ready," Governor Vance, the corpulent politician advised everyone in the room. The President nodded to him. Rumors had been running wild that Davis would be tried for war crimes and would be hung. It was clear that reality was ever-present on his mind.

"Mr. President, you'll have to leave now if you have any chance of making the coast before Sherman gets here."

"Thank you, General..."

At that moment a messenger walked in and handed the President a note.

"Well, the coast is out. We'll have to head south."

"But there's large contingents of Union troops throughout North and South Carolina and in Georgia."

"Well, we have no choice. Get everyone together and let's get out of here," the President said with a pained look on his face. His negro valet began to attend to his wardrobe and bags and he hurriedly rushed them out to the waiting coach outside.

"Where are you heading Mr. President?" Lawrence asked.

"Down to Georgia."

The boys looked at each other and became wide-eyed.

"Any way we could hitch a ride with you, Mr. President?"

"Love to have you along boys but the coach is going to be packed with bags and such. We've got my family, bodyguard, and valet as well."

The boys were dejected and as they looked out the window could see that the President was right. The coach was bursting at the seams and there was definitely no extra room. There were several other coaches for the rest of the President's cabinet and they too were overcapacity. Their next thought turned to horses and they inquired of the General if there were any spare horses. As with coach space, there were no available horses. They didn't know who they were more sorry for; themselves or Jefferson Davis.

As the boys walked out of the house, Lawrence asked the President a question. "Mr. President, was there any chance of us winning this war?" Davis looked down at the floor with a solemn expression. He shook his head. "I tried everything I could boys but there were just too many things weighing me down. If people had only listened to me there might have been a better outcome."

"You couldn't persuade them?"

"Like any government, you have your yes men and your naysayers. In my government, we just had too many cooks in the pot. We weren't unified enough. Not to mention the fact that we didn't have the resources the North did, but still, I think we could have done better. Anyway, we'll never know. I wish you all the best boys. Hope you get home soon," the President winked and then turned to get some of his bags. The boys grimaced thinking of what could have been.

After watching the coaches and men on horseback roar out of sight in a wave of dust, the boys decided to head into Greensboro and see if they could get a hotel for the night. As they got to the outskirts of town they saw many people gathered at the train station. The boys smiled believing that the trains there must be in operation. As they neared the crowd they could see President Davis along with his cabinet about to board one of the trains.

"Sorry, folks there's no more room on the train. You'll have to wait until tomorrow morning for the next one. It leaves at 8 am," one of the attendants announced.

"Sir, are you sure there's no more room?" Lawrence said as he pushed his way through the crowd.

"Fraid not son, all the seats are taken."

"Can we ride on top?" The portly attendant, resembling something more like a walrus than a man, just laughed and turned to walk toward the station. Sully slapped Lawrence's chest with the back of his hand and then pointed toward the train.

"C'mon, follow me," he said under his breath. The two men ran to the other side of the station where northbound trains were boarded. They jumped down onto the tracks and then ran around the other side of the building. They then looked for sections of the train that were unattended like where the cars were joined together. The train was pulling slowly out of the station and the boys began to pick up the pace. They located a section between train cars that they were able to board. The boys began to run as fast as they could and Sully was able to grab onto the railing and haul himself up. The train was now moving even faster and Lawrence was not going to be able to make it. Sully reached out his hand and Lawrence lunged for it, grabbing onto it, and then with one motion, Sully was able to pull him up.

"Looks like I've saved your skin again," Sully said with a wry smile. Lawrence smiled and nodded his head. They were now depending on God's good graces regarding how far the train would take them. Anything at that point was better than walking.

CHAPTER 5
Death in the Queen City

April 22nd, 1865

As they pulled into Concord, there seemed to be a ruckus as the train came to a stop. The boys hopped off and could see there were coaches lined up at the station. Jefferson Davis and his cabinet were quickly ushered into the coaches. Before anyone could react the coaches were gone in a great swirl of dust.

The boys inquired of the conductor what was happening.

"Charlotte is occupied by the Union and so President David has to flee via another route to escape," the conductor said and then quickly whistled for the train to continue. The boys, seeing the conductor was out of sight, quickly ran back to their usual spot on the train car. It was getting later in the day and cool air started to strike them as it whipped around the sides of the cars. They huddled together and kept their coats tightly buttoned. They did enjoy the scenery as the rolling hills, meadows, and forests went by.

They arrived in Charlotte in the late afternoon. The train was due to stop for an hour to take on coal, deboard and board passengers and have a general inspection. It was a large station with a turntable that enabled large locomotives to be moved on to various tracks heading in multiple directions. Charlotte happened to be the site of Confederate shipbuilding during the last half of the war after the Union had blockaded multiple ports, including Norfolk. The Confederate government picked Charlotte as the new shipyard being far enough away from the Union and also having good connections to the railway system.

The boys walked through the shipyard and became mesmerized by all the machinery and equipment used to build anchors and propellers and other parts of ships. There were large lathes, planers, and steam hammers used in forging the necessary pieces. Along the river's edge stood large steam-powered cranes that could move heavy parts. They now stood like giant dinosaurs that were stuck in their tracks. It was a testament to southern engineering and know-how. It brought to mind men like the gentleman from West Point they had met on the third night of their journey. So much potential but the factory now looked like a ghost town, save for some Union troops guarding the main building.

Further down the road, there were buildings with great stores of ammunition and ordinates. Unfortunately, there were also hundreds of Union troops stationed throughout the buildings and factories. They began to marvel at the site and wondered how the Confederacy could have been stopped with such manufacturing potential. It clearly hadn't been enough. As they were scolded by the troops for having gotten too close to the buildings, a loud bang rang through their ears. A shockwave penetrated their bodies. They looked around and could see a pillar of smoke rising from behind one of the buildings. They ran around the main building and could see a large wooden structure in flames.

"A bunch of gun powder just went off!!!" yelled one of the Union officers as he instructed multiple men to run over to the building. Almost immediately there was a large horse-drawn cart that had a water tank and nozzle that was quickly employed. As the boys neared the scene, they could see multiple bodies lying by the side of the road. They soon learned that there was a store of gun powder being kept in the basement of a building right next to a boarding house where many people were staying. The boys ran over to see if they could lend a hand. Before they knew what was happening there were several doctors and nurses from a nearby hospital conducting a triage of the wounded. The boys were quickly employed to help carry the wounded down the street to the hospital. While Lawrence and Sully and the hospital staff tended to the wounded, the Union soldiers did their best in containing the fire.

The scene soon became horrific as several men, attempting to retrieve bodies from the building came rushing out screaming having caught on fire themselves. Lawrence found a water trough and grabbed a bucket of water. He ran over to one of the men and threw the water over them. The man screamed out in pain and Lawrence could see his skin falling away from his upper body. Another man, in a hospital lab coat, grabbed the man and wrapped a wet piece of cloth over him.

"Someone help this man to the hospital!" Lawrence immediately complied with his request and helped the man. Sully also provided help by grabbing the man's arm and placing it over his shoulder to which the man cried out even louder. The boys got him to the hospital as fast as they could where an orderly put the man on a stretcher and with the aid of another man moved him into the surgery.

Lawrence and Sully were numb from all the pain and mayhem. They had not experienced anything like this since toward the end of the war. It was like they were reliving the horror all over again. There was one significant difference between now and during the war; the dead and wounded were civilians. And one body, in particular, drove Lawrence to his knees. Lying on the sidewalk in a pool of blood was a young boy, maybe eight or nine years old. The blast had destroyed much of his upper shoulder and it was clear he was dead. Lawrence felt ill and fell to his side. He could feel the flames whip around him like a hot wind. He tried to scoop up the child into his arms but as he did so, he could see that the boy's arm had detached. His mind began to swim with horror and he started to weep uncontrollably. Another man from the hospital, he wasn't sure if it were an orderly or a doctor, wrapped a blanket around the boy and took him from Lawrence. Lawrence ran to the front yard of a nearby home and then fell on the lawn. He began to convulse and shake with both physical and mental pain. *How could God allow this?!!!* He screamed to himself. Sully ran over and tried to console him.

"Lawrence, come on. There's nothing you could have done for him," came the hollow consolation. Sully put his arm around him and cradled him as Lawrence continued to sob. He had never sobbed for the men he had killed on the battlefield, but this was different. This was something sacred that had been horribly violated – an innocent life. A life that was just beginning and now it was snuffed out. *Where was God in this?* Lawrence wondered. Sully tried to hold Lawrence but his body soon went limp and he fell to the ground. He appeared to have passed out but then Sully could see him rocking his head back and forth in complete agony of what he had witnessed. Sully too had become overcome and sat down on the ground by Lawrence, putting his head down on his knees, also wondering where was the divine.

As the last of the bodies that could be retrieved from the boarding house were taken to the hospital, the fire was slowly brought under control. All of the fire wagons in the vicinity had come to the site and were slowly gaining the upper hand. Eventually, the fire was put out and the two large buildings stood as black skeletons against the smoky gray sky. Steam was rising as if they were cursed places. One of the doctors came over to the boys and tried to lend comfort.

"Thank you boys for your help. You helped save a lot of people today. If you hadn't intervened several of those in the boarding house would be dead. Thank you," again the praise was hollow and there was little that could comfort Lawrence or Sully at that point. They both stared off into the distance, wondering what the point was of their lives. Wondering what was the point of anything if someone so innocent could be immediately extinguished. The pain of seeing dead soldiers on the battlefield had been bad enough, but the loss of this little boy was something that would haunt them for the rest of their lives.

Lawrence was feeling light-headed and the doctor suggested to Sully that they help Lawrence get to the hospital. Once in the hospital, they laid him on a bed. The doctor gave Lawrence a sedative and he immediately went to sleep. For the first several hours he slept soundly. Later he began to dream or hallucinate. He could see a dark figure at the end of the hospital floor. Everything was blurry and he could not make out the features of the man other than he was a negro. He was tall and was wearing a Union uniform. He pointed to Lawrence and told him to come with him. Lawrence fearing for his life began to run.

"Lawrence, you can't run from me!!!" the man shouted. Lawrence ran down a stairwell and came to the lower level of the hospital. He walked outside and could see bodies everywhere. They were negroes. There were several large trees just outside of the hospital and multiple bodies were hanging from them. They looked like slaves who had been lynched. Just then, the negro soldier came through the door of the hospital and began to scream at him.

"You did this!!! You did this, you white devil!!!" At that point Lawrence woke up screaming in his bed, drenched in sweat.

"Lawrence, what is it?!!!" an alarmed Sully said as he rushed over to Lawrence and clutched him in his arms.

"It's okay, it's okay!"

As Sully consoled him, Lawrence slowly calmed down.

"Where am I?"

"You're in the hospital." Lawrence looked around and got his bearings. He tried to remember how he got there.

"Is everything okay?" a nurse asked. Lawrence slowly nodded his head.

"What time is it?"

"It's a little past ten in the morning."

"What, really? Let's get out of here."

"I wouldn't recommend that young man," the nurse advised Lawrence.

"Sorry ma'am, but I can't take up your valuable space. You have real patients to tend to."

"Nonsense, we have plenty of room. Since the war ended there has been more than enough room."

"But what about the wounded from the explosion?"

"Unfortunately we only had about thirty wounded we could treat. Most have passed."

Lawrence sat up in his bed. He was wearing only his long johns and they had been saturated with sweat.

"At least let me have the doctor check on you before you leave."

"No ma'am, I have wasted enough of the doctor's and your time. I'm embarrassed that I've acted this way."

"Embarrassed for acting like a human being? I think we need more men to act with more compassion. Then we wouldn't have these stupid wars. What a waste."

The boys listened to the nurse's words and nodded in agreement. Even in the most sacred cause, was war ever the answer? They were beginning to feel that it wasn't. Even if it meant the loss of their land and property, the death of one person wasn't worth it. Or maybe preserving a country? Fighting for a just and Godly cause? Lawrence began to wonder.

One offer Lawrence did take from the nurse was a hot bath. Both he and Sully took hot baths and it helped relax them somewhat. After their baths, they went to a local inn where they paid a nickel and were able to get a room overlooking the city center. Lawrence wanted to be as far away from the shipyard as possible. The inn was owned by a younger woman named Tess whose husband had been killed in the war, fighting for the Union. At that point the boys didn't care if he had fought for the North, they felt the woman's pain and sympathized with her. They decided the best thing they could do that day was to help her with chores around the house. Sully fixed several cabinets where the doors had come loose and Lawrence varnished some of the floorboards in one of the empty rooms. It was a good way for both of them to forget the horrors of what had just happened.

After completing their chores, the boys were exhausted and had earned themselves a nice home-cooked meal; pork loin and gravy with biscuits and green beans. For dessert, they had apple pie. They were stuffed. After a cup of coffee, Sully implored both Tess and Lawrence to join him at a tavern he had seen earlier that was just down the street. Tess declined, stating that she was tired and wanted to have an early night. Surprisingly Lawrence took him up on his offer and the two men headed down the street and walked over to the tavern. It looked like the owners of the public house were doing a roaring trade. They seemed to cater to all walks of life; vagabonds, misfits, prostitutes, professional men and women of various trades including some of the medical personnel from the hospital, and off in a secluded corner, various officers and enlisted men of the Union Army. Clearly, all were in the need of a drink.

Sully and Lawrence noticed a chalkboard at the entryway that had the prices of drinks scrawled on it in chalk. They ignored the chalkboard and headed for the bar area. Lawrence was feeling somewhat awkward. Having been the son of a preacher, such establishments and especially the drinking of liquor were strictly forbidden. He was also concerned about what God thought. But having been a student of the Bible, he remembered the miracle at the Wedding of Cana where Jesus had turned water into wine. Clearly, Jesus had partaken of wine? If not he clearly didn't oppose its consumption. But he also knew that He wouldn't condone its abuse.

The two men walked up to the bartender where Sully ordered a whiskey. He then motioned to Lawrence to make his order. Not sure what to try, Sully, suggested a beer. The bartender plopped down a glass of whiskey and a large mug of frothing beer that spilled over the edges.

"To sobriety!" Sully joked as he clinked his glass against Lawrence's mug of beer. Lawrence took a swig, hoping so would relieve him of some of the stress caused by the previous day. He swirled the malty beer around his mouth and swallowed. He had tasted beer before when he was younger but it had seemed sour. This tasted nice and he quickly took a much larger gulp of the ale. He could feel the release of pain and pressure and he felt it a godsend.

"Sully, this was a great idea!" declared Lawrence as he slammed down his mug. Sully laughed and was surprised he hadn't broken his mug. Lawrence stared at the foam coming over the top of his mug and became mesmerized.

"Wow, I'm ah sorry barkeep. Allow me to clean that up!" Lawrence gave way to a large burp and he was already tipsy.

"Not to worry sir, I've got a rag right here."

"Thank you, my good man."

Sully could tell that Lawrence did not have his usual serious countenance. While not opposed to humor and making a joke, Lawrence still was more of a serious and internal personage. Soon Lawrence was ordering another beer and as another mug was slammed down before him, a man began to play piano right near the bar area. This caught everyone's attention and soon the entire tavern began to join in with cheery songs, save some of the Union officers and enlisted who had gathered in their usual corner.

The piano player was soon joined by a tall blonde man in overalls who was playing the banjo.

There's a yellow girl in Texas
That I'm going down to see
No other darkies know her
No darkey, only me...

The rest of the patrons in the bar joined in, with the exception of those from the Union…

She cried so when I left her
That it like to broke my heart,
And if I only find her
We never more will part

Lawrence began to walk closer to the piano and started to bellow at the top of his lungs. While at first out of key he soon found the notes and was the star of the chorus…

She's the sweetest girl of color
That this darkey ever knew
Her eyes are bright as diamonds
And sparkle like the dew
You may talk about your Dearest Mae
And sing of Rosa Lee
But the Yellow Rose of Texas
Beats the belles of Tennessee
Where the Rio Grande is flowing

And the starry skies are bright
Oh, she walks along the river
In the quiet summer night
And she thinks if I remember
When we parted long ago
I promised to come back again
And not to leave her so

Lawrence now standing prominently by the piano, had captured the attention of everyone in the bar. Lawrence had been a lead singer in his father's choir in church and now he was letting the stress of the last several years and especially the last several days leave his body. For the last verse, Lawrence, now singing a solo, changed the words to reflect the Tennessee Army's version...

And now I'm going southward,
For my heart is full of woe
I'm going back to Georgia,
to find my Uncle Joe
You may talk about your Beauregard
And sing of Bobby Lee
But the gallant Hood of Texas,
He played hell in Tennessee

The last verse caught the attention of the Union soldiers which prompted a man who had been playing guitar to walk over and start bellowing a northern march...

When Johnny comes marching home again
Hurrah! Hurrah!

We'll give him a hearty welcome then
Hurrah! Hurrah!
The men will cheer and the boys will shout
The ladies they will all turn out
And we'll all feel gay
When Johnny comes marching home.

The man's Union colleagues soon joined in…

The old church bell will peal with joy
Hurrah! Hurrah!
To welcome home our darling boy,
Hurrah! Hurrah!
The village lads and lassies say
With roses they will strew the way,
And we'll all feel gay
When Johnny comes marching home.

Lawrence and the rest of the Confederate patrons took umbrage and had prepared a response. Just as the Yanks had finished, the Confederate side of the house sang their song…

I wish I was in the land of cotton,
old times there are not forgotten,
Look away, look away, look away, Dixie Land.
In Dixie Land where I was born in,
early on a frosty mornin',
Look away, look away, look away, Dixie Land.

Then the battle began as they alternated lines of the songs which eventually turned into a cacophony of noise…

Get ready for the Jubilee,

Hurrah! Hurrah! Then I wish I was in Dixie, hooray! hooray!

We'll give the hero three times three,

Hurrah! Hurrah! In Dixie Land I'll take my stand to live and die in Dixie!!!

What started off as good-natured ribbing soon turned violent when a drunken rebel pushed the guitar player from the North to the ground. The room quickly dissolved into a mass of flesh with arms punching and legs kicking. Tables were pushed over and glasses began to shatter as they hit the floor. Lawrence, feeling a renewed vitality went over to the closest man in blue and swung as hard as he could, sending the man to the floor. Before he could savor the moment however a colleague of the fallen man quickly exacted revenge and the next thing Lawrence knew he was looking up at the ceiling. He rolled over to avoid the collapse of two others engaged in a fevered wrestling match. Sully, a little more soused than usual, remembered his boxing days and began landing punches left and right.

Within a few minutes, the Union police stormed the tavern, and whistles along with shots fired through the roof brought the battle to a quick end.

"Whoever throws another punch will either be shot or thrown into jail. Now which do you want?!!!" screamed a Union officer, who held a shotgun in one hand and a revolver in another. As he continued his tirade, Lawrence and Sully who were now toward the back of the saloon slipped into a separate dining room. Beyond the sight of the Union Captain, they lifted up a window and poured themselves through the opening as if they were made of molasses. They quickly got up and ran as fast as they could to the boarding house, laughing uncontrollably as they did so.

"Well, you boys look a little worse for wear," Tess said as she let the boys in at the front door.

"Much obliged ma'am. We're sorry but we let off a little steam after what happened in town."

"Don't blame you. Do you need anything?"

"No ma'am, we've troubled you enough. We'll just head to our room now," Sully said, tipping his hat to her. The boys quickly scurried upstairs where they got to their rooms and immediately plopped down in their beds. They soon passed out from the exhilaration of the evening. It was one of the few nights that Lawrence had slept all the way through. He had been praying for sleep, but it typically came in fits and spells, no longer than an hour or two at a time. The war had troubled him. The sights, the smells. He was now no longer the innocent boy he had been growing up in Atlanta. Would his family recognize him? He would be the same physically, but he was definitely not the same inside. What Lawrence didn't realize was that he was going through a metamorphosis. And it wasn't just a change from the war, it was a deep change…an ongoing change. A change that would never cease. For the rest of his life, he would continue to evolve.

The next morning, the cock crowed. Lawrence began to think about St. Peter and how he denied the Lord three times before the cock crowed. Would he have done the same thing had he been St. Peter? The thought quickly left his head when Sully threw his pillow at him.

"I couldn't believe you last night Larry!!!"

"Don't call me Larry!" Lawrence threw the pillow back at Sully.

"C'mon, let's get going. There's a train at eight."

The boys collected their gear and headed downstairs for a quick bite to eat. They gave Tess another nickel, expressing their thankfulness to her for her hospitality as well as concern that she would now be hard-pressed to make ends meet with her husband's passing. Lawrence admired her. She looked a little forlorn, but she had beauty. She had southern strength and charm. Would they find the same when they encountered the destruction of Georgia and the deep South?

The boys ran out the door and caught the train just in time, gaining access as they had the previous two trips. As the train bumped and chugged down the track, the boys hoped they would settle in for a long ride home. After a two-hour ride, they came to a halt near the South Carolina border. They were instructed that the tracks had been damaged by the Union troops and they could go no further. There was a make-shift station set up just north of Rock Hill.

The boys were on foot again and they quickly gathered their belongings and headed for the road into Rock Hill. As they made their way into town, they were immediately struck by the lack of southern men around. Union troops were patrolling the streets, but there only seemed to be women, children, and the elderly. They entered a general store where a young woman and an elderly woman were moving goods around the store in a wheelbarrow.

"Let me help you with that ma'am," Lawrence said without waiting for an answer. The wheelbarrow had a sack of cornmeal in it and she was attempting to wheel it over to the corner of the store where there were several sacks piled up.

"Thank you, sir. Much obliged."

"Say, don't you have any menfolk to help you?"

"No sir. They're all gone."

"All gone? You mean they haven't returned from the war?"

"Mostly dead," the elderly woman said from behind the counter.

"Many of our men went off to fight. They'all fought in some of the worst fightin'. Some of the biggest battles. We've lost over eight hundred men."

Lawrence and Sully had a sick feeling rush through them. How would the town survive? It surely couldn't run with only women and children. Lawrence became outraged. His heart turned black with anger. *If those damn niggers hadn't got all uppity we wouldn't have this problem!* Lawrence seethed with anger. His complacency from the past two weeks had turned back to righteous indignation. In many ways, he had just wanted the war to end. He didn't want to see any more bloodshed. But with the explosion in Charlotte and the devastation to Rock Hill, he began to rethink his moral sabbatical. He wanted to help the women but he didn't know-how. He needed to get home. One thing he knew for sure, if he ever became rich, he would rebuild the South. The boys purchased some beef jerky and then bid the women a good afternoon. They found an inn that, like the general store, was now only run by women. They were sisters who had lost both of their husbands to the war. It was a familiar theme.

As with their prior stops, the boys did some chores around the inn to help out. When the roof needed mending, Lawrence grabbed some boards, a hammer, and some nails and headed up to the attic. The attic was dark and full of cobwebs and dust. He took with him a lantern and pushed up through the door leading to the attic. He was greeted by a cloud of dust and it looked like it hadn't been visited in years. Both of the women's husbands had been killed toward the beginning of the war so it probably hadn't seen the light of day in four years. Multiple pieces of furniture had been covered in sheets. There was a desk that hadn't been covered and he could see a picture on top of it. It was of the older sister and her husband. She was a blushing bride and he was wearing his Confederate uniform. Lawrence sighed and shook his head, having a horrid feeling in his gut about the incredible waste of life caused by the war. With each passing day, he wondered what had it all been about.

After nailing up a couple of boards to cover holes in the roof, Lawrence headed down to dinner. The women had put out a wonderful spread; salad, soup, biscuits, and a large roast. The boys along with two other guests took to the dinner with gusto. After dinner the boys immediately retired for the evening, knowing they had a long march ahead of themselves the following day.

The next day the boys bid farewell to the sisters and started on their way. There was no train for them to take from Rock Hill to Atlanta so they knew they needed to make haste. They paid the sisters extra to get some leftover roast and a sack full of biscuits for their journey. With a little kick in their step, they set out for home.

CHAPTER 6
Challenging Beliefs

April 26th, 1865

The boys headed due West that morning and stuck to the dirt and gravel roads. They made it to McConnells that afternoon but found little around besides an old Presbyterian church. As they made their way around to the other side of the church they could see a funeral was in progress. There looked to be a pastor with only four family members standing over a grave. There was a slight breeze that was carrying around a white wispish mist. As the boys approached the site, they stopped short and took off their hats, and bowed. They overheard the pastor commending the man's soul to God. The man had been wounded at the Battle of Columbus on the 16th of April. With the secession of fighting, he was brought back to the McConnells, but his wound had become infected and he had died the evening before.

The pastor appeared to be in his sixties, with white hair and beard, looking worn and weary. He would have been a good model for Michelangelo's Sistine Chapel. He spoke slowly and directly to the family, but he seemed to quickly run out of words to say.

"Lord, we thank you for the life of Jethro. He was a young man but he gave much to this town during his short lifespan. He gave the ultimate gift, the gift of life," the pastor's voice seemed to evoke many emotions; sadness, profoundness, and even a look of disgust. Disgust from losing another young man to the war. As the pastor finished his words, a light rain began to fall. The ladies put up their parasols and turned for a nearby horse-drawn carriage. The pastor started to walk toward the church in the opposite direction as a teenage boy began to trail behind the women.

With the rain starting to come down harder, the pastor ran toward the church. Sully and Lawrence quickly chased after him.

"Reverend?" Sully yelled. The pastor turned and looked at the boys. His expression was as if he had seen a ghost.

"Reverend, do you know of anywhere we can stay tonight?" Lawrence asked as the rain became more steady. The beleaguered pastor eyed the boys up and down. His expression then brightened. "You can stay with me," he said with a bright smile. His countenance seemed to change and he began to perk up. "Let's head into the church for a moment." He motioned for the boys to follow him as they went through the front door.

"This church was built in 1820. It's served us very well."

"Are you the original pastor?" Lawrence asked as a loud clap of thunder could be heard not far off. Everyone turned to look out the window and could see the sky darken further. A bolt of lightning could be seen on the horizon, seeming to shatter a group of tall trees. The pastor put away some books in his office and encouraged the boys to join him as soon as possible at his home which was just across the street.

The three men hurried across the street as they began to be pelted with heavy rain. The pastor quickly closed the door behind them.

"Please come in boys and make yourself at home," the pastor showed them to some chairs around the kitchen table. He took a pot that had been sitting on the table and brought it over to the fireplace. He hooked the handle of the pot to a wire that was fixed over the fireplace. He then put in some wood and kindling and started a fire.

"Mrs. McCready makes a fine stew. I think you'll enjoy it."

The boys were comforted by the fire. The temperature had dropped pretty quickly with the coming of the storm and they were quite content where they were at that moment. The fire had roared into life and the blackened bottom of the pot was soon aglow. The stew smelled delicious.

As the boys settled in, they began to look around the house. Like the home Lawrence grew up in, it was modest, typical of a pastor's abode. He appeared to not be married as the house was a bit untidy, mostly with books and papers lying around in various spots.

"Not married are you Reverend?" asked Lawrence.

"My wife passed away a couple of years ago."

"I'm sorry to hear that."

"The Lord's will. She had been sick a long time and it was better for her to pass into the peace that surpasses all understanding."

The boys smiled and nodded their heads. Lawrence could tell the man had been a pastor all his life. When most sentences ended with Biblical principles or Christian sayings you know the speaker had a long history of liturgical work. And while the wrinkles and cracks were prominent on his face, he still had a youthful enthusiasm for his job.

"Were you impacted much by the war?"

The pastor smiled and nodded as he took his place on a nearby rocking chair.

"Yes, we had our fair share of bloodshed. Not in town but many of our boys lost their lives. Of course, you saw one of them buried today."

"Sorry to hear that."

"And then toward the end of the war, we had to fight off our own Confederate troops for food and supplies. Times were getting desperate for our boys. We tried to give them food but we needed to eat ourselves and there wasn't much left."

"Our own troops were looting you?"

"Fraid so. I can understand it but it resulted in violence. One of our ladies was killed trying to fight off a band of rebels who had been threatening her for her livestock. One night they went to her farm and she tried to hold them off with her shotgun. She killed a soldier but was killed herself. Very tragic."

"Makes you wonder where the Lord was in all this?" Sully asked, questioning to himself. The pastor began to look at Sully, realizing he wasn't the most faithful of men.

"I don't suppose you have any whiskey?" Sully continued.

"No, I don't subscribe to the use of alcohol."

"Didn't Jesus drink wine?"

With a knitted brow, the pastor began to contemplate Sully's reference.

"You know? At the wedding of Cana."

"Yes, I'm sure he did, but for me, it can cloud my thinking so I abstain."

"Even a sip clouds your thinking?"

"Well, it's not the sip. It's what the sip leads to."

Lawrence nodded his head and began to think back to the last night in Charlotte where he had imbibed a little too much. He wasn't sorry for what he had done but he knew he would need to prohibit future lapses of sobriety. In his mind, he confessed to the Lord his failing and vowed not to let it happen again. He had officially repented.

Sully continued to push his point, "but you judge others who enjoy spirits?"

"I don't judge, I merely encourage others to avoid its use. There are not many who can handle the power of alcohol. It's like all humankind. We never can seem to find balance. Things would be fine if we could have a glass of wine, but what is often the case? We become drunk. We try and erase our past or remove problems by drinking. We think that by drinking it will resolve a problem. But when we wake up the next morning…we have the same ol' problems."

Sully nodded his head and began to fumble with his backpack. He produced a small whiskey bottle. Lawrence racked his brain thinking where he might have gotten it from. Had he stolen it from the sisters at the inn? The pastor went back into the kitchen and quickly returned with a glass for Sully to use, fearing his continued slugs from the bottle would spray its contents onto the floor.

"Thank you, Reverend! Would you like some?" The pastor shook his head. His expression showed agitation that Sully hadn't heeded his advice.

"Is there anything or anyone you do judge Reverend?" Sully asked as he took another swig from his bottle. The pastor was silent as he rocked back and forth in his chair.

"For example, Abraham Lincoln?"

"Never met 'im."

"No, but he was responsible for this war don't you think?"

"Naw, we as mankind are responsible for the war."

"But don't you think we had the right to defend the Confederacy?" Lawrence now joined the conversation.

"We are all sinners. We are fallible. I learned that the Confederacy was only as good as its men and the men I knew were not very good at all. Robbing women and children. I understand that they were hungry but they needed to show some dignity. They could have hunted for food."

"But what about our way of life?"

"I never owned any slaves. Did you own slaves?"

Both Lawrence and Sully shook their heads. "We had a maid that was given to us by the parish but I don't think technically she was a slave," Lawrence offered. The pastor nodded.

"Boys, the South had an elite group of people...certain families that made money. But for the average man and woman, they didn't make money. It's only the 10 or 15% of the population that made money. They owned the plantations that made the cotton. They had the slaves. It was them that wanted this war."

"But didn't we all benefit from the cotton? Maybe we're not all plantation owners but we enjoyed a strong southern economy. That economy produced jobs in farming, transportation..."

"But was it worth fighting a war over? Was it worth all the bloodshed?"

"When a foreign power comes in and tries to tell you how to live your life, then yes it's worth the bloodshed."

"It's not a foreign power – it is the United States of America. We could have made things work without slavery. We could have had a strong economy producing crops under the same government. But it was corrupt men who wanted to keep their money, keep their slaves. Boys, it's inhuman to keep people captive! They are not livestock for us to do with as we choose. They are God's creation. Flesh n'blood like you and me. Five fingers on each hand, five toes on each foot. Two legs and two arms. A head, a heart, and a mind. A mind that can think and feel like you and me!"

"Here, here!" said a drunken Sully. Lawrence was not so accepting of the pastor's words.

"Slavery is a necessary thing pastor. We can't do the work we need to do in the South without slaves. The institution of slavery has been around forever and it will always be around. Even the Lord talked about slaves and their need to obey their masters."

"Young man, please do not distort the words of Jesus. As you have said, slavery was an institution. Slavery in the time of Christ was a form of people paying off debts but wasn't a means of exploiting people. You need to study your history."

"Well, I live with my mother who is a widow and no one ever helped us. There was many a night we starved. We never benefited from all the cotton and textiles mills. My mother had to work her fingers to the bone working the looms at the textile mill. And old Byron Johnson just stood there watching all the money trickling in. Had a fancy house there in Decatur. We had a one-bedroom apartment by the mill. She was yelled at and basically mistreated. Made pennies."

"I thought you were pro-war when we left for the front?"

"I was pro-living. They shot people for deserting. But as the Rev says, there were too many people benefitting from this war at the top; plantation owners, politicians."

"Boy, you two have a negative view on life. Didn't the Yankee forefathers say we should have life, liberty, and the pursuit of happiness? I mean, did we not have the right to determine our own futures?" Lawrence argued.

"I think the best thing to do my boy is get to know who the slaves are. Did you know any slaves?"

Lawrence shook his head. He was from a pastor's family with moderate means and they did not have any slaves per se, except their maid. Some of his friends and neighbors did. They were the wealthier parishioners of their church.

"No, I never met any of them other than our nanny."

"As a preacher, I've learned that God created all men, and as you reference the Yankee forefathers so we have the right to pursue happiness, doesn't that apply to all people?" As the preacher asked the question, he rose from his rocking chair and then went over to the cupboard where he produced three plates that he placed on the nearby table. From the same cupboard, he retrieved silverware for the trio. He placed the plates and silverware in evenly spaced areas like he had buttled before in a past life.

"The war is over and for better or worse we need to get along. We need to get along with the northerners, we need to get along with the government, we need to get along with all people. The thing I've learned about life is we are all the same. White, black, brown, yellow...we all have a beating heart and a mind. A mind to think. That's how I know God exists, through the mind, the brain," the preacher pressed his index finger against his temple multiple times.

"There's this fella in England. Came up with the theory of evolution. There was no divine creation. Everything just evolved from some primitive life form. Single-celled creatures turned into pollywogs. Pollywogs turned into salamanders. Salamanders turned into fish. Fish turned into lizards. Lizards turned into birds. Birds turned into monkeys. Monkeys turned into men."

"Sounds like hogwash!" Lawrence exclaimed.

"It's scientific fact!" Sully retorted.

"Maybe so, but you can't have the human mind comin' from nothing cause that's what they're basically sayin'. Nothing like the human mind can come from nothin'. Maybe God created evolution, I don't know, but God gave us a brain to think. We need to use it. It's clear that God created all of us. He didn't make any mistakes. If you are saying he made a mistake by making negroes then I think you are wrong. Like all colors in nature, he created multiple kinds of people."

As the preacher finished his thought he carried the pot from the fireplace over to the table and began to heap scoops of the stew onto the plates. The boys' mouths began to water. Lawrence began to think less of theology and more about his stomach. He conceded the argument for the moment and took his place at the table.

"For what we are about to receive we give you thanks oh great and merciful God. For from your bounty you choose to give us this wonderful food. Amen."

"Amen!" Sully said as he grabbed his fork and began to dig in. The boys had not had beef in a while and they enjoyed every bite. The stew was very savory with carrots, celery, and potatoes. Next to the fire was a basket that was covered. The reverend retrieved the basket and offered the boys warm biscuits. As they tucked into the fluffy dough they thought they had died and gone to heaven.

After dinner, the boys played some cards with the reverend. He smoked a pipe and continued to rock in his chair. The conversation had turned less philosophical and more practical.

"How long will it take you to get to Atlanta?" the reverend asked.

"Not sure. I'm hoping only a week or so more. I hear all the trains are down between here and there so it'll be pretty much on foot."

"Speaking of which we may want to have an early night and hit the road as early as possible," Sully suggested. Lawrence agreed and the two men were shown the other room in the house that had two beds in it. After the wonderful meal, they were soon sound asleep.

The next morning a cock crowed and the sun was back out. The ground was damp and the bushes and trees glistened with the previous day's rain. As the boys bid farewell to the reverend they walked down the silent empty street heading out of town.

"Good luck boys. I'll be praying for you."

The boys turned and saluted the reverend. Lawrence had taken the preacher's words to heart. He began to think about how he would now view negroes. Were they really equal? The reverend was right, why would God create something that wasn't good or equal? But had the reverend ever needed labor? Having grown up in Atlanta there was no way the economy there would have thrived without slavery. He didn't own slaves but his family benefited indirectly from slavery. The congregants at his father's church made sure they gave generous tithes which, while not luxurious, provided a solid income with good food on the table and a roof over his head. It would also pay for his training as a preacher when he got back home. His father and mother wouldn't have used the money generated from slavery if it wasn't right? His mother and father were good, honest people who taught the word of God. It was just the way it was in the South. It was a way of life and slaves were a part of it. "Slaves obey your masters," the Lord himself said that. Was the reverend saying Jesus Christ was wrong? The reverend just didn't truly understand the way of life of the true southern man. He was a noble thinker but clearly, he was wrong and his thinking didn't belong, especially in a place like Atlanta.

Now that Lawrence's thinking was clear and his rationalization was completed, he could move forward with a happy heart. It didn't matter that the world was falling down around him, it was after all the next world that was important. God was the most important thing and God would help and support him and his family.

CHAPTER 7
Revolt in Anderson

May 1st, 1865

After walking all day and all night, the boys arrived in Anderson. That afternoon, as they walked into town, there was a great commotion going on. The boys ran toward the center of town and hid behind some trees when seeing some Union soldiers. It looked like the soldiers were rustling up some of the townspeople. As they slowly made their way toward the town square, they could see two men being strung up and about to be hanged. The soldiers were busy either pushing locals out of the way or shooting their guns and rifles into the air to try and bring some order.

The boys were able to get further into the crowd and Sully asked one of the onlookers what was going on.

"The Union troops killed one of our boys today Billy McKenzie. He was so frustrated that he pointed a gun at some troops and they fired on him. An innocent boy!"

"Why are these two being hung?"

"They were trying to help..." as the man said those words, the two men were hung and were soon squirming, their bodies dangling from the branch of a large oak tree. The crowd gasped in unison. The boys were horrified and enraged. This is what life under Yankee rule was going to be like? Sully and Lawrence looked at each other and mutually decided they would do something. But what? They ran back in the direction where they had originally come and stopped at a house at the edge of town.

"I can't believe those bastards."

"I thought the war was over?" Sully said as he picked up a rock and threw it as far as he could. He would have strangled anyone who would have walked in front of him at that moment, he was so angry.

"We need to find some guns."

"Don't worry gentleman, we'll give you those guns," the boys turned to see a young Confederate cadet. He had blonde reddish hair and a thin, wispy beard.

"We are taking back Anderson," he turned and pointed to what appeared to be a platoon of young cadets.

"Who are these kids?" Sully asked.

"We were just finishing up training at the military academy down the road. We heard what happened and headed over here."

"I don't think you have enough men to fight the Union troops," Lawrence said wearily. Having spent the past several years fighting battles where the enemy typically outnumbered his compatriots.

"No, we probably don't. But we're here to fight for the honor of the South. We won't let these northern bastards strip us of our pride!!!" The young man who held the rank of lieutenant looked back at the rest of the men and yelled at them to follow him. As he began to move forward he told one of his aids to give Sully and Lawrence a couple of pistols. The boys grabbed them with enthusiasm and were soon marching with the cadets. Before they knew it they were in the center of town and all hell was breaking loose. The boys had also been given two cartridge boxes they could use to reload their pistols.

As they reach the center of town the fighting intensified and the boys had to rely on their experience on the battlefield. Both Sully and Lawrence had learned to anticipate the actions of the enemy. As if in a dream, things immediately began to slow down. It felt like the Union troops were stuck in the mud, they moved so slowly. Sully quickly fired several rounds hitting his mark. Lawrence coming right behind him did the same with deadly accuracy.

The boys and their cadet colleagues pushed down Main Street and quickly forced the Union troops out of the town square. Sully and Lawrence fired upon several Union soldiers who were trying to hang another man. Lawrence wounded one of the hangmen and the northerners were soon on the run. The man who had the noose around his neck was on a horse. It was a miracle the horse hadn't been spooked into running. Lawrence put his hand on the horse's main and began to stroke his head, hoping to not stir him. Sully climbed onto the horse and quickly removed the noose from around the man's head and untied his hands which had been bound behind him. Once released the man jumped off the horse and took the reins from Lawrence. It was the horse's owner.

As the dust settled, several men from nearby Pendleton arrived in the town square. They reported to the commander of the cadets that they had been in a firefight with some Union troops that were heading into Anderson. They also reported that Union troops had been thwarted in their attempt to blow up a railway bridge on the Saluda River.

As the scene began to calm down, many of the townspeople emerged from their homes and gathered with the victorious cadets.

"Thank you boys, you saved us," a middle-aged woman cried.

"It won't be for long ma'am. There are more Union troops on their way here. They think there is liquor and gold that we are hiding."

"Along of course with Jefferson Davis," one of Lieutenant Lewis' men said with a smirk.

"What do we do?" a man with a horrific look on his face asked. The lieutenant was silent, shaking his head. With no response to the man's question, the lieutenant yelled to his men to move toward the west of the town to root out any Union stragglers. For the rest of the night, there was periodic gunfire as the nervous cadets thought they saw phantom northern soldiers.

The boys settled in for the night with the woman who had commended the cadets. Her name was Mrs. Molly Thompkins. She was 63 and had recently lost her husband; not to the war but to natural causes. She had a home just off of Main Street and the boys were able to take a spare room there. Mrs. Thompkins was able to make the boys some potato mash with some gravy. She had not had meat in over a month, with very little being available.

"Thank you for the meal ma'am. It's much appreciated."

"Oh, my pleasure boys. You deserve it for saving our town from those devils."

Lawrence nodded his head and smiled. Sully smiled, knowing that she was not completely in tune with reality. She refused to believe the Union troops would be back.

"I'm sure Jefferson Davis will send reinforcements and we will win this war after all."

Lawrence struggled with the need to comfort her but also the need, to tell the truth. With Lee's surrender and Union troops now occupying much of the South, what had just happened was a mere skirmish that would soon result in the town being handed back to the Union. How the boys would extricate themselves from the situation they were unsure about.

After dinner, Mrs. Thompkins showed the boys to the spare room and they soon bunked in for the night. As the boys lay in bed staring at the ceiling, they began to contemplate the situation.

"Is there any hope we will get out of here unscathed?"

"I don't know. Once those troops get here tomorrow…we might end up like those two men that got hung earlier today."

The thought of hanging from the end of a rope was sobering.

"Should we just get out of here now? Run while we can?" Sully suggested. Lawrence blew out a deep breath of air. Shaking his head he continued. "For the past few weeks, I've felt like I've been on the run, like a man without a country. It's time to stop and fight like a man."

"Fight for what?" Sully asked in his usual dissenting tone.

"Our way of life."

"Our way of life. You're the son of a preacher. My mother lives in poverty. What 'way of life' are you fighting for?"

"Didn't you learn anything from today? Don't you see how these bastards are going to treat us after the war? They don't care about us. They've been looting all the houses and stores around here. These people are animals. Do you want to be enslaved by these wretched heathens!"

Sully rolled over in his bed and contemplated what Lawrence said. He didn't know whether the treatment under Union rule would be any worse than what he and his mother had already experienced, but it was clear there would be no arguing with Lawrence. He was entrenched in his beliefs and there would be little to change them, at least for now.

Having been completely exhausted, both men passed out quickly and were soon awakened to the sound of a cock crowing. They gathered their belongings and headed out to the town square. Mrs. Thompkins had baked some biscuits for the boys for which they were very grateful. They wished Mrs. Thompkins well and continued outside. As they gathered with the rest of the troops, a bugle was heard in the distance and a small figure on the horizon soon turned into a larger image of a terrified boy who had seen the Union troops marching toward the town.

Before anyone could think, bullets were flying everywhere. Bullets could be heard ricocheting against barns, water barrels, horse troughs, anything that could withstand the piercing of hot metal. The Union troops, with several horse-mounted officers, were almost toward the center of town. Sully and Lawrence gathered themselves and hid behind a large building. They began exchanging fire with the Union troops.

While Sully and Lawrence held their own, their comrades did not fare as well and the tide quickly turned due to the sheer numbers of Union troops. The cadets fell back toward the east, while the boys headed west, taking shelter behind various houses on the south side of the city. As they turned to see what was happening it was clear it was a complete rout and so the boys decided to head to the western outskirts of town. They found a hill that they quickly ran up and hid behind.

As the noise subsided and the dust settled, the boys looked over the hill to find that the Union had restored order. The cadets had either been killed or taken prisoner. Lawrence and Sully then decided to hide in a nearby wood and wait and see what might happen. Was the war really over? Were there Confederate troops secretly waiting to unite with other units and continue the fight? How could that be though with their supreme commander having surrendered three weeks earlier?

For the rest of the day, the boys hid out in the woods. From the town, they could hear occasional shouts and loud discourse from the Union troops. Later in the evening, they could hear their frivolity and the celebration of their victory with ample amounts of alcohol. The boys rested their heads on their backpacks, trying to ignore the din of Yankee hubris. Lawrence had managed to get a new backpack from kindly old Mrs. Thompkins who had an old one her son used to use. As the sky darkened, Lawrence and Sully just stared up at the stars between the tall pine trees wondering if they should just leave at that point. Before they could make a decision they were sound asleep.

The next morning, the boys mounted the hill and looked down upon Anderson. It looked peaceful and numerous Union troops were strolling the streets. The minor uprising had been put down and it was time for Sully and Lawrence to make a quick exit. They were within a few days trek to Atlanta and it was time to get home. Life on the road had been long and arduous and it was time to settle into a new life. At least that's what was in Sully's mind. Lawrence wanted to settle into a new life but in a country that was run by the Confederacy. While he had dreams and ambitions he also had a practical side and the events of the past couple of days in Anderson soon ended any hope he had of a southern uprising. It was time to get home and settle into his career.

Later that afternoon the boys were able to cross into Hartwell, Georgia. They had finally arrived in their home state. With it now being May, they could feel the humidity and heat rising. They could tell their pace was somewhat slowed by the elements but they were glad to see their first Georgia town. They stopped for a drink of water at a well near the town's end and were soon on their way. Like the many towns they had visited before, the inhabitants looked like restless spirits with no place to go. Many more in Hartwell looked impoverished and that scene would play out over and over as they got closer to Atlanta. By nightfall, they had made it to an area known as "Eagle Grove" where they decided to bed for the evening in a small wood. As they tried to sleep they could hear a commotion in the distance and got up to see what it was. There was a group of several small buildings that were lit up with people milling about. Having not seen such life for a while they decided to pick up their gear and head into the small town.

As they passed several of the townspeople, the inhabitants appeared to be bright and upbeat, waving and acknowledging the visitor's presence. Quite a change from the lifeless faces they had been running into previously. One man, who was shuffling along at a quick pace raised his hand in a salute.

"What regiment you boys in?"

"Twelfth battalion."

"Oh, artillery eh?"

"Yes sir."

"You boys should grab some refreshment from Stoller's over there. They've got beer and food and some great entertainment," the man said after saluting again and then shuffling off into the night. The boys agreed and quickly headed to a small brick-covered building that looked like a small factory. As they entered, the place seemed to burst into life. It was like a saloon that one would find in Atlanta. There was much celebrating going on which seemed to be in juxtaposition to everything they had seen over the past several weeks.

"You boys thirsty?" a man from behind the bar asked.

"Sure, can we have a couple of beers?"

"Absolutely!"

"This place seems awfully lively given…"

"Given the end of the war?"

Lawrence nodded his head as he placed his cap on the bar and his bag on top of a stool.

"I think everyone has been depressed long enough. We decided to open the old bar a couple of days ago and everyone from Royston to Lavonia has been coming here. You boys want some food?"

"Sure, what'ay got?"

"My wife has some roast brisket in back. Want me to fix you a plate?"

The boys stared at each other with watering mouths and nodded in unison. It was like they had entered paradise. As they grabbed a table they could hear a group of musicians tuning their instruments and then immediately jumping into a song. There was a young man on banjo, with an even younger man playing spoons, an older woman playing the piano, another young man on an upright bass guitar, and a beautiful red-haired woman on fiddle. In the corner, laying on the floor was an elderly man playing a small bass drum. They played an Irish folk song, and the entire tavern was captivated by the group. It was upbeat and everyone was soon joining in.

One step over the line sweet Mary
One step over the line sweet Jesus
Hoping for to reach our heavenly home
Hoping to see your sweet smiling faces

One step over the line sweet Mary
One step over the line sweet Jesus
Tired of our earthly dwelling here
And hoping that our death frees us!

It was as if the building was coming apart as the room began to tremble. The boys thought there was an earthquake happening. Everyone was jumping and dancing and clapping. Sully and Lawrence thought maybe they were possessed. Everyone who was seated was stomping on the floor and the floorboards were moving up and down. The inhabitants seemed to care little if the entire place would crumble to pieces. The song finally ended in a big burst of applause and as it did the boys were greeted by a comely woman who was a little older and a size that suggested that she enjoyed a little too much of the brisket. But she was jovial and placed the full plates before the two men. The silver plates were full of brisket and sweet rolls. There was another plate full of butter to put on the rolls.

"Wow, what is this place?"

"I don't know. It's like paradise sprung up in the middle of nowhere."

After weeks on the road and seeing suffering throughout the South, it seemed so odd that there would be somewhere that hadn't been affected by the war. Or maybe they had been affected but they had now determined they would move on. Is that what Lawrence would have to do? He would have to settle for the resilient southern spirit but with the yoke of Union government.

The band continued to play into the wee hours of the night and the boys were surprisingly riled up by all the music and fun. They had experienced this from time to time in Atlanta at their various church functions, but this was something out of the ordinary. When dawn came the boys, somewhat exhausted, decided that they should keep on with their journey. The townsfolk all gave them a hardy goodbye and gave thanks for their service to the Confederacy. Both Sully and Lawrence pledged that they would return one day to thank them again for the hospitality.

As the boys began to walk down the dusty road, the red-haired fiddle-playing girl came running after them.

"Hey boys!!!" she shouted, causing the sleep-deprived men to turn with a jump.

"Say, I really want to thank you for your service to our country," she said, flashing her beautiful light green eyes. She was probably the most beautiful woman Sully had ever laid eyes on.

"No problem ma'am," Sully said, doffing his cap. She then planted a kiss on each man's cheek and then began to blush.

"By the way, in the barn over there they're having a meetin' if you're interested." She started to walk toward the barn and then waved for the men to follow her. Inside there was a group of men meeting. One of the men was at a makeshift podium and banging a gavel calling the meeting to order.

"Gentlemen, thank you for attending our first meeting of the Order of the Knights of the South. I want to thank Ben Bradley for the use of his barn and the ability to meet here weekly. I think we can all take heart for what happened a couple of days ago in Anderson. Our boys fought bravely and I know with a little organization we can continue the fight."

Sully and Lawrence looked around and saw mostly middle-aged men. There was no one younger than the mid to late thirties. Clearly, any of their young men were either dead or had no taste for war at that point.

"Anyway, if not all-out war, with our group we hope to grow and help with insurrection on a level that will make the Union troops go back home. We want to have a free South where we can make our own decisions."

All the men in the audience began to clap, except for Sully and Lawrence.

"With this new movement, we hope that we can enlist all the men of the county. We will be putting pressure on government entities and only voting for those government leaders that truly represent the southern man. We know it will be an uphill climb but we will do our best to put pressure on the powers that be to make sure our voices are heard in this new world we find ourselves in."

At that point, Sully and Lawrence tried to slip out unnoticed.

"Gentlemen, leaving so soon?"

"Ah, well we need to get going back home. We're from Atlanta."

"Okay, boys. Thank you for your service!"

The boys raised their caps and then soon departed. Sully and Lawrence began to discuss what they saw and heard and wondered if it were a new movement within the South. It seemed harmless and perhaps they would start their own chapter in Atlanta. Little did they realize there were several already brewing in many parts of the city.

Despite their lack of sleep, the boys seemed to be renewed in spirit knowing they were within days of being in Atlanta. They rested in Danielsville and early the next morning were in Athens, walking through the town and college campus which looked like a ghost town except for a few maintenance workers that were milling about, seeming to have no task in mind. Lawrence walked up to one of the workers and asked when the college might open again. The worker wasn't sure but asked his supervisor who told Lawrence that they were hoping to open again toward the beginning of the following year. This was of great interest to Lawrence because he was hoping to take classes at the university during the fall.

With the help of the supervisor, the boys were able to find shelter for the night at one of the temporarily abandoned dorm rooms on campus. They found a woman in town who would make them a hot meal for a nickel and were soon back on campus with some stew and plenty of bread. Lawrence found the campus very reassuring and hoped he would be a student there someday. He found one hallway that held various statutes and paintings of past teachers and faculty of the school. It wreaked of academia and he loved it. That night, while fast asleep, he began to dream of being in school, being challenged by teachers, and commiserating with fellow students in the great halls of learning. The dream soon turned into a nightmare however when the school seemed to explode into flame. Union troops seized the school and forced everyone to leave. There was one vocal officer who derided the students and he yelled and screamed at the top of his lungs. He seemed to be speaking for the North. The cry was that no one from the South would ever be allowed the opportunity for education again.

CHAPTER 8
A City Lay in Ruins

May 4th, 1865

The following day, the boys rose early and were able to reach the town of Monroe by early afternoon. The town was silent. There was a textile mill that was idle with no one doing any work. They could see inside the main building and the looms appeared abandoned. Monroe was a big producer of cotton and it now looked like it would be a while before the mill would be up and running.

At that point, the boys were so close to Atlanta that they decided they would just finish their journey. By mid-afternoon, they made it to Between.

"Huh, 'Between,'?"

"Yeah, it's halfway between Atlanta and Athens," Sully instructed Lawrence with pride.

"Looks like it should be called 'Nothing,'" Sully nodded his head and they began their final push in earnest. They grabbed a quick bite to eat at a small shack in Buncombe (present-day Loganville) and then continued to walk all night. The roads and scenery became more familiar which made the boys very eager to make it home as soon as possible. By dawn, they could see the outskirts of Atlanta and picked up the pace even quicker. As they neared the city they could see the ruins. Most buildings were destroyed. Telegraph poles and cable had been torn down with many of them laying across the road. They could see that much of the railway system was destroyed as well. It looked like a giant bomb had gone off in the center of the city.

As they neared the heart of town, there were Union soldiers everywhere. Many were directing traffic or telling locals to clear out the rubble. There were horse-drawn wagons moving piles of rock and wood debris. Seeing the destruction, the boys began to trot through the town which caused concern from some soldiers patrolling the city. They were cautioned to slow down several times. When they reached Sully's house he was relieved to see the mill and the associated tenement building still intact. He ran up the stairs of his apartment and pushed through the front door. His mother was sitting alone in the dark in a rocking chair knitting.

"Mama, it's me."

Sully's mom peered through the darkness, somewhat blinded by the light. Thick dust could be seen through the shaft of light that emanated through the open door. Much of the town was covered in it.

"Is that you my son?"

"Yes, mama." Sully ran over to her and clutched her. He buried his head in her arms and she began to shake, her whole body trembling.

"I thought I'd never see you again!" she practically yelled. Lawrence stood at the door watching the scene. His heart was warmed. It was the one good thing he had seen so far of Atlanta. As the reunion continued, Lawrence began to look down the street toward his home. He could see the post office that was near the house, but it looked like it had been destroyed. Was his home in the same shape?

"Good to see you Mrs. Sullivan, I best be off."

"Good to see you, Lawrence. Thanks for keeping my boy safe."

"Do you want me to go with you?" Sully asked.

"No, you take care of your mama. I'll see you soon," Lawrence said, doffing his cap to Sully and his mother. Both of the men exchange glances that indicated they would miss each other but were very glad that their ordeal was now over. Or was it?

As Lawrence began to walk down the street, he found it difficult to avoid the piles of rocks and stones, and other debris. *Surely the city would have been cleaned up by now?* He thought. As he walked near the post office he could see the roof had been shorn off and all the windows shattered with little of the glass left. He looked inside and could see water and burnt wood all along the floor. Clearly, things did not bode well for his home if the post office had been torn apart like that.

As Lawrence turned the corner he was shocked to find his home laying in complete desolation. It was a brick home but it seemed as if no brick had been left on top of the other. They were strewn throughout the lot, much as if a tornado had struck. As he walked through the remains, it was clear that his parents and sister were nowhere near. The only structure still standing was the chimney. As he looked at it he could see what looked like an envelope attached to the brick. He walked closer and could see it had been nailed into the mortar. He pulled it out and looked inside to find a letter…

Dear son, we hope and pray you are still alive. We have relocated to Irbyville up north. Please come as soon as you can.

Love from your family

Lawrence pondered journeying up to Irbyville. It was probably twenty miles. As he began to walk northward he could see several factories in the downtown area completely destroyed. They looked like they were smoldering still from the earlier destruction but it was probably swirling dust and debris. If he could imagine what hell was like this was it. The great industrial might of the South had been pushed to its knees. *Why had God allowed this?* he again asked himself. He tried to ignore the ruins but he imagined how many people must have lost their lives in the final battle for the city. His stomach churned and he began to look at the Union soldiers with hatred and contempt.

Lawrence trudged the twenty-mile journey to Irbyville and arrived in the late afternoon. It was a small town with a post office, a church, and a textile mill as well as a mix of small homes and cottages with the odd plantation or mansion here or there. As he walked down the street he inquired of an elderly woman if she had heard of the Ambrose family.

"Oh yes, Reverend Ambrose and his family live in the white house right next to the church. Fine man that reverend. He does a nice job each Sunday. Glad we were able to find such an experienced preacher."

Lawrence thanked the woman and headed toward the far end of the town where the church was. The church overlooked a river where further down the hill was the textile mill. As he arrived at the house he could see the mill was in full swing with much activity. There was a multitude of employees running to and from the buildings. It looked to be a very profitable enterprise given the current state of the country.

Lawrence walked up to the house and was impressed by its size. This was quite an improvement from their house in Atlanta. There was a tile pathway leading to the house with shrubs and bushes lining the front entryway. The house looked to be two stories with white paneling and a black roof with matching window shutters. As he neared the front door he could see that behind the shrubs was a nice patio with a table and chairs for anyone to relax on. It was quite the setting.

As Lawrence knocked on the door, it seemed to open almost immediately. There standing at the door was his baby sister Martha.

"Hey, kiddo! How are you?" Lawrence asked. Before he received an answer, Martha immediately bolted into his arms. Lawrence could feel her grip as she began to tremble. After several minutes he pulled her up and carried her inside. He put her down in the front entryway. The two looked at each other. Martha's eyes were wet with tears and as she tried to wipe them away only more came in their place.

"I missed you so much, Lawrence. We thought…we thought something happened to you."

"No, I'm here. I guess you never received the letters I sent?" Martha shook her head with a confused look.

"They might have gone to the other house but nothing came here."

"How long have you lived here?"

"About a year."

As Martha finished her sentence Lawrence's mother appeared at the kitchen doorway. She gasped and then ran as fast as she could to Lawrence. Her mother grabbed onto him and held him as tight as she could. She never wanted to let him go.

"My son, my son!!! We thought we had lost you!"

"No mama, thanks to God I survived."

No sooner had those words left his lips than his father appeared from around the corner. He had heard a commotion from his study.

"Lawrence?" he asked incredulously. He raised his bifocals up and then could see him more closely.

"Son, it is you?!!!" he cried and immediately ran over and embraced him. Soon the entire family was clasped together in a large embrace, with ever-tightening hands and arms grappling each other. Tears and laughter were all intermingled in the encounter.

"How did you survive all these months?" his father asked.

"God's good graces. Just the thought of coming home to mom's peach pie was enough to keep me going."

The still interlocked bodies somehow managed to make their way to the kitchen as one entity and finally disengaged for everyone to sit around the table.

"Did you see a lot of people get killed?" Martha asked.

"Unfortunately yes."

"Let's not talk of that now Martha. How about something to eat? I'm making my fried chicken with collards, mashed potatoes, and biscuits!"

"That sounds mighty fine mama! I think I've had my fill of squirrels and other rodents. It will be great to have one of your home-cooked meals again!"

The family sat in silence for a while with expressions of relief. The Reverend Ambrose, his wife, and his daughter all had silly grins on their faces. They weren't sure if they were seeing a ghost.

"How come you didn't write?" The Reverend Ambrose repeated Martha's question.

"I did. Martha thinks that maybe your change of address caused them to get lost. Speaking of your change of address, how did you come by this place?"

"God's providence…that and William Fuller."

"Who's William Fuller?"

"He's the owner of the textile mill."

"How is it that the mill is running?"

"Mr. Fuller had a mill in Atlanta but that was destroyed. He had been in the process of setting up one out here. After the Yankees came through and burned up everything he moved all his operations up here. He knew that I was looking for work and said I could preach at his new church."

"The Union is letting him run a factory up here?"

"Yes, apparently he knew some politicians which allowed him to get to know the local officers. I'm guessing there's a little palm greasing going on."

"Oh, I'm sure you can count on that."

"Well whatever it is, everyone within ten miles has employment and we have a brand new church!"

Lawrence smiled and hugged his father. A few minutes later his mother had placed before the family a feast. The family had been reunited and there was tremendous relief and happiness that their son had returned.

CHAPTER 9
Home Sweet Home?

June 1865

For the next several weeks, Lawrence got accustomed to his new home. He rested a lot, read, and caught up with his family on the latest news and gossip. After convalescing for a spell, Lawrence finally decided to reintroduce himself to society by attending church. He had watched from his bedroom window the previous two Sundays and noticed that it was an enthusiastic crowd that walked up to the church. While cajoling his son to attend his services, he didn't push Lawrence as he could see he was a little fractured spirit-wise.

Initially staying off the subject, his family finally asked Lawrence what the war had been like. Lawrence had avoided the topic as he was doing his best to bury the memories. But after his father pushed him to "get it off his chest," he finally relented.

"There was one battle where we were in a trench with mud and rain coming down. The Union had us trapped against a hillside. The captain of the battalion thought it better that we fight our way out than to just sit there. I had my doubts but he seemed sure of himself. We were under constant attack by their artillery. You could smell the gunpowder in your nose. It was an acrid horrible smell. There was smoke everywhere…death was everywhere.

We finally decided to make our way toward the southern flank where there was an opening in the lines. The captain then raised his sword and gave the signal to move. As we charged up the side of the trench, the bullets and cannon fire just got worse. It was like a wave or surge of hot air that just blew against us, like hurricane winds. I could hear cannonballs whizzing all around; one split a tree open right next to me with chards of wood splinters raining down on us. The sound was awful, like metal being bent or torn apart. We eventually had to fall back and as we did so, canon fire caught my friend Pete. I had just leaped what felt like thirty feet back into the trench and came splattering down into the mud and was then stuck. And as I sat there, Pete's head came flying over the edge of the trench and right into my lap. I had never had something so…so…" Lawrence began to tremble and his mother ran over to him and began to rub his head and shoulders.

"It then became somewhat of a blur. I remember screaming, not like the natural screaming that someone does when they are shocked by a large bear or someone surprises them, but this horrible screaming that has no sound. You just hear your head vibrating and your body vibrating in such a way that you think you are coming apart. The other men looked at me like 'what the hell are you doing with Pete's head?' I wanted to throw it as far away from me as possible, but I somehow managed to get up and I put it onto a blanket that had been spread over some other dead soldiers. The captain then came running down the trench to see what was all the commotion. My buddies just pointed out what I had done. The captain looked at me like I was crazed like I had decapitated Pete. He later realized what had happened and then tried to console me. While all this was happening, a regiment of Union troops had pushed toward our trench. We managed to return fire and force them back. I was completely numb and can't remember how I did anything. I remember shooting at a couple of Union soldiers coming up over the top of the trench. Luckily, the other Confederate battalion that was to the west of our position was able to push the Union forces back toward the north and we were able to escape the next morning."

With that story, Reverend Ambrose realized that his son needed time to recover. It would be a while before he would be ready to attend church or any other social gathering.

As nighttime fell, Lawrence walked toward a barn that was near the river. The barn was lit and there appeared to be something happening inside. As he walked near the barn door he could hear a man shouting. As he neared the entrance, he could see a Union officer barking orders to a group of soldiers. As he came closer he could see men lying on the floor of the barn in what appeared to be Confederate uniforms. They were lying face down with their hands behind their heads. The Union soldiers were standing around with their rifles poised.

"Fire!" the officer said and the soldiers began to shoot the helpless men on the floor. There seemed to be no end to the shooting and blood was everywhere.

"That ought to teach these rebel pigs!!!" the officer shouted. Lawrence, being completely numb from what he was seeing, somehow retrieved his nerve and ran inside the barn.

"Stop, stop!!!" he cried. The officer turned to look at him. His face became blurry and soon seemed to morph into an image of a skull. A skull with eyes moving around inside of it.

"Ah, another lousy reb. Kill 'em boys!"

As the men raised their rifles toward Lawrence, his feet felt like they had been cemented into the floor. He tried to turn to run but couldn't. As soon as the men shot at him he awoke with a horrible scream that caused his parents to come running to his room.

"Dear what is it!!!?" his mother asked trying to calm him down. Lawrence was trembling and in a cold sweat. He was completely out of breath and he thought his heart would explode. The Reverend Ambrose could see his son would need time before he could do anything productive. He hoped that being able to go to school might help him restore peace to his mind.

After his mother brought him a cold cup of water, Lawrence seemed to calm down and was able to later get to sleep. Eventually, he was able to sleep soundly. After he had come back home, the peace and quiet had started to bring back memories of the war. During his journey from Virginia back to Atlanta, the ongoing anxiety of the trip had seemed to block out the horrible past. Now that he was home, the past seemed to come roaring back to life.

The following morning, Lawrence arose late. Although lunchtime, his mother made him bacon and eggs. He came down a little disheveled but a bit more upbeat than he had been.

"Doing okay dear?"

"Yes, mama. Sorry about last night. Had a bit of a nightmare."

"Not to worry. With everything you've been through it's no wonder you don't have more of them."

Lawrence was a little concerned that there might be more on the way. He decided that the best thing was to go to work to get his mind off the past. After breakfast, he headed out to the barn and began to chop wood. It seemed to do the trick with the exception that he became a little weary of the barn and what might be in it. He forced himself to go in and he realized that there was nothing to fear. He continued his work until the late afternoon when his father appeared.

"Hello son, would you mind if Mr. Fuller came over for dinner tonight?"

Lawrence stared at his father in silence, seeming not to comprehend what he was saying.

"Mr. Fuller is our main benefactor and we typically invite him for dinner every other week or so."

"No that's fine pa…it's fine."

"Why don't you rest now. Get yourself a bath and get some clean clothes on."

Lawrence nodded and looked at his father with a worn smile. The Reverend Ambrose put his arm around his shoulder. Lawrence never remembered his father doing that before. Not that Reverend Ambrose was unemotional, but he did have a tight rein on his feelings, typically not letting things get to him or exposing his true thoughts. After all, it wasn't becoming of a preacher to let his feelings get the best of him.

Wilberforce Edward Fuller was a large man. When he laughed, whatever building he was in it would seem to shake. He was the ideal southern gentleman and he knew how to get things done. He knew everyone that one needed to know to get what he wanted. Everyone called him "W.E." which most thought was his way of getting people to think that he was all about the people, all about "we," but what he really wanted was for people to think about "W.E." He typically wore a large brim white fedora style hat that covered his mostly bald head. He had enough hair on the side to comb it over, but it was clear that he was devoid of natural head covering. He always wore overalls and was typically dressed in a tan-colored suit with a western-style tie at the collar. His appearance would often conjure up the image of a Mississippi riverboat gambler. He had a gruff exterior and unusually oily skin. His cheeks were often red and ruddy and his overall countenance was a mixture of Fallstaff and Father Christmas. To say people were intimidated by him was an understatement. While some of his business practices were suspect, he attended church faithfully every Sunday and was the biggest contributor to the Irbyville Baptist Church. He in fact was the one who had built the church at his expense. He expected everyone who worked for him to attend church every Sunday. Most did willingly, but others began to resent the command.

When the Fullers arrived that evening, the Ambrose family greeted the Fullers; William, Margaret his wife, and four daughters, as if the King of England had arrived. The Reverend Ambrose and his wife spared no expense to make sure the Fullers were comfortable. Lawrence began to look around for the red carpet.

When Lawrence was introduced to Fuller, he was greeted with a bear hug. When finally released Lawrence thought he might be permanently paralyzed.

"Welcome home my boy. I want to thank you for your service to your country."

Lawrence began to think of which country he was referring to. The North, the South, the Union, the Confederacy?

"We hope things will get back to normal soon, especially for our boys who fought so hard. But now we need to think about the future. Let's forget about the past and move forward, eh?"

Lawrence nodded and followed his father's motion to sit down.

"Your father tells me you're are going to follow in his footsteps and become a preacher?"

"Yes sir, that's the plan."

"You'll be attending school in the fall I take it?"

"Yes sir. I will be going to Franklin College."

"Ah yes, on the University of Georgia campus. That's a fine school. I just want to let you know that I have told your father that I will happily pay for your education."

Lawrence, sipping on a glass of water, almost choked when he heard the news...

"Well, that is mighty kind of you, Mr. Fuller." As he said this he noticed his daughter Sarah just to the right of him. Sarah was eighteen and a very pretty girl. She was smiling at Lawrence with a little twinkle in her eye that signaled that she was looking for a potential mate. For Lawrence that was far off in his mind. He could barely absorb what was happening with his career. As he had journeyed from Virginian to Atlanta, his mind had been more focused on how he would function in a Northern-run world and even how he might instigate a possible rebellion. In what shape or form that rebellion would take he had no idea. His mind would wander from time to time about having a career, having a wife, having a home and family, but he thought those things to be a long way off in the future. Now all of sudden those aspirations seemed to be right in front of him.

The rest of the evening went fairly well. Fuller droned on about the new South and shoveled out a plethora of platitudes, basically stating that he would be responsible for the "New Atlanta." For Lawrence, what Fuller said was the least of his concerns. He was focused on getting his head right and getting ready for his career.

As the summer went by, Lawrence recuperated by helping around the house, fixing windows, fixing the barn, digging a new well, and planting new trees at the back of the property toward the river. Lawrence took great joy in gardening; it was creating life rather than destroying it. He also began to help restore the local library that had been destroyed during the war. He had gone through the town asking the wealthier neighbors (wealthier being a relative term since most were now destitute), to donate books. He would also use the library to start helping him to prepare for college that fall. Besides the occasional trip into Atlanta to stop by and see Sully, Lawrence made sure to keep himself busy.

On one of his trips to Atlanta, he stopped for supplies at one of the major general stores that the Union had helped open back up to the public. While there was a general store in Irbyville, the general store and market in downtown had almost everything one could possibly need. When he had finished his shopping he began to walk down the street to his horse-drawn cart, happily donated by W.E Fuller, when he spotted a black man that looked familiar. He was across the street on a ladder fixing a sign. If he didn't know better it was the soldier from Appomattox who had embarrassed him in front of the other soldiers when they had surrendered their weapons. It was a face he would soon like to forget, but could he? Thoughts of revenge began to fill his head, but this wasn't the place or time for such a thing. And even if he had found a place or a time, what would he do? Was this not a time to heal? A time when he needed to think about becoming a minister? Honorable people like pastors and ministers didn't seek revenge, did they?

CHAPTER 10
Spiritual Renewal

September 1865

That fall, Lawrence began his classes at Franklin College. It took him just over an hour via horseback to get to the school. There were not too many students and there had been multiple rumors that they might have to cancel that semester, but Professor Thompson, who would be his advisor told Lawrence "not to worry," and that it would all work out.

Reginald Willard Thompson had been a dean at Franklin College for the last ten years. He had been a chairman for the Southern Baptist Convention. The denomination was in a lot of turmoil at the moment as it tried to reconcile the results of the war, abolition, and how races would be integrated into religious faith. While there were no negros at Franklin, as it was not permitted, the professor was keenly aware that his students would want to know how they would deal with the "New South," and how they would interact with the former slaves.

For the first few months of the so-called "Reconstruction" period, things were quiet. The Union presence in Atlanta and other Georgia towns and cities kept things moderately peaceful. Deep down however something well below the surface was beginning to brew. For many northern politicians, the key would be to assimilate southern men into northern life as soon as possible. Recruiting ex-rebels to the armed forces, police, fire brigades and other civil and municipal works would be a priority. For the average Union soldier, it had been a long war and they wanted to get home as soon as possible.

Whether the Confederates wanted to assimilate was of little interest to them.

For Lawrence, the Union presence seemed to be everywhere. There was a garrison in Irbyville and there were troops stationed on the main campus of the university. They were using many of the buildings as barracks. As best as he could he tried to get used to it. The only thing that seemed to help was his faith in God. It was a faith that had laid dormant for the past four years. It was a faith that was almost non-existent on his journey from Virginia to Atlanta. But now, being back home, he would reach out to God again. Professor Thompson, not only an academic, he was a profoundly spiritual man as well. Lawrence looked forward to many deep conversations with him about theology and life. Professor Thompson was in his late sixties and it was clear there was much to learn from him.

There are those times in life when you least expect it when you encounter and reencounter your spiritual side. One afternoon while waiting for class, Lawrence sat in the chapel of Franklin College. He could see through the windows that the wind was blowing crisply through the trees and he began to imagine the scene on the Day of Pentecost. Were there really flames that appeared on the disciple's heads? Was there really something called the Holy Spirit? If there was he hadn't been around Irbyville lately. As Lawrence labored and labored to increase his faith, he began to think that he would just have to give up and submit to God. He looked around and noted there was no one else in the chapel, he walked up to the altar and got on his knees.

"Lord, I know you must be there. Sometimes it is so hard to see you but I know in my heart you must be there. I guess after everything that has happened to me over the past couple of years I have lost...to some extent, my faith. Please help me to believe Lord. Help me to believe like that little child I was that never doubted for a minute in your existence. But now, with all the death and evil I've seen, I have lost that childlike faith. Please help me O God!"

For the next several minutes, it felt like God had reached down and touched him. Not in a calming manner, but like His hand had reached down through him, grabbing his heart. There was a burning sensation in him, a renewal and tears began to flow down his cheeks. He quickly regained his composure and got to his feet. He began to look around to see if anyone had entered the chapel. He didn't know if what he had just felt was real, but he smiled and thanked God for the reassurance. He quickly left for class.

The following Saturday, Lawrence rose early and began his chores. He scoured the property for broken tree branches that he could chop for firewood. It was a warm day so he took his shirt off as he began to chop wood. While lost in his own world, he was suddenly aware that someone was observing him. He turned around and could see Sarah Fuller.

"Sarah, what are you doing here?"

"Oh, my dad had some business at the mill so I came along with him."

Sarah was a beautiful girl. She had dark brown hair with deep blue eyes. She wore her long hair in a braid. She was not a "Southern Belle" per se, preferring to help with a lot of the chores around the house. Given the now lack of slave labor, it was mandatory. It was good for her though and she had a faint suntan that gave her a robust look to her face. Almost a bronze look that for Lawrence gave the appearance of something resembling a goddess.

"I wanted to see how your studies were going?"

"Ah well…I am enjoying my classes and think that it will be a good course of study for me."

"So, a career as a preacher then?"

"That's what my father wants."

"What do you want?"

"Well, it's hard to say. I want to grow closer to God but I don't know if I will be any good at preachin'."

"I think you'll be great."

"How do you know? You've never heard me speak…at least in public."

She smiled a coy smile and began to play with her white dress. Her dress was flowing in the breeze and he began to feel something inside. He started to feel a little nervous. He had thought about one day being married but those thoughts had been fleeting. Was this the girl the Lord wanted him to marry?

"I can tell you're a good talker."

"'Good talker' eh? Well, that's good enough for me. How 'bout you, what do you want to do with your life?"

"Well, daddy just wants me to find a man, settle down and have children."

"Is that what you want?"

"I don't know. I thought that I would like to teach."

"Why don't you?"

"I'm thinking about it. Trying to convince my father is the thing. Plus now he's paying for your tuition, I'd hate to ask him to pay mine."

"He seems pretty wealthy, couldn't he afford it?"

"I suppose. We'll see. I'm just waiting for the right moment."

"Sarah! Time to get back home!" Mr. Fuller could be seen on the other end of the property shouting out to Sarah.

"I got to get goin'. Good talkin' to you Lawrence."

"Likewise," Lawrence doffed his cap to Sarah and gave a slight bow. She smiled a bright smile, her cheeks seeming to blush. Lawrence watched as she walked toward the other end of the property. W.E. waved to him and he responded back in kind. He wondered what it would be like to have Mr. Fuller as a father-in-law. The family was already indebted to him, how would it be if he eventually became his son-in-law?

As Lawrence continued into the afternoon working around the house, he received another guest; it was Sully. They embraced and held each other tight, recalling their ordeal.

"Sully, what brings you all the way up here?"

"Lawrence, I hate to ask you but my mama and me are looking for a new place to live."

"What happened. I thought you were set up at the mill down there?"

"I was, but now they are needing fewer people and so next month I will be out of a job. Do you think you could get me a job up here?"

"I'll check with Mr. Fuller."

Sully was very appreciative of whatever Lawrence could do. He helped Lawrence around the yard for a couple of hours before he had to head back to Atlanta. As he left, Lawrence felt great pity for Sully and the rest of the folks in Atlanta. It would be a while before there would be plenty of jobs available.

The next day, Lawrence attended Sunday services. He had started going back in July but had felt a little uncomfortable, especially when his father had introduced him to the entire congregation. He received a standing ovation for his service during the war and he was embarrassed by all of the attention. He guessed if he was going to be a preacher he had to get used to it. The one thing that seemed to get him through it was the beaming face of Sarah in the front pew with her father and the entire family. He didn't really notice anyone else, just her.

"These continue to be difficult times," his father's sermon began.

"Changes are coming that I don't know how we will be able to manage…but God will help us through it. We will meet people we never thought we would meet before and we have to be ready for that. The Lord said that the gospel would be a light unto the Gentiles. He warned His people the Jews that they could not rely on the law. As it says in the book of Romans chapter two, verses 28 and 29, 'For he is not a Jew who is one outwardly; neither is circumcision that which is outward in the flesh. But he is a Jew who is one inwardly; and circumcision is that which is of the heart, by the Spirit, not by the letter, and his praise is not from men, but from God.'

"My brothers and sisters, we need to be on the lookout for who is a real child of God. There will be false prophets and evildoers that will come in many different forms, many different races or different religions. We must protect ourselves. We must band together and fight this evil. I thank Mr. Fuller for creating this wonderful town, this wonderful church, this wonderful community where we can be free of the world's evils. I urge each and every one of you to watch out for each other. Let's make sure we do not let any evil come to our beautiful community."

A loud "amen" came from the corpulent Mr. Fuller who was fanning himself from the heat. Everyone soon joined in with the amens not wanting to look out of place, and definitely not wanting to look like they didn't support the Reverend Ambrose and Mr. Fuller. Lawrence however was not necessarily of the same accord. He had wanted the South to be separate but he was now cautious of thoughts of segregation. Was segregation the way to heal all the wounds of the past? Maybe that wasn't even the message that his father was preaching. He knew his father well, however, and he knew what the underlying message was. Whatever his point, he consoled himself that he would see Sarah that night at the family dinner.

After dinner that evening, Lawrence slipped out into the back patio and started walking in the nearby field to get some fresh air. He hadn't realized it but Sarah had been following him.

"Beautiful night isn't it?" Sarah said, causing Lawrence to jump out of his skin.

"Why Mr. Ambrose, did little ole me frighten you?"

"Why of course not Miss Sarah," Lawrence said, catching his breath, rolling his eyes, and giving her a rebuking smile.

"Trying to get away from my father I see?"

"No…yes. He tends to get on my nerves. I appreciate what he's done for this town but he sure does let everyone know it."

"Yeah, it's part of the curse if you want to live in Irbyville. The mill pays well but you have to pledge your eternal allegiance to the great W.E. Fuller."

"How did you grow up under such a man?"

"Despite everything you see, he has been very good to my mother, my sisters, and me. He has always taken care of us, provided for us."

"Is material wealth enough?"

"He's different with us…" Sarah said as she navigated herself around a peach tree branch. They continued to walk in the cool, now somewhat damp evening air.

"I remember him as warm and gentle, especially when I was little. He often came and read to us girls. He would sit on a large rocking chair in our room, some of us would climb on his lap. He is so large, almost all of us girls could sit on his lap when we were younger. He would read us all kinds of stories and he would do all these funny voices and sounds, it was great fun. He always made time for us, taking us to holiday events or apple picking…by the way I wanted to ask you something."

"Yeah?"

"Would you escort me to the apple orchard tomorrow for the apple picking?"

"Uh, sure, why not."

"I'll pack us a picnic basket and we can talk further."

With that Sarah turned and walked back toward the house. Lawrence was starting to have feelings for Sarah. While young, she was mature and confident. She knew what she wanted. Was it him? He was beginning to hope so.

The next day, Lawrence called upon Sarah at 12:30 p.m. Lester Milton was going to have his apple orchard open at 1 p.m. for all of Irbyville to come and pick apples. It was an annual event that almost everyone in town turned up for.

Sarah as always looked her beautiful self, wearing a yellow summer dress and matching parasol. Lawrence managed to find a nice jacket and trousers that were hidden way back in his closet. The fit was a little tight but he still looked presentable.

Lester Milton and generations of Milton's operated apple orchards near Irbyville for over a century. Lester, while not dependent upon W.E.'s good graces, still liked to keep in his favor for no business in Irbyville did well without W.E.'s endorsement. And so, once a year, at W.E.'s behest, Lester would open his orchard up to the public. It was a goodwill gesture that he learned paid dividends. People from other counties would come and get the delicious "Milton Apples." For W.E., it was just another avenue to which he could throw his weight around and create publicity for his altruism.

As the apple picking began, Lester lined up multiple horse-drawn carts that people would jump into the back of and sit. Lester provided burlap bags for each person. Once they reached various parts of the orchard, the cart would stop and there would be a free for all with people running through the orchard laughing and screaming as they picked apples. For Lawrence and Sarah, they were content helping children get their fair share. Lawrence would often pick up the littlest of the children and help them reach high up into the tree to pick their choice of apples. Sarah liked how Lawrence would at first get on the child's level and speak to them directly. It was one of the many ways in which Sarah learned about the character of Lawrence.

Later as the day progressed, Sarah suggested to Lawrence that they have their picnic lunch. Lawrence was more than ready for lunch after all the picking he had done, mostly of course for the children. The couple found a solitary spot on a small hill that overlooked the orchard. Lawrence laid out a large blanket and Sarah began to pull out various dishes she had made from the basket. She was quick to point out that she had done all of the cooking. It was a feast for the eyes; fried chicken, potato salad, boiled eggs, pickles, green bean salad, fresh milk, and peach pie. Lawrence's mouth began to water. As he grabbed a chicken leg, Sarah was quick to slap his hand.

"Why Mr. Ambrose! I thought you were studying to be a pastor? Also, I thought you a gentleman?"

"Oh, yes, please forgive me." Lawrence took off his hat and then bowed his head.

"Bless us Oh Lord and these thy gifts that come from your bounty, through Christ our Lord, Amen."

"Amen," Sarah said emphatically, then smiling a little smile that Lawrence took to mean that he had been forgiven.

"Wow, Sarah, this chicken is delicious."

"I should say so. I was up cooking all last night," she said with a coy smile that let him know that it was not true.

"Well, however long it took you and whenever you did it, I very much appreciate it."

"You are quite welcome."

As the couple ate their meal, they could feel a nice breeze that had originated over another nearby hill. It caused the apple trees to lightly shake and then came up their hill like a torrent, sending both of their hats into the air. They both laughed with glee and Lawrence quickly got up, running around in a frenzy trying to retrieve the errant headwear.

As they began to dig into the peach pie, they looked at each other with an expression of contentment.

"What are you thinking about Mr. Ambrose?"

"Well, Miss Sarah, how at one time I was running for my life during the war and now here I am having this great meal, on this beautiful day with one of the prettiest girls I've ever met."

"Why Mr. Ambrose, that is awfully forward of you," she said comically batting her eyes.

"Well, I can only speak the truth ma'am."

"Well if that is the case, I will need to put that to the test."

"I welcome it."

Sarah smiled and accepted the challenge. With a wrinkled nose, she began to think up some questions for the truthful soul. She then began…

"What is the worse grade you received in school?"

"C-. That was my first year of algebra. I was a little distracted by Becky Sanders that year."

"Ok, let's see. Oh, have you ever kissed a girl before?"

"Yes, my mother!" Lawrence smiled a coy smile and then they both burst out into laughter. Sarah began to think of some way she could trap him into divulging something juicy.

"Did your parents ever spank you?"

"Oh Lord yes. I used to get into all kinds of mischief when I was younger."

"What was the worst?"

"Oh, let's see. It probably was when I threw a rock through Old Man Lemmon's back porch window. Man, I got a whoopin' for that!"

Sarah laughed and then sat back admiring the view. Lawrence began to study her expression and then a bright smile developed on his face.

"And now it's my turn. What do you really think of me, Miss Sarah?"

Sarah began to think and smile. She would pretend to think of something and then shake her head. She would then do the same but this time nod. She smiled and then confided.

"I think you are a responsible, mature young man. Based on what you tell me you also are respectful of women."

"Oh, how so?"

"Well, you encouraged me to go to college. That means you respect me."

"Of course I do."

"And you think I am your equal."

"Without a doubt."

"Well then. I'm beginning to think you are mentally handicapped!"

Lawrence was taken aback. He studied her face and could not tell if she was joking or not.

"Why do you say that Miss Sarah?"

"Well, given that every man in the South thinks men are superior to women, I would have to think you are plum crazy," she said then starting to laugh. Lawrence began to laugh and started to lean toward her, thinking he would kiss her. When Sarah realized what he was doing she became serious and began to purse her lips.

"Oh, this is where you two got to!" Elizabeth, Sarah's younger sister yelled as the couple was about to kiss.

"I hope I didn't interrupt anything?" Elizabeth said with a sly smile. Both Sarah and Lawrence rolled their eyes and laughed. Elizabeth as usual had thwarted her older sister's plans.

For the rest of the day, Lawrence looked for opportunities where he could be alone with Sarah but unfortunately, none were coming.

After ignoring the professor's requests for a month, Lawrence finally gave in and decided to go into Atlanta one Saturday morning. Professor Thompson wanted Lawrence to apply what Christ was teaching him at Franklin by helping the poor of Atlanta. He liked his students to help with the "AMA," the American Missionary Association, and help them with their efforts to support the needy. When he arrived he was met by Walter Fanning who was in charge of the local branch of the mission. Mr. Fanning had a northern accent so was immediately suspect by Lawrence. He was white though and so he took his instruction. Most of the people in the main office were negro so he was somewhat relieved that Mr. Fanning was there. His relief soon turned to horror however when Mr. Fanning introduced him to a young negro woman.

"Lawrence, this is Callie. Callie this is Lawrence. Callie, can you help Mr. Ambrose to set up for the food hand-out?"

"Yessir Mista Fanning. Mr. Lawrence, right this way if you don't mind," the young, attractive girl who looked to be in her early twenties, motioned for him to follow her to the back storage room where the food supplies were kept. She explained that there was a food handout every Saturday at 1 pm to give out bags of rice and corn and other dry goods. The poor of Atlanta, which was a good portion of the population would line up early that morning to get a place in line for the handout. Callie asked Lawrence for help with taking grain out of a large barrel and placing it into burlap bags. While a bit tedious, Lawrence found the work somewhat uplifting. He could see just outside of the main door the line of people, their faces anxious for the hand-out to begin. Maybe this was true religion versus what he was studying? After all, Jesus wasn't an academic but a servant.

"Miss Callie, ya ready for me?!!!" came the loud gruff voice of a tall black man coming in from the nearby backdoor. He stood against the bright light so his features were not visible, but his voice was unmistakable. It was the negro soldier from Appomattox who had embarrassed Lawrence. Lawrence dropped his scooper back into the barrel. He trembled slightly with anger, at the man's appearance.

"Mr. Lawrence, this is Thaddeus Brown or 'Thad' for short."

"Mighty nice to meet you, Lawrence," Thaddeus held out his hand for Lawrence to shake. There was an uncomfortable interval between the time that Thaddeus offered his hand to the point where Lawrence eventually shook it. Thaddeus, not recognizing who Lawrence was, just grinned a large grin. While this grin was a grin for the sake of pleasantries, for Lawrence, it was the same grin of rebuke and humiliation that Thaddeus had given him at Appomattox. Thaddeus quickly got onto his task which was to take the burlap bags that Lawrence had filled and put them into a large wagon that was out on the street. It was there that he would be dispensing the goods to the people.

After recovering from his initial shock, Lawrence regained his composure and started work again on the bags. For the rest of the afternoon, he kept his head down on the barrel, praying for humility and the ability to not seek revenge. It would be hard, however, but he soldiered on.

Near the end of the day, Callie had instructed most of the workers to go home save herself, Lawrence, and Thaddeus. There were only two people left in line, both were elderly. Callie handed a bag to an older black gentleman who was beaming from ear to ear to receive his bag of grain. He slowly shuffled off down the street. The last person was a quite elderly white woman who had a cane. There appeared to be no means for her to take even a small bag of gain. As she approached the stall, she stumbled forward. Callie quickly reached out and grabbed onto her before she took a tumble to the ground. The woman turned to look at Callie, and with her withered and lined face, broke out into a deep smile.

"Are you okay ma'am?"

"Yes dear, thank you."

"Are you close by ma'am?"

"No, I'm afraid I'm all the way down the other end of Peach Street."

"Okay, let me help you, ma'am."

Callie grabbed a small wheel barrel, put a large sack of grain into it, and began to push it down the street with the old woman in tow.

"That's our Callie for you," Thaddeus said smiling as he watched her go down the street.

"Yes, that was very nice…"

"Given everything she's been through I would say she is a saint," Walter Fanning said as he joined the conversation.

"Lawrence, can you help me bring the cart up onto the loading dock?"

"Certainly."

As the two men walked down to the cart, Mr. Fanning explained what had happened to Callie.

"Callie grew up on a plantation near Macon. Her master was Miles Van Guilder. He was a cruel man. Five slaves died under his care or lack thereof. When Callie got into her teens, Van Guilder tried to rape her. She tried to escape. She got away for a day or two, but Van Guilder tracked her down. When he caught her he treated her horribly. He left her in a smoke shed for days, often beating her. If it hadn't been for the end of the war, she would have died. And yet, she is the most loving, forgiving soul I have ever met. How could anyone be treated in such a way and still love? I know I couldn't."

After wheeling the cart back onto the loading dock, Lawrence turned to see Callie coming back up the street. A welling up of warmth seemed to fill his soul. He thought that God was about to open the heavens and speak to him. It was like St. Paul being knocked from his horse to the ground. But instead of a booming voice from above, it was the small figure of a former slave girl who was making his soul tremble. Feeling somewhat tongue-tied, Lawrence tried to speak.

"Thank you, Callie. Thank you for letting me help you today."

"No, thank you, Mr. Lawrence. And you are welcome any time here at the mission."

She smiled an angelic smile, patted him on the shoulder, and then headed back inside. Lawrence thanked Mr. Fanning for the opportunity and bid him goodbye. With his renewed sense of faith, he began to look around for Thaddeus to say goodbye but could not locate him. He untied his horse and started to head up the main street toward home. He began to think about what had just happened. Was it an epiphany, a vision? Whatever it was it left him chocked up with a stream of tears running down his cheeks. He then began to laugh with pure joy. It was like some sort of burden had been lifted from his shoulders. It was like a sickness in his soul had been removed. He had been healed, even liberated.

That night, after dinner was completed, Lawrence, having had to endure the endless platitudes of Mr. Fuller, asked Sarah to join him on the front porch swing. Her siblings would giggle whenever she was alone with Lawrence.

"Beautiful night tonight," Sarah said staring up at the night sky.

"Yes, it's incredible. I don't think I have seen so many stars."

"By the way, I talked to my father about becoming a teacher and he has relented."

"Wow, that's fantastic!"

"I'm late for this semester but pa said I could start in the Spring."

"That's great. Which school?"

"Well, there's really only one open to women it's the Georgia Female College, down in Macon."

"Macon. So you would obviously have to move down there?"

"Yes, there are dormitories. I would have to live there full-time," Sarah looked at Lawrence with a coy look as if to see what type of reaction would come.

"Hmmm...well you have to do it. It's a great opportunity."

"Yes."

"You may not get another chance like this again."

"Yes."

"You can't..." before Lawrence could say another word, Sarah planted a kiss on his lips. He pulled back slightly and began to look into her eyes. They both smiled simultaneously and began to kiss again. Lawrence, somewhat concerned about Mr. Fuller's location, began to look through the front porch window. Sarah could see he was a little distracted and began to scold him while the kiss continued.

"What are you doing?" she said in a mumbled rebuke.

"Looking for your father." Lawrence pulled back slightly. "Do you think he will approve of this relationship?"

"And what relationship is that pray tell Mr. Ambrose?"

Lawrence laughed at Sarah's sly attempt at entrapment. He began to study her face and smiled broadly.

"Why of engagement Miss Fuller."

"So your intentions are honorable then?"

"Oh yes, ma'am. I have nothing but the deepest respect for you and your family."

Sarah smiled and pulled him by the collar closer to him and they began to kiss again. This time with a little more passion. Lawrence resigned himself to the fact that if Sarah was fine with the relationship then Mr. Fuller would be. Before they could continue, the very man in question came barreling onto the porch.

"There you two are!"

The two immediately went back to their original positions which was a polite two feet apart. Mr. Fuller eyed the pair up and down and suspected that there had been some light petting occurring. Although being a little suspect of his politics, W.E. had come to respect Lawrence. While five years older than his daughter, he found him a deeply thoughtful and considerate young man. Someone he wouldn't mind having as a son-in-law.

"Ah, Mr. Fuller. May I speak with you in private please?"

"Why certainly my boy."

Lawrence motioned for him to join him on the front lawn, somewhat outside of earshot of the curious Miss Sarah.

"Sir, I have come to respect your daughter quite a bit and as I enter the clergy, I would like a woman as bright and strong as your daughter to help me on this journey…" W.E. stared at Lawrence with a blank face while Sarah, on the edge of the swing was about to fall off trying to hear what was being said.

"...anyway, I would like to ask you for her hand in marriage. There would of course be a sensible time period for the engagement." W.E. looked Lawrence up and down as if to inspect him. A lump grew in Lawrence's throat and his heart began to race. W.E.'s brow became knitted and he began to squint at Lawrence like he was looking at him through a microscope. He then all of sudden began to burst out into laughter.

"Of course my boy, of course. You have my consent. Now have you actually asked your intended?"

"No sir. I wanted to get your permission first."

"Well done, well done my boy. You have my permission." W.E. then retreated back into the house, doffing his hat and giving a wink to his daughter as he went through the front door. Lawrence looked at Sarah from the front lawn and smiled. She was wearing a yellow dress and as usual, had her hair in a long braid with a large yellow ribbon. She was also wearing a white locket around her neck that was given to her by her grandmother. The white locket set nicely against her lightly tanned skin. He gave her a coy smile, pretending not to know what was on her mind. He beckoned her to come over to him but she shook her head and beckoned him to join her on the swing. He smiled knowing that this girl had a mind of her own and that she would be no one's servant. Lawrence liked that and never imagined being with a woman who felt differently. He assuaged to her request and immediately came up to the porch and got on one knee, grabbing her hand.

"Miss Fuller, I would like to extend to you an offer of marriage if you would be so amiable."

"Why Mr. Ambrose, I think that would be agreeable."

Lawrence smiled at Sarah's control of her emotions. She was probably the most down-to-earth and practical girl he had ever met. With her agreement he kissed her hand and then rose up onto the swing, pulling her into him. She broke out into laughter and the two began to kiss. After several minutes of embrace, the two ran back into the house and made their joint announcement of their pending nuptials to the rest of the family. Everyone in the house was pleased with the news and they looked forward to the wedding which was planned for the following summer.

With the announced engagement, Lawrence had a new lease on life. His faith in God and Man had been renewed and for the first time in a long time, he felt positive and productive. His studies at Franklin College were going well and his professor was pleased with his study habits and progress. In an effort for Lawrence to receive a practical application of what he was learning, Professor Thompson encouraged him to continue going to Atlanta once a week to help the American Missionary Association with some of their work. Lawrence was more than agreeable to the idea, having had his mind truly opened for the first time by Ms. Callie.

CHAPTER 11
"Rise of a New South!"

April 1866

Lawrence smiled as he looked at the calendar. It was a year to the day when the war had ended and he and Sully had begun their epic journey from Appomattox to Atlanta. It seemed like it was just yesterday, but in other ways, it seemed like a century ago. So much had happened. After all, he had been through, God had pulled him through. Not only saving him from a stray bullet, but bringing him all the way home and now studying at one of the best schools he could ever imagine attending. He was betrothed to a beautiful girl and he had a renewed energy to become the best pastor he could possibly be.

It was on a cool Sunday morning when Lawrence felt ready to give his first sermon. It was a packed congregation and his father, mother, and sister sat beaming in the front pew. The entire Fuller family was also present with Sarah practically gushing she was so proud. He just hoped he could live up to their expectations. In many ways, he had come to a point where he didn't care what their expectations were. The only thing that truly mattered was God. And where was God? For Lawrence, he had felt His presence ever since the meeting with Callie several months earlier. He had continued to go down to the mission one Saturday a month, and it had helped him to see God was at work in the lives of all people. He had gone from the confused, disillusioned rebel soldier to a more settled, more open, more believing Christian soldier. It was appropriate that the choirmaster had in fact chosen "Onward Christian Soldier" as the opening hymn that morning.

After the opening hymn and prayer, one of the church deacons motioned for Lawrence to head to the pulpit. Lawrence took his Bible in hand and approached cautiously as if he had been ushered into the "Holy of Holies."

"Good morning everyone. I hope y'all had a great work week and a fine Saturday." There were various nods and mumbles of agreement throughout the congregation. The church was quite a large building. There was the main floor where over three hundred people could be seated. There was a balcony above the front entrance where another one hundred could sit. On either side of the main floor, there were large glass-stained windows with depictions of various biblical events. All in all, it was a triumph for Mr. Fuller. There were various plaques, signage, and artifacts that bore the Fuller name. Everyone in Irbyville and the surrounding areas knew who had built the church. After all, it was he who provided the area's main source of income. While Lawrence often felt he should be intimidated by W.E.'s wealth, influence, and renown, he somehow wasn't. As he grew in his ministry and thus closer to God, he knew exactly whom he served, and it wasn't Mr. Fuller. If only everyone else felt the same way he thought.

"I want to speak to you today on the Apostle Paul and specifically his conversion. We read in chapter nine of the book of Acts about the conversion of Saul of Tarsus. Prior to this, we get a picture of who Saul was. He was a zealot for Judaism. He saw Christianity as a threat to Judaism. It was a threat to all that he had believed in. Having been raised as a good Jew, he would have abided by the commandments. He would have faithfully attended the synagogue. He would have obeyed every precept of what was taught in the temples. He was in short, a devout man.

"What we've learned about Saul is that his mind, his heart, his whole being was striving for God. And when he saw a threat to his entire way of life, he with complete passion went after the threat. He didn't do it half-heartedly, he did it with all his being. He went to the council in Damascus asking for letters to bind any man or woman who professed the name of Jesus Christ. These "letters" were actually arrest warrants from the high priest. Saul was basically the new sheriff in town. He was going to bring all of the outlaws and bad guys to justice. He truly believed he was doing the work of God.

"Saul believed with all of his heart that he was doing the right thing. He believed in Israel. He believed in the Levitical structure with the priests and the Sanhedrin. He believed in his country and its twelve tribes. And what might have driven him to such lengths? Clearly, the Roman occupation would have had some influence on him. The great Roman Empire was a threat to everything he knew. While he couldn't control the Roman threat, he was going to do everything possible to control the Christian threat.

"And so the Lord sees the heart of Saul. He knows what drives Saul and He knows that Saul is good. Saul is just disoriented. Saul has been clinging to the Old Covenant not realizing that God has made a New Covenant with all people, not just the 'Chosen People.' So God intervenes as He often has to because we human beings can be a little thick-headed. We can be a little confused. And that's okay, as long as we are open to God's word and God's direction for us."

Lawrence could see Sarah smiling brightly as he continued. He hoped the next part of his sermon would go over well.

"We here in the South, during the war, we were a lot like Saul. We had a belief, we had a drive and purpose. We wanted to continue to live in our country as we had always lived. And why not? Life in the South used to be great. We were a great Confederate Nation. We all believed in God. We were a Christian nation...weren't we? And now like Saul, we have to become Paul. We have to convert. We have to change to a new way of thinking. But I believe the South will rise again. Not as the way we want in terms of a material or a physical country. Just like the Jews with their continued waiting for the Messiah; they expected the Messiah to come and overthrow the Roman Empire and I am sure that is exactly what Saul was waiting for as well.

"We southern men and women today may be hoping for a physical reconstruction of the South, but ladies and gentlemen, God is calling for a spiritual reconstruction of the South!" Lawrence said as he pounded on the pulpit, something he copied from his father who often did the same thing. He received various smatterings of applause and shouts of "Amen."

"Ladies and gentlemen, I invite you all not to look for a physical reconstruction of our previous life here in the South, but a new life. A life filled with wonder and awe. A life filled with wonder and awe at the great things that God has done for us. We have a great God who believe it or not has delivered us. 'Seek ye first the kingdom of God and all these things will be added unto you.' Ladies and gentlemen, let us together seek to renew the spirit of the South from within. Let us meet every Sunday. Let us have prayer meetings and Bible studies on Wednesday nights. Let us commit ourselves to spiritual renewal. Let us rise again!" Lawrence smiled and then headed to his seat next to the deacon. Deacon John Cole was an older man who was on the finance committee and held a lot of sway with the church and the community. He did not look exactly pleased with the sermon. Lawrence did look over to Sarah who wore a proud smile on her face and gave him a little wave. As for his father and Mr. Fuller, they both looked a little perplexed. But as for Lawrence he felt content and smiled broadly at the congregation. The deacon said some closing words which Lawrence didn't pay attention to and then was called up to close the service with prayer.

"Dear God. Thank you for this wonderful day. Please help us to remember that each day we need to be converted like the Apostle Paul. That we need to put to death the old self and put on the new. Thank you, Lord. Keep all of us safe this week and bring us back together soon. In Jesus' name. Amen."

After the service concluded, Lawrence walked to the entrance of the church to greet the congregation. The first to meet him was the Fullers. As W.E. went to offer his hand, his daughter Sarah rushed in and placed her arms around her future intended.

"Excellent sermon Mr. Ambrose. I thought it very apt."

"Well thank you, Miss Fuller. Those are very kind words."

W.E. finally wedged his way between the two and offered his hand to which Lawrence shook.

"Interesting concept Lawrence. I think there were some hidden meanings?"

"No, not at all. I think we as southerners can rise again but we need to focus on the spiritual rather than the material."

W.E. began to squint with one eye, giving the appearance that he was being hoodwinked. He was beginning to see Lawrence for who he truly was, a thinking man. He was not one who would easily bow to the yoke of the Fuller empire like almost everyone around. It was now going to be a game of who was truly in charge. For Lawrence, it was no game and W.E. could play as many as he wanted to, but for Lawrence, a new life was what he looked to.

Once the Fullers had left, he was then greeted by his father, mother, and sister.

"Interesting topic son. I thought it rather peculiar."

"Oh, how so father?"

"It left a lot to the imagination. Not the practical, everyday living type of sermon I would have thought you would have made. You know, 'love thy neighbor and who exactly is my neighbor' type of thing."

"Oh, I thought it had a practical application. We are to focus on the spiritual and not the material, nothing more than that."

His father with a similar expression of suspicion and knitted brow gave an insincere smile and then walked back to the parsonage with his wife and daughter.

As he continued to shake hands for another twenty minutes, he could see a familiar face toward the end of the line. When everyone else had been satisfied with their congratulations and questions, the last one in line stood before Lawrence. It was Sully and he looked a little worse for wear.

"Sully, how are you? I thought that was you in the last row of the balcony. Trying to be inconspicuous I see."

As Lawrence grabbed his hand to shake, he could smell the whisky on Sully's breath.

"Are you okay Sully?"

"I guess I am as good as I will ever be."

"What's the matter?"

"Ah, I really thank you for the job but we are not doing too well as far as ends meeting."

"Didn't you get set up in the apartments near the mill?"

"No, there were no more available. Instead, I'm living with my mom in a tent near the river."

Giving Sully a once-over it was quite true that he had found hard times. Not only did he wreak of alcohol, but he looked emaciated, nothing but skin and bones.

"Why don't you come back to the house with me. Ma will cook us up a nice supper."

"Thanks, Lawrence but I'm not dressed to come over to the parson's house."

"Hey, my parents will understand. Now c'mon."

The truth is that Lawrence's parents would mind but he didn't care. They needed to see what was happening to the everyday southern man. Thanks to the Fuller's ivory tower, he could see his parents had no real clue as to what the true state of the South was. It was time they were awakened to the reality of what was going on. Besides, this was Sully. He was the guy that helped him get through the war and the journey back to Atlanta. He was not going to forsake his friend.

Back at the house, Lawrence's parents were greeted with the sight of Sully.

"Ma and pa, this is William "Sully" Sullivan."

"Just call me Sully." Sully reached out his hand to the good Reverend Ambrose who shook it with a stunned look on his face. Mrs. Ambrose smiled and bowed her head and motioned for him to come into the house.

"Is there anything I can do for you, Mr. Sullivan?"

"Please ma'am, just call me Sully."

"Okay, Sully. Would you like anything?"

"Well, I think he could use a good bath, hey Sully?"

"No Lawrence, I bathe in the river every day."

"Well, let's get you a bite to eat anyway. Ma can we give Sully some vittles?"

"Yes, dear. We have some leftover venison meat and some potatoes. I'll warm that up."

"Great ma. It is much appreciated!"

Both the Reverend and Mrs. Ambrose retired to the kitchen, each in a state of shock, having been exposed to Sully's noxious odor. After a few minutes, both the Reverend and Mrs. Ambrose returned with a feast. The Reverend Ambrose pushed a cart that had the venison, roast beef, mashed potatoes and gravy, green beans, biscuits, and honey. Sully's eyes widened by what was being presented.

"Ma and pa, we have a very honored guest with us today. If it'were not for Sully, I wouldn't be here."

"Oh, how so?' the Reverend Ambrose asked.

"At the Battle of Cumberland Farm, he saved me. There was cannon fire whizzin' over our heads all night. One of them would have hit me if it were not for the quick action of Sully pushing me out of the way. I landed on a hard rock but hey, I'm not complainin'."

"Why, that was very good of you Sully. Thank you," Mrs. Ambrose said in a quiet and demure fashion.

"Thank God for 'im. We lost a lot of good men that day."

Everyone became quiet as Sully and Lawrence began to remember all of those who had fallen during the war. Trying to break the silence, Lawrence continued.

"Where's squirt?"

"Ah, she's at the Fuller home. She was invited to have supper and play with Becky." Hearing the name "Fuller" seemed to put Sully off his food.

"Sully, what's the matter?"

"Oh, nothin'. I'll tell you later." Sully regained his appetite and continued on with his lunch. After the meal, there was plenty of coffee and dessert. Sully sure could use the coffee. When the meal was done, Mrs. Ambrose offered to do any wash that he and his mother might need. She also packed up a large bag full of food that he could take with him back to the tent. As Lawrence walked Sully outside, he could see that there was a lot of worry in Sully's eyes.

"Hey Sully, I'm sorry for everything that's happened to you. Aren't they paying you anything at the mill?"

"It's a dollar a week. I can get some bread, milk, and cheese but between two people, it's not enough."

"Well, look. I'll start pestering Fuller to see if we can figure out an apartment. I'll come by with some food. Do you like the work okay?"

"Yeah, it's fine. I think I can work my way up to foreman and that will pay a little more. But it will be a while before that will happen." Lawrence put his hand on Sully's shoulder and smiled at him.

"I know it sounds trite, but God will come through. He helped us get out of the war alive and he'll help us through this."

Sully gave Lawrence an expression of "It's easy for you to say," before giving him a pained smile and then turning to walk back home. Lawrence felt a pang of helplessness, watching as his good friend walked away. As with the mission, he would need to not only speak in platitudes but live what he preached.

While Sully was walking, he suddenly stopped and turned back to look at Lawrence.

"Oh, by the way, Phillip Asquith was with me the other night."

"Really, Phil was with you? How's he doing?"

"Not well…he's dead."

"Whadya mean? What happened?"

Sully began to walk toward Lawrence. Lawrence could see Sully's body almost go limp as he walked up to him.

"I had been trying to help him. When he lost his job at the Atlanta mill, he was really depressed. Remember how during the war he threatened to kill himself?"

Lawrence nodded silently, remembering the several times that he and Sully had to convince Phillip not to kill himself.

"Well…he finally did it. Blew his brains out last night. He came by the river looking for me. My mother told him I was at the mill. He apparently, stood by the river, shot himself in the head, and floated downstream. They found him this morning."

Sully began to cry thinking not only about the pain Phillip was going through but feeling guilty that had he been there when he came by the tent he might have somehow saved him. Lawrence walked over to Sully and clutched his friend and tried to console him. He wondered how many good southern men had taken their own lives. So many had suffered from the stress of war and although the South might have surrendered, the war continued on for thousands of men on both sides.

CHAPTER 12
A Devilish Demand

May 3rd, 1866

The following month, the Ambrose family was invited to a gala at the Fuller home. It was going to be the "party of the century," according to Sarah. There were going to be several politicians there including the Governor of Georgia Charles J. Jenkins. As predicted it was a grand event and everyone who was anyone was in attendance. The Fullers spared no expense. There was a string quartet that was playing very upbeat and traditional southern tunes and hymns. There were numerous waiters providing guests with food and drink. The house was well decorated with bunting on all the railing with red crushed velvet carpeting laid down everywhere. It was a sight to behold.

In the middle of the main dining hall was a buffet table that seemed to be "endless" in Lawrence's estimation. It could have fed half of Atlanta he reckoned. At the beginning of the proceedings, Lawrence kept a low profile and stayed mostly in a corner with Sarah trying to avoid being noticed. He watched as W.E. mingled with his guests, especially speaking at length to the Governor. Lawrence began to wonder at the machinations going on between the two and how the Governor was surely giving W.E. all the tax breaks and other credits possible. All with the idea of having a little extra put aside for the good Governor.

Sarah of course looked her beautiful self and was clearly in full form. She took the arm of her fiancé as they strolled around the front hallway, introducing themselves to the various guests. They met the chief of the local constabulary, a gruff man who matched W.E. in corpulence. They met one of the farmers who provided the town with most of its fresh dairy products. They met the man who owned one of the main lumber mills. He had ruddy cheeks and was clearly drunk and it was almost impossible to speak with him without being dispatched by his breath. He seemed to have a cheery disposition but little control over what he said. Sarah was surprised that her father had invited such an uncouth man to their house. From Lawrence's point of view, he would often say, "he is one of God's children," which irritated Sarah as just an excuse to forgive anyone regardless of their manners or behavior.

Sarah Fuller, while having a high moral standard and a sense of etiquette and formality, did have a soft side for her fellow man. She was always one to interact on the same level as their maids during the time of the Confederacy. While expecting much from everyone she met, she still did have a kind streak that served her well. No one in the community thought of her in an unkind way. Her father on the other hand was clearly despised. She understood that and tried to mend whatever ill will he had created.

Later on, they met Cedrick Phillips who owned a paint supply shop. He provided W.E. with the paint and dye for his fabrics that the mill created. Phillips was a timid man and was apt to apologize for any misstep or any word that could be deemed contrary. Sarah and Lawrence could see he was visibly nervous, sometimes such that his hand would tremble. He practically jumped out of his skin when W.E. and the Governor joined their conversation.

"Governor Jenkins, I'd like you to meet my future son-in-law, Mr. Lawrence Ambrose. A former veteran of the war and currently studying theology at Franklin College."

"Wonderful to meet you, my boy. I've heard a lot about you," the Governor said with a chuckle.

"All good I hope?" Lawrence queried as he shook the Governor's hand.

"Yes indeed. And please know that we appreciated your service to our country. And know we will want to call upon you again as the South rises back up." Lawrence smiled with a look of mild bewilderment.

"I understand Governor and I will be ready to offer a prayer and a sermon or any charitable act that the good people of the South may need."

"Excellent my boy. I know W.E. will be calling upon you with some local events and such that you will want to be involved with. Any support for my gub'ment will be appreciated."

"Of course Governor."

"So what else have you been doing with your time?"

"Apart from school and helping with the chores around here I have been helping out on Saturdays with the American Mission Association."

The house seemed to go completely silent. Had he said something wrong? He began to look around the room at people, thinking that he must have lost his mind saying whatever it was he had said.

"The AMA is doing great work to help the good people of Atlanta. It's God's work."

At that point, the Governor with a furrowed brow and frown nodded and walked away. W.E. gave Lawrence a look of horror as he pursued the Governor. Lawrence looked at Sarah who offered him a similar look of confusion. Lawrence's father walked up to him and shook his head in disgust.

"What did I say?"

"What in the world were you thinking?" the Reverend Ambrose asked and then joined W.E. and the Governor in a corner of the room. They were apparently discussing what Lawrence had just said.

"What was wrong with what I said?" Lawrence asked Sarah.

"I have no clue but you have sure rattled a few cages here. I never knew I was marrying a rebel. Well, I guess we were all rebels at one point," Sarah said ironically.

The rest of the evening Lawrence kept his distance from everyone else. He would only speak or dance with Sarah and mainly kept to himself. When everyone had left, W.E. called him to the side.

"My boy, I know this is going to sound harsh but I can't have you associating with the AMA anymore."

"Why not?"

"They are a Yankee organization that is bent on destroying our ways. The leader is from Massachusetts and he wants to feed and educate every freedman in the South. If the South is going to rise again as you said in your sermon, it will have to be on our own terms. Not the terms that the North is forcin' on us. Do you understand?" Lawrence was unsettled and was frozen. He could neither nod nor shake his head. He just stared at W.E... The whole thing had caught him off guard and he didn't know quite what to do other than pray.

Taking Lawrence's silence and blank stare as an accord, W.E., with a large grin on his face slapped Lawrence on the back and walked away. Lawrence, still in shock was greeted by Sarah.

"What ya gonna do Lawrence?"

Lawrence silently shook his head. He had no idea. A year earlier he would have sworn an oath to such an idea, but now he was not of the same mind. He knew he had changed. The Holy Spirit had come into him and changed him. God was revealing His truths to him and now he couldn't go back. Like with Callie's story, it now hit him like a ton of bricks what his position now was. While maybe not an abolitionist, he could no longer support slavery, nor discriminate against freedmen. What was he going to do? The first thing he did when he got back home was get on his knees and prayed to God for wisdom.

CHAPTER 13
Wedded Bliss

June 23rd, 1866

The day of the wedding came like a locomotive barreling out of control. Lawrence had kept the date in the back of his mind while staying focused on school. When he woke up he began to tremble at the thought of what was about to happen. With what was now his first step of each day, he rolled out of bed, onto the floor, and onto his knees to pray. He had now become accustomed to praying. He recognized it as a way of communing with God. Apart from prayers for meals with his family growing up, he had never really prayed. He knew now that prayer would be essential to everything he did. It was one of the Lord's commandments and Jesus had established an easy prayer for everyone to start their day with; the Lord's Prayer.

Our Father, Who art in heaven
Hallowed be thy name
Thy Kingdom Come
They will be done
On earth, as it is in heaven
Give us this day our daily bread and
Forgive us our trespasses as we forgive those who trespass against us
And lead us not into temptation but deliver us from evil
For thine is the kingdom, the power, and the glory forever and ever. Amen

As he raised his head, he looked out of his bedroom to the field in the backyard of the house. The sun was rising and beams of sunlight were pouring through the window. He thought it a good sign. He washed up and then headed down to breakfast. A sumptuous meal had been prepared by his mother with grits, honey and biscuits, bacon, eggs, and griddle cakes.

"Wow, looks like you are sending me off to war again. Is there something else I should know about marriage?" Both his parents gave each other a coy look and began to smile.

"No, nothing to worry about son. You will love married life."

Lawrence began to smile knowing that his mother was concealing information about the marital state. At that point, it was too late and he knew he would have to find out for himself.

After completing the meal, Lawrence headed upstairs to get himself dressed. He had a gray suit and bow tie that his father had used on his wedding day. It fit him surprisingly well and he was soon physically ready. As for being mentally ready, well that was another story. He waited in the downstairs foyer for his parents and sister to get ready and began to get nervous thinking about the endeavor he was now facing. Would he be any good at playing husband and father? Was he really ready for such a responsibility? All he knew was that he loved Sarah very much and he hoped that would be enough. That and a lot of prayer. The one good thing was he knew that Sarah was of like mind when it came to spiritual matters. They should be good at helping each other during the hard times, which he knew were coming.

The wedding was set for 1 p.m. at the Fuller house. Like with the gala the previous month the house was again decked out. Lawrence's father would perform the ceremony and W.E. would provide everything else, including a three-night honeymoon in Savannah. The ceremony was to be held in the Fuller's backyard with again the cream of the crop of society being in attendance. It had become a perfect day, with marginal heat and clear blue skies. Again Lawrence felt it might be a positive sign of things to come.

In a small field about 200 yards from the main house, on a small hill, Fuller's men had constructed a beautiful arbor where the pastor and bride and groom could stand. There were one hundred chairs that had been lined up perfectly with rope stretched out as a guide. As the groom waited with his father under the arbor, from the house he could see a horse-drawn carriage pull up to the back door. He could make out Sarah and her parents getting in and the carriage soon leaving in a cloud of dust. As they arrived at the base of the hill, Mrs. Fuller helped her daughter get out of the carriage. She was immediately greeted by her three sisters who were acting as bridesmaids. Mrs. Fuller then, in a slight gallop, made it quickly up the path to the front row of seats. Sarah made it toward the back row on the arm of her father, her sisters clutching onto her train.

As the same quartet who performed at the gala began the wedding march, everyone in attendance began to stand. The bride, her father, and her sisters began to walk down the path in coordination with the music. As Sarah approached, Lawrence had a lump in his throat. She was the most beautiful woman he had ever seen. She had the typical, slightly bronzed glow about her, but today it looked even more angelic. He could see her face as her veil was quite sheer and an occasional breeze would move it to the side. Her wedding dress was a beautiful white color with lace on the upper neckline. The fit of the dress was snug and it highlighted her curves which he thought a bit unusual for the time. Although for Lawrence, it was the perfect vision.

As W.E. gave Sarah's hand to Lawrence, he gave his soon-to-be son-in-law a somewhat sinister look. Lawrence became concerned. What expectations would W.E. now have for his new minion? Would those expectations now be even higher? He tried to shake any thoughts of obligation to his new father-in-law and again refocused on his beautiful Sarah.

"Dearly beloved, we are gathered here today to join this man and this woman in holy matrimony." Lawrence looked over to Sarah and the two shared a knowing smile.

"In our glorious Christian tradition, going back to the Old Testament, it was pleasing to God when he created the institution of matrimony. Seeing that man was alone, he created from Adam's rib a woman and the two were to cleave to one another and become one," again Lawrence and Sarah shared a knowing look.

"This is the Lord's commandment that as man and wife they shall become fruitful and multiply. As they cleave together, they will be providing each other love and support along this journey," the Reverend Ambrose smiled at the couple and then gave a glance to his wife who was also in the front row. While their marriage had known difficult times, they had always done their best to support each other. The road had been rocky at various points, but they managed to put those difficulties behind them and move on, choosing not to blame each other or hold grudges which can often end a marriage.

"And so, we again join together with this couple and pray that their coming together as husband and wife will be a blessed union. Lawrence, do you have the ring?" Lawrence nodded and pulled out a gold band from his suit pocket.

"Repeat after me. With this ring, I thee wed," Lawrence became slightly nervous as he realized that this was it.

"With this ring, I thee wed."

"And with it I bestow…"

At that point, Lawrence seemed to go into a dream state. He could barely focus on what his father was saying. He hoped he mouthed the words correctly and that Sarah could see his sincerity. She seemed to smile and nod as if he were able to understand and comprehend the words he was saying. With relief, his father then looked to Sarah and more or less repeated the same words. She looked so beautiful. She could have been repeating the constitution in Japanese and it wouldn't have mattered. They were then asked to kiss which he dutifully complied. There was cheering and the presentation to the crowd that they were now "Mr. and Mrs. Ambrose!" At that point, Lawrence regained his nerve and they both walked down the path together hand in hand. The carriage took them back to the house where they had a wonderful chicken dinner and an incredible wedding cake at the end. Given the wealth of W.E., they were one of the few weddings around that had a photographer capture much of the glorious moments. The rest of the afternoon zoomed by and before they knew it, the bride and groom had changed into more casual clothing and were being shuttled via the carriage to the Irbyville railway station where they would take the late afternoon train to Savannah.

When they arrived in Savannah, the happy couple checked into The Marshall House which had been recently occupied by the Union Army. Lawrence's previous trip to Savannah had not been a good one with the Confederate Army having to abandon the city and head north. While the city itself was beautiful with its tropical feel and wide range of flora and fauna with large oak trees draped in Spanish moss, the site brought bad memories for Lawrence. But in the spirit of the "New Lawrence," as he now referred to himself, he would make some new memories.

The newlyweds were checked-in and headed up to their room. Lawrence picked up Sarah and carried her over the threshold of the doorway, laying her gently onto the bed. He then opened a window and looked out over a lush courtyard filled with dogwoods and Lagerstroemia. He breathed in the fresh air and then turned to see his stunning bride looking at him. She had a coy look in her eye and she extended her index finger and motioned for him to come hither. He quickly complied and grabbed her, pulling her into him. This was new as they previously had only kissed with little physical contact. He had been craving more. Had she? He assumed so. With one motion he picked her up and carried her in his arms. She broke out into laughter at the gallant gesture. He smiled and then plopped her on the bed which caused even more frivolity.

As he sat on the bed next to her, he leaned over her and smiled. He brushed a long curl out of her eyes and began to stroke her cheek. She became serious knowing that something was going to happen. She had dreamt of this time since she was an adolescent but now it was becoming a reality. She wore a peach sundress that buttoned from behind. She lifted herself up against one of the pillows by the headboard. She then gathered her long flowing hair in her hand and moved it over one shoulder, allowing Lawrence easy access. Seeing her compliancy, he moved in close, bringing her body into his. He gave her a long passionate kiss and then began to feel for the buttons at the back of her dress. He was quickly successful in unbuttoning her dress and began to pull it toward him revealing a white slip. Once the dress was removed, he then pulled at her slip revealing her breasts which she quickly covered in a feigned attempt at being modest. Lawrence smiled and kissed her passionately again. Both were virgins and had never been this intimate with anyone else in their lives. Many a time Lawrence had been tempted during the war. Sully had tried on several occasions to have him go to local brothels but Lawrence had declined. One night though in Southern Virginia he had been tempted. Sully invited a "local girl" to Lawrence's room but Lawrence had passed out by that time, not knowing how close he had come to losing his virginity.

Now things were different. Now he was with the woman he loved and wanted to be with. The feelings were natural and not forced. As he pulled the slip completely off of her, she kicked off her shoes, leaving her in a completely natural state. He then stood up and gained a full view of his wife. He removed his jacket and shirt and as he climbed onto the bed, she helped him with his pants. The two were now as unencumbered as Adam and Eve, and they felt as if they were the only inhabitants in the world. There was no one else who existed. Lawrence slowly fondled her breasts and then again passionately kissed her mouth, rubbing his hands all over her body.

For the rest of the evening, they made love and enjoyed each other. They were content and had no other agenda or place to be at that moment in time. It was everything they had imagined and looked forward to a long life together, expressing their love to one another. Later, as they lay looking up at the ceiling with utter contentment, Lawrence began to think about how the Lord had blessed him. But why? With all the suffering he had seen around him for the past several years, why was he now being rewarded? Had he done something good? Had he somehow avoided sin more than anyone else? How could God be heaping so much love and reward on Lawrence Ambrose? He felt he didn't deserve it. He felt like a sinner, like anyone else, punishment was his due reward. But as he turned his head and looked at the beautiful woman lying beside him, he decided that he would not refuse the Lord's grace. He would accept every gift the Lord would bestow upon him and he would do everything in his power to help those who had not been so blessed.

For the next several days, the contented couple enjoyed Savannah and each other. They took many strolls through the beautiful streets and vowed that one day they might live there. Maybe that would be Lawrence's first pastoral assignment; Savannah Baptist Church. They began to dream of their future together and couldn't wait to get back to Irbyville to start their new lives as man and wife.

CHAPTER 14
Dark Forces Arise

July 4h, 1866

When the newlyweds arrived back from their honeymoon, they were given a small house to live in on the Fuller's property. It was a small quarters, but the Ambrose's decided to make it their own happy little home.

For the third month in a row, the Fuller's played host to another grand event - a fireworks display on the far western end of their property where there was a small lake and island. The fireworks would be set off there and would provide the mill workers with an opportunity to forget their cares as well as to be told of another thing they needed to be grateful to W.E. for. Before the events that night, W.E. had invited Lawrence to a "community meeting," that he felt the young preacher should attend.

Earlier that morning, one of the mill workers came to the "little parsonage" to speak with Lawrence. A young woman named Molly Sanders wanted Lawrence to come with her urgently to help her with her sister. Lawrence gave Sarah a peck on the cheek, grabbed his coat, and headed out of the door. The walk into town from the Fuller's was about ten minutes. Molly and her sister lived in one of the mill's apartments right on the river. Molly worked for the mill but her sister Elizabeth did not. She had a different profession entirely.

The sisters lived on the third floor of the tenement building. Lawrence breathlessly tried to keep up with Molly as she scaled the two flights; then was quickly ushered into the apartment. Molly looked around and called out to Elizabeth but there was no response. She headed toward the bathroom and found Elizabeth leaning over the bathtub. She was vomiting. As she lifted her head and wiped the residue from her lips, Molly could see that she had a shaving razor in the other hand.

"No, Elizabeth don't!!!" Molly screamed. Lawrence ran into the bathroom and pulled the razor from Elizabeth's hand and put it into his pocket. He then grabbed a nearby bucket of water and a towel. He put the towel in the water and began to dab it on Elizabeth's face. Once she was cleaned up, he helped her to her feet and then walked her to the bedroom, laying her on the bed. She was clearly intoxicated. He grabbed a nearby chair to sit next to her.

"How long has this been going on?" he asked Molly.

"About a year now. She was fired from the mill and has never really been able to recover."

"Who fired her?"

"W.E."

"What was the charge?"

"That she was stealing thread from the mill."

"Was it true?"

"I don't know. I don't think so. She'd never done anythin' like it before. At that point, her life seemed to spiral out of control. She had to move in with me and couldn't find work. Not much work in town besides the mill. So she took to prostitution."

"Has the doctor looked at her?"

"No, he typically only sees people that can afford to pay him."

"Has she tried to take her life before?"

"Yeah, once she tried to drown herself, jumpin' off Sutter's Bridge. Luckily a guy from the mill found her in time and brought her back."

"Is there anything else besides the loss of income that's bothering her?"

"Isn't being a prostitute enough?" Lawrence nodded. Molly then walked over to a nearby window to open it, hoping fresh air might help.

"She's been beaten up a couple of times, been robbed, and wasn't paid for her...her work. It seems like it's got worse since the past couple of months."

"I'll see if Doc Withers can come by."

"I don't think that'll help. She needs something more. Religion I guess. That's why I came to you."

"I see. Well, there's not much I can help her with while she's in this state. I'll try and come by later and see how's she's doing."

"I'm much obliged, Reverend Ambrose."

"Well, I'm not officially a minister yet. Still have to finish my schoolin'."

"Well, I've heard a lot about your sermons. People are takin' notice."

"Oh, have you been to our church?"

"Well no, but my other sister Becky has. She says you are a smooth talker."

"Well, I'm not sure smooth talking will help your sister, but I will try and help.

The next stop for Lawrence was the meeting in downtown Irbyville that W.E. wanted him to attend. It was close to the mill so he was early. The first to arrive after Lawrence was Harry Clay. Harry Clay was the owner of one of the most prosperous quarries. If anything was to be built in Atlanta, the raw materials and stone would come through his quarry. With the money the federal government would be pouring in to rebuild Atlanta, Clay would be an even wealthier man than he already was. Lawrence admired him for his white hair. He had never seen anyone with such hair. Most older men with white hair would have streaks of gray or maybe lines of beige but his hair and handlebar mustache were solid white as if he had just walked in from a snowstorm.

Next to arrive was Augustus Hauser, the local magistrate who was rumored to live in W.E.'s pocket. Anyone who found themselves on the wrong side of the law but was a friend of W.E. would find himself quickly exonerated. The price however was eternal allegiance to W.E. Augustus, whose family had arrived from Bavaria a generation earlier, still had a faint German accent.

As the rest of the meeting attendees arrived the whole scene began to smack of an underground club for the rich. There were even a couple of W.E.'s men from the mill that served as waiters for the meeting, bringing the exclusive invitees any kind of drink they desired. When W.E. arrived it was as if the entire assembly turned and gawked. W.E. was a man of great stature throughout Georgia and it was clear he was a major force behind whatever this meeting was about.

"Gentlemen, why don't we begin?" Augustus asked as each member began to find their seat.

"Brothers of the South, we welcome you here today. I see we have a couple of new members. Lloyd Williams our town's city clerk. Lawrence Ambrose, the Reverend Ambrose's son who we hope will eventually take over for his father. Welcome gentlemen. Also, it's good to have our town's mayor back, Henry Wedgeworth, who recently went to Illinois for this year's mayoral convention. Welcome back, Henry.

"Now we all want to discuss the recent arrival of the AMA into Atlanta. Clearly, this is something we need to rectify. Does anyone have any ideas?"

"I've got some sticks of dynamite we can use to take care of 'em," Frederick Gross said as he then burst into laughter along with just about everyone else in the hall. Lawrence couldn't believe what he was listening to and began to look over at W.E. W.E. met his gaze and it was clear that his father-in-law was trying to send him a message. At that point, he didn't know whether he wanted to stay or protest by leaving. He thought though that it might be a good idea to pretend to be sympathetic and listen to their plans.

"Thank you for that Mr. Gross, but I think we can come up with another solution. Although, things might come to a point where we may need to provide some intimidation if other methods do not work."

Lawrence became quite concerned about what the meeting was truly about. But the agenda soon turned to another subject entirely; providing for widows and orphans in Atlanta. The rest of the meeting was spent discussing an office that was to be set up in Atlanta that would distribute money, food, and clothing; apparently in competition to the AMA. It would all be funded by the "Sons of the South," or SOS, which primarily consisted of all the men there. Everything sounded fine until the last closing remarks by Mr. Hauser.

"So it is agreed, we will set up an office and begin to do the distribution sometime next week."

"How do we prevent the coloreds from coming in?" the now-famous Mr. Gross asked, raising his hand and rising all in one motion.

"Well, we plan to contact those who are in need through a list that W.E. has."

For the next several minutes questions flew around the room with various members answering them. Lawrence was in a state of confusion. While having grown up a proponent of slavery, now his faith was telling him something different. Was it time to stand up to these men? Would it do any good? These were mostly old men set in their ways. Would they really ever change their minds?

"So with that, I think we'll conclude the meeting. Remember brothers that we want solidarity. This is a movement that will truly help the South to rise again. We do not want to remain under the North's yoke. They are tyrannical people and they seek to destroy everything that we have built up over the years. Stay strong. We will not let our good country fall!" Hauser's words were greeted with cheers and applause. Lawrence looked to make a quick exit but was stopped at the door by Mr. Hauser.

"I hope we can count on your support Lawrence?" he said with W.E. and other pillars of the movement standing behind him. He smiled and tipped his hat and walked as quickly by them as he possibly could while not seeming to be in a hurry.

Later that night, everyone from the mill gathered at the Fullers. The fireworks display was incredible and like their grand explosions, were a testament to W.E.'s personality, influence, and self-absorption. While they sat on a blanket watching the show, Lawrence told Sarah about the girl from the mill who was down on her luck. Sarah thought it might be a good idea if she came along as well to help. Lawrence agreed.

"By the way, I went to that meeting your father wanted me to attend today. Kind of an odd thing."

"Oh?" Sarah said as she handed Lawrence a piece of peach cobbler she had made earlier.

"Yeah, it almost seemed like a rally of sorts. They are creating some kind of charity in downtown Atlanta…competing with the AMA."

"What's wrong with that?"

"Nothing except that they want to discriminate against freedmen."

"Hmmm," Sarah said as she took a bite of her cobbler. She began to rock her head back and forth as if thinking about the implications.

"So what do you think about that?"

"Well, shouldn't the charity be for all people?"

"I think so, yes."

"So you don't support slavery?"

"I used to, or I think I used to. For me, it was more like something I grew up with. Something that was always there, like a tree in the front yard, or a favorite book on my shelf. It was always there and I never questioned it."

"But now?"

"Well, I've learned that we are all God's children. Why should one child be enslaved to another?"

Lawrence looked down at his pie, shook his head, and laughed.

"What?"

"It's kinda funny that we've never had this conversation before."

"I guess it's a brand new world. It's all new to us. What are your thoughts?"

"Like you, I once just thought of it as part of my life, my culture. Now it's becoming more and more abhorrent. The Lord has been giving me revelations over the past months while working downtown for the AMA. Now that I think about it, He's been giving me little revelations since the war ended." Lawrence began to think about the dream he had at the house he and Sully first stayed at after Appomattox. A horrible dream about African people in slavery. He realized that the Lord had been speaking to him for a while on the subject.

"But, how do we get the older generations to see?" Lawrence asked with a loud sigh.

"That's a tough question. I don't think my father will believe in any world without slavery. Where the white man is not the boss and in charge of everything."

"Sounds like we've got a lot of work to do."

"But trust in God. Ask God to help you. He will," Sarah smiled her usual sweet smile. Her eyes glistened in the night air. If there was ever one correct decision Lawrence had made in his life, it was to marry Sarah. He gave her a peck on the lips and then put their plates away in a nearby basket. He stood up and then grabbed her by the hand and raised her up. They began to look in each other's eyes and soon began to giggle. He gave her a long passionate kiss. She pulled back and looked into his eyes with a large grin.

"Well, Mr. Ambrose. You seem to be in a romantic mood."

"I am Mrs. Ambrose. I wish we could head home now," he said with a wink.

"C'mon, you got work to do Reverend Ambrose."

Lawrence smiled, grabbed the basket and blanket and the two walked hand in hand back to the house. When they returned to the house they were immediately greeted by W.E.

"So what did you think?" he said in his usual blast of hot air.

"Fantastic daddy. You did it again!" Sarah said with a bright smile as she passed him into the house.

"Great show sir, I haven't seen fireworks like that since the war." At that point, W.E. grabbed Lawrence around the shoulder in an attempted bear hug. He clearly had been drinking.

"Oh my boy, I hope you know I've placed a lot of trust in you. My daughter. My church…the people of Irbyville. Don't disappointment."

"I'll try and not sir," Lawrence said as his teeth vibrated from the shaking W.E. was giving him. He looked into W.E.'s eyes and they looked like they were lit up. Maybe the drink was firing him up but Lawrence didn't like this side of him.

"Ok daddy, we'll see you later," Sarah said as she returned back outside.

"Where are you two going?" W.E. asked.

"Going to see a friend. We'll see you later," Sarah said as she grabbed Lawrence's arm. W.E. stared at the pair as they walked out of sight. He had a look of suspicion on his face and began to rub his chin.

Lawrence knew he was a lucky man when he walked with Sarah over to the mill. She wore a white summer dress and sandals and looked like a flower. It was appropriate that when walking down the street, Sarah had strayed such that she brushed up against a magnolia tree.

She was lost in all the beautiful leaves and emerged as if a goddess being born. If God wasn't blessing Lawrence then who was? He knew that God was giving him things he never dreamt of.

When they arrived at the Sanders apartment, they were greeted by Molly who looked like a wreck. Elizabeth was lying on a nearby bed and Molly had been putting a wet cloth on her forehead.

"Hi Molly, this is my wife Sarah," Molly immediately bowed her head to Sarah fully aware of who she was.

"How's Elizabeth?"

"There's something wrong. She would be sober by now but she's been in some sort of trance since you left. She's been mumbling, she sometimes speaks and it sounds like a foreign language."

"Foreign language?"

"Latin or Greek, I'm not sure what. And she has these violent convulsions and I have to hold her down. I'm exhausted."

Sarah patted Molly on the arm to reassure her and then walked closer to Elizabeth. She was sweating profusely. Although it was July, it was an unusually cool day, with several thunderstorms passing through the area. With the temperature being lower Elizabeth shouldn't have been too warm. But when Sarah felt her head it was clear she was burning up with fever."

"Shouldn't we go for Doc Withers?" Sarah asked.

"He won't come. I would send my sister over there but he says he's 'engaged.'"

Just then Elizabeth began to scream and howl. It was a reverberating, skull-shaking sound that seemed to emanate from hell itself.

"This seems like something beyond our calling. Molly, has your sister been involved with witchcraft?" Lawrence asked.

"Has she seen a palmist or been involved with anyone who does palm reading or seances...the occult?"

"She does have a friend who calls herself a 'fortune teller,' like a gypsy. She's a very strange person. She took my sister to a graveyard the other day to see if they could conjure spirits."

"Conjure spirits?"

"Something must have happened. You don't play with the occult."

"What can we do?"

"The only people I know who can deal with this are Catholic priests."

"Catholic priests? We don't have any here."

"There is one I know in Atlanta."

"How do you know any priests?" Sarah asked puzzled.

"He teaches at Franklin College. Can y'all hang on while I get him?" Sarah urged him to rush. He ran out of the apartment as fast as he could and ran all the back to the Fuller farm. He got his horse and began to make for Atlanta, all the while praying along the way. He made good time and was in the city within twenty minutes. When he arrived at the Church it was past ten o'clock in the evening. He tied up his horse and ran around back to where the priests lived. He knocked on the door and with luck, Father Thomas O'Reilly received the distraught Lawrence. Father O'Reilly was famous for having persuaded Sherman from destroying many of the churches in the burning of Atlanta. Now Lawrence prayed that he would be able to perform another miracle.

"Father, you have to come with me."

"Why my boy?"

"There's a woman in Irbyville. I think she's possessed. You have to help us."

The priest stood puzzled trying to comprehend what Lawrence was saying. Once it sunk in, he told Lawrence to wait. He went inside, grabbed a prayer book and a bag, and was soon back outside ready to leave. Lawrence helped him onto the back of the horse and the pair were soon galloping up Peach Street toward Irbyville.

When they arrived at the Saunders apartment, there were several neighbors gathered at the front door. Lawrence, thinking something had happened immediately rushed up the stairs to see what was going on.

"Lawrence, thank God you're here! Elizabeth tried to throw herself out of the window!" Sarah was frantic with a look of terror in her eyes. Lawrence moved back toward the stairwell and then ushered Father O'Reilly into the main room, quickly closing the front door from prying eyes.

Upon entry into the room, Father O'Reilly placed his bag and prayerbook on a nearby table. He then stood back and looked at Elizabeth. He could feel a presence. He then tried to talk with her but she just grunted and began to stare at him. Her eyes appeared to be inflamed. From the bag, he quickly produced a robe which he placed over his head and pulled his arms through. He then pulled out a rosary and what looked like a small vial. The whole scene looked odd to Lawrence, Sarah, and Molly. Being Southern Baptists they had never seen such a thing. Lawrence did remember though that when he was a teen, there had been a troubling disturbance in his father's church. There was a woman who they had never seen before, who started attending services. She would always sit in the front pew. She had been fine for a couple of services but on a later visit, she became quite belligerent and would interrupt his father's sermons. She would yell swear words and sometimes speak in another language, all with the intent of disrupting his father's sermon. The ushers eventually had to remove her. They later commented that she was very strong and that it took three large men to handle her. They never saw her after that and most just regarded her as mentally ill, but Lawrence suspected there was much more going on than that.

"Has the girl been to a doctor?" Father O'Reilly asked.

"No, he wouldn't come."

Father O'Reilly frowned and began to shake his head. He typically did not like to perform an exorcism unless as a last resort and that the person had at least been checked medically. He knew however that as soon as he stepped into the apartment, he could feel a sinister presence.

At that point, Father O'Reilly produced the vial of Holy Water and began to shake it in the air, with droplets hitting everyone present. As soon as the water hit Elizabeth, she began to convulse uncontrollably. He then took one end of the stole from around his neck and placed it around Elizabeth's neck. He motioned for Lawrence to hold her down as she began to flop back and forth. Father O'Reilly then made several prayers and then he began to entreat the being inside of Elizabeth.

"Tell me thy name, the hour and the date of thy going out, by some sign." Elizabeth continued to be agitated and began to spit at the priest, yelling something in Latin. Father O'Reilly then helped Lawrence keep her down and placed his right hand firmly on her forehead. He said several more prayers and then began to encourage the spirit to leave.

"I exorcise thee, most vile spirit, the very embodiment of our enemy, the entire specter, the whole legion, in the name of Jesus Christ, to get out and flee from this creature of God."

At that moment, Elizabeth began to relax and soon was completely calm and lucid.

"Elizabeth, are you okay?" Molly came running to her side. Elizabeth was in a daze as everyone helped her up.

"Lawrence, please give her some water." Lawrence walked over to a nearby dresser where there was a pitcher of water on top. He poured a glass of water and gave it to Elizabeth. She drank it in one gulp, wiped her mouth, and then looked at everyone present.

"What's going on?" Everyone was relieved to see that she was back to her normal self. It had been a stressful couple of days, especially for Molly and she was so happy to have her sister back.

"Thank you, Father, we are indebted to you," Molly said as she grabbed the priest's hand.

"No my dear, this is part of my work. I am only too happy to help every soul the Lord puts in my life. Now if you like, you're welcome to come to Mass every Sunday," he said with a bright smile. Lawrence laughed and patted the priest on the back. He began to think about Catholicism and how it had not been that popular in the South. And now with new organizations that seemed to blame everyone but Southern Baptists for their troubles, would the Catholics be next?

Lawrence gave Sarah a kiss and then escorted Father O'Reilly downstairs to his waiting horse. With a good sprint, Lawrence had Father O'Reilly back home just before midnight. Lawrence thanked the priest profusely for what he had done for Elizabeth. He then headed back north to Irbyville to pick up Sarah.

CHAPTER 15
Unfortunate Souls

September 1866

Lawrence was excited to get back to school that fall. Both he and Sarah would be in school full-time and they were both exuberant for what their futures held. They now were both working toward the day where they would run their own private Christian school and church. Where that would be they had no idea but they were happy with their new dreams. What they didn't know is how this dream would play out in the new South with the rumors that there were many white people unhappy with the way reconstruction was proceeding.

More and more rumors were going around that there were militant white mobs forming, all with the intent of intimidating the newly freed slaves of the South. While many in the South were aspiring to a new, different, and better way of life, there were also many who wanted the old South and all of its previous benefits, no matter how immoral they might have been.

The good thing was that both Lawrence and Sarah were of like mind. They wanted a new future not only for themselves but for all of those around them. And with that in mind, on the first Saturday of the new semester, they both went down to Atlanta and helped with the AMA food drive and distribution. It was a glorious day with both Lawrence and Sarah taking real joy in helping all of those who needed help. Sarah even took a liking to Thaddeus, despite all of the previous things that she had heard from Lawrence. But Lawrence had now come to the realization that he needed to give up everything in the past and move on, and with that thought, he and Thaddeus became good friends. Lawrence even helped him repair the fence around his mother's home on Peachtree Street.

And while things underground were becoming a concern, above ground things couldn't be better for the newlyweds. They were becoming the fixture of Irbyville. Lawrence's hands-on approach to ministering to the people was having a real impact. People like Molly and Elizabeth Saunders were now full-fledged members of the church and were at every meeting and function they could attend. It wasn't only the Saunders who Lawrence and Sarah had had an effect on, but almost everyone in Irbyville.

One Sunday afternoon, after church and the couple, had finished lunch, they decided to take a walk down by the river. As they walked a couple of miles upriver from the mill, they came upon a campsite. The occupants looked to be mainly women, in fact, they were all women with the exception of one male teen. The couple stopped and greeted them and as they talked to several of the women it was obvious they were prostitutes. They told Lawrence and Sarah that they were just there temporarily, having lost their homes during the war. While it was possible that was their reasoning for such a sparse life, it was clear what their occupation was. Clearly, they were supplying the men of the mill with sexual favors.

"Have you thought about working at the mill?" Lawrence asked Dorothy, the woman who appeared to the camp's leader.

"We have but they're not hiring at the moment."

"How do you obtain food?"

"We get handouts and we fish. We also have a rifle to hunt squirrels and rabbits."

Lawrence and Sarah had grave concerns for the women's safety, not to mention the hygiene of the camp. While they would bathe and clean their clothes in the river, it was safe to say that they were suffering from various sexually transmitted diseases.

While Sarah spoke to the women, Lawrence went over to the teen boy who was sitting on a stool at the entrance of one of the tents.

"What's your name?" Lawrence asked.

"Samuel, but you can call me Sam."

"Hi Sam, how old are you?"

"I'm seventeen. Turning eighteen in a couple of months."

"How did you end up here?"

Sam explained to Lawrence that his mother used to be a member of the group. She had died however and being alone with no one else in the world to help him, he decided to stay with the group. He had been with them since he was fifteen.

"Do you help out with chores?"

"Yes as best as I can."

Lawrence noticed the boy was somewhat effeminate and who could blame him given the company he kept.

"I see the ladies here make their living a certain way."

"Yes, they basically sell their bodies to the men at the mill."

Lawrence was a little taken aback by how Sam nonchalantly explained their occupation. He could see in Sam's eyes a look of resignation. A look like life had beaten him and he had little to look forward to. While he had seen that look in many an adult, he didn't like seeing it in someone so young.

"And you, what about your occupation?"

Sam shrugged his shoulders. "I find money wherever I can find it."

Apart from a few passages in the Bible, Lawrence had never encountered homosexuality. He knew that it existed but thought it was found in other places like in Europe or within the wealthy or artistic communities. He seldom found anyone of that persuasion in the South.

"Wouldn't you rather go to school or have a real job?"

"A real job....like what?"

"I don't know, a doctor or lawyer."

"I'd have to get an education for that. I haven't been in school since the war began."

"It's never too late to get an education. If I can find a school for you will you go?"

Sam looked down toward the ground shaking his head. He then looked toward the horizon with a forlorn expression.

"I don't know...maybe."

"Look, Sam, I know things may seem hopeless now but you have to believe that God has a purpose for you."

"Huh, I think God abandoned me years ago, especially with how I live my life now."

"No, that's not true. We were not creatures that just evolved out of nothing. We have a loving God who created us with a heart and mind to use. You have a heart and mind and you need to use that for positive and productive things, not what you are doing now."

"Easy for you to say. You're a fancy preacher ain't ya. Alls I got is the shirt on my back," Sam's eyes began to water thinking about the life he was trapped in. Lawrence stared at him with a look that said he would not give up on him.

"Look, why don't we do this. I get you a job at the mill and then when I get my school together I will get you enrolled. It may take a year or two but it will be worth it."

Sam stared at Lawrence to see if he really meant what he said. He then nodded. While still sad, he now had a somewhat hopeful look on his face. Lawrence patted him on the shoulder and turned to find Sarah.

As with everyone she met, Sarah had all the women in the camp stirred up to repentance and wanting to change their lives. She too had vowed to get them jobs at the mill. Now all she had to do was beg and plead with her father to create ten additional jobs. It would soon be eleven after she had spoken with her husband.

After their encounter with the women by the river, Lawrence sought out a medical doctor near the university. He was introduced to doctor Sydney Rhodes who was the physician on staff at Franklin College. Lawrence advised him of the poor conditions of the mill and the women by the river and asked if the doctor would take a look. He would pay him for his services. As there was little need to provide medical services at Franklin except for the odd check-up of the faculty which was only ten at the time, he agreed. Dr. Rhodes was young and eager to put what he had learned into practice. As a doctor at Franklin College, he was also a devout Christian and eager to help where he could. Lawrence, Sarah, and the doctor quickly became good friends.

As Lawrence's sphere of influence continued to grow in Irbyville, he soon came to know almost every person in town. There was Clare Philpot who was the town's gossip and supplier of all the latest news. Sandra Pillsbury was the quiet but careful eye on all the movements of everyone. She was either visible from her front window or on the street just outside her house inspecting everyone who passed by. There was Sadie Sandberg, who while no one suspected she was a prostitute was definitely flirtatious with any man who walked by including Lawrence. She was one of the funniest people Lawrence had ever met and it was always a pleasure for him to be in her company. The duration of the interactions would have to be kept to a minimum, however, otherwise, they would be under the hard gaze of Miss Pillsbury. Doc Withers, while not one of Lawrence's favorites due to only catering to the "rich," had the most gregarious and witty wife Pauline. She was always the first to show up if they needed help at a church event or service. She was also not shy about what she thought and that even included how her husband handled his occupation, much to Lawrence's delight. Despite people urging Dr. Withers to be more inclusive, he would merely shrug and say he already had too many patients. Lawrence would later learn that was by design of W.E. W.E. wanted the good doctor to be on call for the Fullers and a small circle of friends.

As for menfolk, Lawrence had become quite close to Harry Rodgers, the town barber. Harry was amiable and provided a great ear for Lawrence to bend. Nathaniel "Nat" Collins, the owner of the general store was the salt of the earth and Lawrence could always count on him to provide any help he needed. Besides Sully, Lawrence's best friend was Kyle Stanton. Kyle was the city supervisor and worked on the town council. He was working on a degree in engineering from UGA and was one of the most intelligent people Lawrence had ever met. He was Lawrence's age and so had a similar view on life; that the old ways were not necessarily the best ways.

As Lawrence's social network grew, he was able to understand what drove the people of Irbyville and how he might best meet their needs. Was preaching a sermon every Sunday going to meet those needs? He knew that it wouldn't and had to make himself more visible to the townspeople. So each day after breakfast, prayer, and a Bible reading with Sarah, he would march out to the town and interact with as many people as possible. He wanted to know what everyone was doing; not so much as to pry but as to help.

With his new outlook on life, Lawrence was able to put his ear to the ground and hear what was happening with almost everyone in town. It was this new line of communication that helped him reach out to Ned Walker. Ned had lost his wife and daughter during a typhus outbreak in Tennessee the previous year. He then moved to Irbyville to get employment at the mill. He had taken a dark turn however and had been on a drinking binge. He had been absent from work the past couple of days and the foreman was threatening him with termination if he didn't start showing up. Lawrence heard about Ned's plight from Clare Philpot. He had begun to rely more and more on Clare as a good source of Irbyville news, even more so than the local newspaper.

Ned lived in a shack just outside of town. Lawrence decided to visit him and see if there was anything he could do to help him. The shack was upriver and looked to be overrun by tree limbs and brush. Clearly, nothing had been done to clean the shack. Lawrence walked up to the front door and knocked several times with no response.

"Ned, are you in there?!!!" Lawrence yelled out. He then walked around to the back of the shack to see if there were any windows. He found one but it was overgrown with shrubs. He pushed them aside and began to peer into the window. It was dark inside and he could just make out someone lying on a bed. He rapped on the window. He could see Ned looking up but then lay back down. He rapped again and this time Ned stood up and came to the window.

"What do you want?!!!" he yelled through the window.

"I want to talk to you!!!" Lawrence yelled back. Ned shook his head and then walked toward the front door. Lawrence quickly ran around to the front.

"What'ya need?"

As Lawrence walked to the front doorway he was greeted with a smell like no other. It was a mix of alcohol and body odor and it practically knocked him to his knees. He looked at Ned and felt compassion. He was in his mid-thirties but stress and drink made him look more like he was in his fifties. He looked like a man who had the weight of the world on his shoulders.

"Hi, Ned. I just wanted to see if you need anything?"

"Who are you?"

"I'm Lawrence Ambrose. The preacher's son."

Ned, through his drunken haze, began to look Lawrence over. As Lawrence peered around the room he could see one cot, a small table with dirty plates and cups, and on the floor was what appeared to be either rags or dirty clothing.

"I don't need anything, bye."

"Stan Buford from the mill says he's gonna fire you if you don't show up."

"That's fine. I quit."

"Are you sure about that?"

"Yeah," Ned said as he slammed the door shut. Lawrence thought the door was about to come off of its hinges. He began to look closely at the shack and the yard. Maybe if it were clean and respectable Ned would become motivated.

The following day, Lawrence and Sarah, and some of the congregants came to Ned's shack with yard equipment, tools, and paint. They spent the whole day raking and clearing tree limbs and brush, fixing loose boards and trim, and giving the shack a coat of paint all the while Ned was passed out on his cot.

Before they departed for the day, Sarah left a box for Ned that had dried food, a canteen of water, some clean clothes, and a Bible. She knocked on the door to alert Ned and then the group left for home. Ned was still passed out and did not hear the knock.

The next morning, before checking in on Ned, Lawrence decided to pay Sam a visit down by the river. When he entered Sam's tent he was concerned by what he saw. Sitting on one of the cots was Sam. He had a faraway look in his eyes and had a pistol on his lap. As

Lawrence got closer he could see that Sam had a bruise on his left cheek.

"Hello, Sam. How are you?"

Sam did not respond. He continued to look straight ahead.

"I hope you're not going to use that?"

Sam finally acknowledged Lawrence's presence.

"Oh, ah…I was just going to kill some rabbits for dinner."

Lawrence thought it was a cover-up, but he didn't know if he was intending to use the gun on himself or maybe one of the men he had prostituted himself to.

"Look, I brought you a couple of books. One for grammar and vocabulary and one for basic math. We can go over these if you like. I would like you to be one of our first students over at the AMA. We just got approved for the funding of the school. We are going to build an elementary, middle, and high school there in Atlanta. If you can get up to speed then we can eventually get you into college. Get you out of the situation you're in."

Sam looked catatonic, almost in a trance-like state.

"How did you get that bruise?"

Sam shook his head and didn't respond. Lawrence then sat down on the other end of the cot. He sat in silence along with Sam, hoping he would finally open up and speak. Sam eventually did take a closer look at the books. Lawrence, seeing his interest, handed them to him.

"You really think I can go back to school?"

"Well, we can certainly try. Why don't I go over these books with you and we'll see where you're at."

Lawrence spent the rest of the afternoon and early evening going over the books with Sam. While a little rusty on his basics, Lawrence could tell he was intelligent and had a lot of potential. Before he left for the day, Lawrence gave Sam some encouragement.

"Listen, I want you to take this. It's not a lot but you can feed yourself for a few days. Maybe a few of the ladies, although I think they have full-time work now thanks to Sarah. I want you to avoid contact with the man from the mill. I want you to think about your life. It's not good what you are doing to your mind and body. You are God's creation. You have God's spirit in you. Do not degrade yourself by resorting to this way of life. I will help you with your education but you need to promise me you will turn away from what you've been doing to yourself. Do you understand?"

Sam perked up and nodded his head, "yes, I will do as you say. Pastor…"

"Yes, Sam."

"Do you really think there is hope for me?"

Lawrence, who had been standing halfway outside of the tent, turned and came back in. He stood by Sam and put his hand on his shoulder.

"All of God's children have hope. All of God's children have great potential. Sam, if you want you can become anything you want; a doctor, a lawyer, you could even run your own mill one day. But you need to think about God. You need to pray to God. I will stop by with a Bible and a prayer book you can use. Once you know the grace of God you will not want to turn back to your old ways. He will liberate you from this way of life."

Sam smiled and nodded his head. Lawrence patted him on the shoulder and then turned to walk out of the tent.

"Pastor Ambrose! Thank you."

Lawrence smiled. He could tell there hadn't been much in the way of assistance given to Sam over the years. He was glad he could help him.

After his visit to Sam, Lawrence went over to Ned's shack to see if he had gotten the supplies. The box however was still on the porch. Lawrence knocked several times on the front door but did not receive a response. He went around back to look through the window and could see Ned on the cot. He looked lifeless. Lawrence ran back around to the front and turned the doorknob to the front door. The door was unlocked but seemed stuck. He then pushed a little harder and the door finally opened.

"Ned!!!" Lawrence ran over to the cot. He looked over Ned and could not see any movement. He could not hear him breathing. He felt for a pulse but there was none. He could see there was saliva on his lips along with something else that he had regurgitated. It looked like he might have choked on his own vomit. With all the smells emanating from the room, it was hard to distinguish if it were vomit. He tried to get closer but the smell was so pungent he had to turn to get some air. He stood up and looked down on the lost soul and began to cry. With all, he had seen during the war, and with the exception of Charlotte, this struck him the most profoundly. He was a lost sheep and Lawrence had not found him in time to save him. He began to feel guilt for not having done something sooner for Ned. He hadn't really known about his plight but yet still felt he should have known.

Sarah walked in and could see what had happened. It was clear Ned was no longer. She tried to console Lawrence but he continued to anguish over his death.

"You couldn't do anything more my love."

Lawrence nodded but it still didn't seem to help. His image of Ned, from the day when he last spoke to him, was one of profound pity. He looked like a man who had been crippled physically and emotionally. What had he done to deserve the fate he had experienced? What was the Lord's will in all of this? What would happen to Ned's soul? He turned to Sarah and he asked her to pray with him. They both knelt down beside Ned and began to pray.

"Lord, I don't know what your will is in all of this but we pray for Ned's soul. We pray that you deliver him from his pain and bring him to your kingdom. Please have mercy on your servant Ned." Lawrence began to shake his head and with tears in his eyes looked over at Sarah. Her eyes too began to water.

"We ask this in the holy name of Jesus Christ. Amen"

After spending four years seeing death on the battlefield, he could not process the death of Ned. Somehow the war was holy and heroic; something of legend where men fought with bravery and courage and many other noble attributes. But this? This was a defeated human who had just literally dissolved into nothing. His pain had brought him to a terrible end and there was nothing noble about it. It was something that should never have happened and he began to hate himself that it could happen in the town where he was a pastor. A pastor? Isn't a pastor supposed to watch over his flock? Isn't he supposed to account for every sheep?

Before Lawrence and Sarah left the shack, they found a couple of photographs of Ned's wife and daughter. Emotions began to well up again in Lawrence's heart. He grabbed onto Sarah and they quickly left the shack, walking over to the nearby funeral home owned by Kendall Fog. His family had a funeral home in Atlanta until the fall of the city two years earlier.

"Mr. Fog."

"Oh, Pastor Ambrose, how can I help you?"

"Ned Walker has passed away."

"Oh, I'm sorry. How can I help?"

"Would you be able to fetch his body from his shack and…"

"And?"

Lawrence choked up when he started to think about what might be done to Ned's body.

"Whatever you need to do to prepare the body for burial," Sarah quickly interjected.

"I can help with the embalmment but somcone will need to fetch him. I don't have anyone free at the moment."

Lawrence nodded his head and began to leave.

"Who will be paying for his embalmment?" Lawrence turned and looked at Fog with a scowl wondering how he could be worried about payment at a time like this. He shook his head and grabbed Sarah by the arm and walked out of the funeral home. He walked over to the city council building and asked Kyle Stanton if he would help him with Ned's body. Luckily Kyle was free and he grabbed a stretcher from the nearby fire brigade office. They retrieved Ned's body and covered him with a blanket. They brought him back over to the Fog Funeral Home and laid him on a nearby table.

"Mr. Fog, I will cover Ned's expenses."

Mr. Fog nodded and then proceeded to look Ned over.

"Ok, thank you, Pastor Ambrose. We should be ready by Monday for the burial."

"Ok, thank you," Lawrence managed a forced smile and then bid Mr. Fog goodbye. As he began to turn for the door he noticed a large gathering of men toward the back of the funeral parlor. It was toward the rear of the building and obscured by a wall, but through the back doorway, he could see the men who had made up the "Sons of the South" meeting. As he focused on the assembly he could make out the corpulent silhouette of W.E. He was laughing and joking with the other men. Lawrence decided it would not be in his best interest to interrupt the proceedings and headed out of the parlor with Sarah.

The following Tuesday, a sparse group of mourners gathered for Ned Walker's funeral. They were not able to locate any relatives of Ned's or anyone who had struck up any kind of relationship with him so apart from Lawrence, Sarah, and a few ladies from the church's grieving committee, there was no one else in attendance.

"Dearly beloved, we are gathered here today to celebrate the life of Ned Walker," as Lawrence said those words they seemed to ring hollow. He looked down at the pinewood box that looked hastily assembled. There was one lily on top of the coffin and nothing else. As Lawrence began to speak again, he could feel a rumbling under his feet. Soon the entire church was shaking and felt as though the entire building was coming apart. As the violent shaking began to subside, Lawrence could see the lid to Ned's coffin starting to shift. Was it from the earthquake or whatever had caused the building to shake? The lid continued to move and up popped Ned Walker sitting up and looking around dazed. Had he not really died? He started to shake his head and look around the church. Lawrence could not believe what he was seeing. Had the Lord resurrected Ned or had he not really been dead?

"So this is how you show your appreciation Irbyville? Are you the only ones sending me off? Maybe had you all known about my plight we wouldn't be any of us here anyway!" At that point, Ned pulled himself up and then jumped out of the coffin. He then started to walk up toward the sanctuary and the pulpit where Lawrence was.

"Why didn't you help me sooner?!!!" Ned said, pointing and yelling at Lawrence. Lawrence began to tremble and shake uncontrollably.

"My dcath will bc on your hcad!"

Lawrence began to scream and soon the scene changed from the church to his bed back home at the Fullers.

"What is it, honey? Are you okay?" Sarah said trying to calm Lawrence. She grabbed onto him and began to hug him as he pulled himself up against the headboard of the bed. He began to pant and was completely out of breath.

"What is it…a nightmare? Was it about the war?"

When Lawrence finally calmed himself, he latched on to Sarah. As she held him tight she could feel his heart pounding through his chest. She quickly jumped out of bed and poured him a glass of water from a nearby pitcher and gave it to him. He gulped it down and then put his arm over his forehead as if shielding himself from some great light. He finally relaxed and settled back down.

"What is it, Lawrence? What were you dreaming about?"

"Ned."

"Ned Walker? What about Ned?"

"He was accusing me of not doing enough for him."

"Honey, that's ridiculous. You did everything you could."

Lawrence began to shake his head.

"Maybe I should have been paying attention to the townsfolk sooner. I told myself I was busy with school and the church..."

"You were. You are not going to be able to find all the lost souls around here. You just do the best you can to find them. The Lord will lead you to them."

"And Ned?"

"Sometimes there are going to be people that you are just not gonna be able to help. They've chosen a path and you will not be able to change that path. Ned was going down a dangerous road."

"But was that his fault?"

"He needed to pray to God for guidance."

"But would you if you lost your entire family?"

Sarah stopped and pondered his question. Apart from several older grandparents, she had never lost anyone close to her. Would she have kept her faith after something so catastrophic?

"You know, I don't know. Yes, it's easy for me to say to reach out to the Lord in times of pain when I haven't really experienced pain, but all I know is that it would be my only option. I couldn't forsake the Lord in times of trouble."

Lawrence looked at Sarah and nodded. She gave him a kiss on his forehead and then lowered herself onto his chest. His heart was still beating hard but he was slowly calming down. She hoped and prayed for her husband that he would be up to the task of leading a church. He had been through a lot with the war. He had seen a lot of death and bloodshed and she wondered if maybe not now but later down the road, would he lose his ability to control everything that had happened to him. She knew the only thing she could do was to encourage him and to pray.

The following morning, in an effort to not have a repeat of his nightmare, Lawrence went around town encouraging everyone to come to Ned's funeral the next day. He started his mini-crusade with Clare Philpot.

"Miss Philpot, would you be able to come to Ned Walker's funeral tomorrow?"

"Who?"

"Ned Walker. He used to work at the mill. He had recently come here from Tennessee. He had lost his family to the typhus epidemic there. Doesn't ring a bell? You were the one who first told me about him."

"Oh, yes, now I remember."

"Would you mind coming tomorrow…to show your respects?"

"Well, I didn't really know him that well. I don't see the point. Does he have family coming?"

Lawrence smiled and then went over to Sandra Pillsbury's house to ask her to attend the funeral.

"Ned Walker? Never heard of him."

Lawrence shook his head and looked down at his feet. He began to ponder how it was that she didn't know who he was. Was it her fault? She seemed to keep an eye on everyone. How could she not have known about Ned?

As he made his way through town he was met with similar resistance. It was as if no one had known that Ned had lived in Irbyville. Apart from the five ladies on the funeral committee, it looked as though the service would play out just like his dream with relatively few in attendance. To say the least, Lawrence was concerned.

The following day, all the members of the funeral committee, two ushers, Kyle, Sully, Sarah, and Lawrence were the only ones in attendance. As Lawrence walked by the coffin to start the service, a chill ran up his spine. He hoped there wouldn't be a repeat of his nightmare.

"Good morning everyone. Thank you for coming. We didn't really know Ned Walker very well. Some of us knew that he had lost his family before coming here. He worked at the mill and...and basically kept to himself. Was it his fault or our fault for not knowing his pain?

"Did we see him around town? Did we interact with him? Did we go to his house? Maybe there was nothing we could do for him, but I think the message here is that the Lord is giving us is to reach out to one another. Even if we know the person, we need to ask, 'how are you doing?' 'What's goin' on with ya?'"

Lawrence looked down at the coffin, wondering if the lid would pop off. He looked around at the church and it was still intact. The Lord had not brought his wrath down upon the town, though Lawrence began to think he would at some point if they didn't start showing more compassion.

"We lay to rest the soul of Ned Walker. The Lord said 'I am the resurrection and the life. The one who believes in me will live, even though they die.' Was Ned a believer? We do not know, but we pray for his soul. We pray the Lord will have mercy on His servant. And may the Lord have mercy on our souls."

Lawrence motioned for Kyle and Sully to come forward. Two other men who were acting as ushers came down as well to help remove the coffin. They all then walked outside to the church cemetery where they buried Ned's body.

CHAPTER 16
"Slaves, Obey Your Masters"

October 1866

As the fall in Atlanta continued, it brought long shadows both figuratively and literally. On the first Saturday in October, Lawrence and Sarah went into Atlanta to work at the AMA. After getting much of the food prepared for the day, Thaddeus pulled Lawrence aside.

"Lawrence, I wanted to talk to you for a moment," Thaddeus said as he looked around, concerned that someone might be listening.

"I just wanted to let you know that I was walking down Peach Street the other day and I saw a group of men moving furniture and other items into a building. When I took a closer look I saw your father-in-law, W.E. Fuller."

"Oh yeah, they are creating their own charity in Atlanta to help the poor."

"Well, that place is no charity. They are KKK."

"KKK, what's that?"

"Ku Klux Klan. It's a group of ex-Confederate soldiers who have created a 'club,'" Thaddeus said as held up the fingers on both hands in a way to indicate quotation marks.

"It ain't no club. It's a gang of terrorists. They want to intimidate us negroes from betterin' ourselves; education, jobs, politics. They have an agenda to bring back the old ways."

"But my father-in-law referred to the group as the 'Sons of the South,' a group that would help provide for people in need."

"That ain't what they do. They're 'part of that group that started in Tennessee. They have been setting fire to people's houses, beatin' up people and have killed people, lynched people."

"How do you know all this?"

"Well, there are a lot of rumors flyin' around. Eventually, I decided I had to see it for myself. Their office backs up on the McMillan Grocers. I work in the backroom where I keep stock, sweep up. No one comes back there. I was on my break last week and I could hear almost everything they were talking about. The wall is thin and their stage is right in the back...right up against the wall that separates the two stores. Anyway, they are talkin' 'bout anarchy and they want to take over the democratic party and put politicians in who help restore white rule, keep the black man down."

Lawrence was stunned at what he was hearing. How could this be true? How could his father-in-law be involved in such a thing? As he began to think about his father-in-law he started to realize that it wasn't too far-fetched.

"Look, come back here on Thursday night and then you'll see for y'self."

Lawrence nodded his head in stunned silence. He couldn't believe that such a group existed. Wasn't it time to forget about the past and embrace the new future, the new South? He began to realize that it was only months earlier that he too had been a proponent of restoring the old South. It seemed though with each passing day he realized more and more the evils of slavery and how the treatment of negroes had been an abomination.

The following Wednesday, Lawrence led a Bible study of a small group of church members. He tried to get the entire church to come out but while the numbers were initially good, it now dwindled to a small group of twelve core members who Lawrence deemed as 'true seekers of God,' congregants who had a thirst for knowing the truth. He admired this group. After an opening prayer, Lawrence began the study,

"Ok, we finished Ephesians chapter five and we are moving on to chapter six. In this chapter, St. Paul is talking about family and other relationships and how we are to behave. It can be quite controversial…

Verse 1: Children, obey your parents in the Lord, for it is right.

Verse 2: Honor your father and mother (which is the first commandment with a promise)

Verse 3: That it may be well with you, and that you may live long on the earth.

Verse 4: Fathers, do not provoke your children to anger; but bring them up in the discipline and instruction of the Lord.

"Okay, as most of you are parents with grown children, it may not be as applicable but yet it is still valid. Even as mature adults we need to be obedient to our parents or at least respectful of our parents. The key like all relationships that we've discussed and will discuss is using our authority with love and discernment. Whether, a husband toward his wife; as we discussed in chapter five, a father, and later we will look at slaveowner, the Lord entrusts certain people with responsibility. As parents we are responsible for loving our children..." as Lawrence said this he looked over at Sarah who had a loving look in her eye and a smile that seemed to indicate more than what it usually meant. He continued..."that love is not meant to just order our children around like slaves. That love is meant to instruct and to discipline. As parents we can go too far; discipline too hard, too often. A father needs to be strong, but also gentle toward his wife and children.

"And that leads us to the next relationship, that is of slaveowner and slave...

Verse 5: Slaves, be obedient to those who are your masters according to the flesh, with fear and trembling, in the sincerity of your heart, as to Christ;

Verse 6: not by way of eyeservice, as men-pleasers, but as slaves of Christ, doing the will of God from the heart...

"So doesn't that mean that slaves are supposed to obey their masters? Shouldn't all these 'freedmen' go back to their masters?" Thomas Wilson asked. Lawrence looked at "Tommy" and could discern that how he asked the question was not so much as to re-enslave people but to truly and honestly understand the passage.

"Well Tommy, it's a good question. You have to remember the cultural setting of the times. A 'slave' was typically not someone who was forced into slavery. Their slavery was a part of repaying a debt they were unable to pay back to someone. They had to work off their debt in the form of servitude to the debt holder..."

"But how would we know that? We're living almost two thousand years later. How would we know what God's intention here is? Aren't we to read the Bible literally?"

"I don't think so. Yes, we are to accept the Bible as the word of God, however, there are many things that are not necessarily meant to be taken literally. The 23rd Psalm for instance; 'The Lord is my shepherd, I shall not want. He makes me lie down in green pastures.' I don't think he means that we are literal sheep lying down in a pasture, but he leads us as if we were. Likewise, there is strong scientific evidence now that the earth is much older than we originally thought, so the first two chapters of Genesis which contain the creation story may not mean that God created things in literal days, but rather thousands or millions of years..."

As Lawrence said this a hush came over the assembled. Was what he just said blasphemy?

"Look, maybe God did create the heavens and the earth in six days, but we need not worry about that. We need to worry about what the Lord is communicating to us and the message is clear. Parents, slaveholders, you need to love those who are entrusted to you. They are not for your use, for you to use as how you see fit, but as the Lord sees fit."

The Bible study discussion continued for another twenty minutes. After a long day, Lawrence was glad when the study finally ended. He closed in prayer, said his goodbyes to the members, and then went over to his wife who was in the last pew. She would often sit in the back to give him an idea of how everyone was receiving his talks. She would also use it as an opportunity to catch up on her knitting without it being too noticeable.

"Hello, Mrs. Ambrose."

"Hello Mr. Ambrose," Sarah said as she gathered her things and then gave her husband a hug.

"You had an interesting look on your face earlier."

"Oh, you noticed did you.? I liked how you talked about being a father without really being a father. Well, guess what?"

"What," Lawrence said starting to get a sense as to what was happening.

"You're going to be a father!" Lawrence was stunned. He wasn't comprehending what the news was. As it started to settle in, his heart began to well up and he grabbed Sarah and pulled her into him giving her a bear hug.

"Hey now, you're gonna squeeze the baby," Sarah said with a laugh. Lawrence pulled back with shock not getting the joke at first. He then smiled and gave her a passionate kiss. They then hugged and clung to each other. So many thoughts began to whirl around Lawrence's mind. *Is this a good time to have a baby? How will I be as a father? Will I be a good father?* He was elated and at the same time a little fearful. Was it a good time to be raising a child with everything that was going on? What would it mean to Sarah's career? They talked it over and Sarah felt that after having the baby she could go back to school. She would have to delay it for a while but she was fine with that. Lawrence could not get over the news and was already a "proud papa." The two went home with their feet seeming not to touch the ground. They were madly in love with each other and soon there would be another member of their little family to love.

The next day, Lawrence met Thaddeus at the McMillan Grocers at 9 o'clock. They quietly moved to the back office and sat near the wall, getting themselves positioned so they could hear what was going on next door. The back wall was made only of a few pillars and then boards running horizontally. It made for very easy listening into the next room. The sound would travel freely between each store and so it was important for Thaddeus and Lawrence to not make any noise.

The meeting opened with Mr. Hauser reading the minutes of the last meeting. He then handed the meeting over to W.E.

"Good evening gentlemen. While we have a general idea of what we plan to do with regard to the disruption of freedmen's aspirations, the most important thing we need to do is make sure we are influencing politics. We need the democrats in our pockets. But not only do we need them in our pockets, but we also need our members to run for office. I have some ideas of who should run and one of those is myself!" Applause rose from the men assembled.

"Gentlemen, I'm not one for violence," he said with laughter and soon the rest of the men joined in.

"I want to avoid bloodshed as much as possible so the best way to effect change is through the law. We need politicians of like mind, like beliefs." W.E.'s words were again met with applause.

"We already have a good relationship with the Governor, but we need to get in good with the other politicians; Alexander Stephens and Herschel Johnson.

We know that the ratification of the thirteenth amendment back in December was abhorrent to all we know. The general assembly wanted to get on the Union's good side; get funding etc. But from the standpoint of right and wrong, it was a sign of their weakness. They crumbled under the pressure of the Union. So, what's done is done. But that will not stop us from our holy crusade to put things back to the way they were. We just need to be a bit more subtle. We need to be invisible in some ways. Soon though we will need to take other action. We have some weapons over at Muller's house, but we will need more." Lawrence and Thaddeus turned and stared at each other after the last comment W.E. made and began to shake their heads in fear. Why did they need so many weapons?

"Gentlemen, we intcnd to rctakc thc South. The freed negroes will not taste true freedom; the right to vote, taking political office, education…what do they need with all of that? They do not have the mental faculties to attain to such things. They are better off working in the cotton fields as God intended their kind to do; heavy labor!"

Lawrence pulled back and began to think that at one time he thought just the same way as W.E. How in the world could he have deluded himself in such a way? What was the point of trying to subjugate a whole race of people? It was insanity, but how was he going to reason with such people?

"W.E., how are we gonna intimidate these nigras? There's almost as many of them as us here in Atlanta."

"We can't worry 'bout that son. We need to be brave. It won't be easy but we need to have courage. Our descendants are going to look back at this time and wonder what we did to preserve the white race. To preserve our sovereignty. It will be difficult but with a little sweat and know-how we will take back our rightful place." At that point, the meeting was adjourned and the men quickly departed the building. Lawrence looked at Thaddeus with a forlorn expression.

"Well, you've opened my eyes, Thaddeus. How do we stop them?"

"Well, I think we need to alert the government."

"The Union?"

"Yes. We need to get more troops to help us fight this thing."

"Isn't there anyone else we can go to?"

"Well, I don't think Alexander and Herschel are gonna hep."

"What about the Freedmen's Bureau?"

"Yeah, that's a possibility. You would need to get in touch with General Tilson. He oversees the bureau."

"My guess is it will be difficult to get General Tilson to exert any pressure on the Sons of the South."

"Well, you don't know 'til you try." Lawrence nodded. He patted Thaddeus on the shoulder smiled and headed out the door.

"Lawrence, what are doing here?" W.E. said as Lawrence walked out the front door. Startled at W.E.'s appearance, Lawrence responded in haste, "Oh, ah, I, I was picking up some powders for Sarah. She's been having headaches."

"Hmmm, awfully late to be here ain't it?"

"I know one of the clerks. He lives close by."

"And where's your bag?"

"What bag?"

"The bag they normally put items in...a paper bag."

"Oh, I just put it in my pocket."

"Can I see it?"

Lawrence became perturbed with W.E.'s request and began to stare at him. W.E. held his gaze and the two began to understand where the other stood. Lawrence started to shake his head.

"I think you're overstepping your boundaries W.E.."

"Really, my boy. And after everything I have done for you?"

"Still. It's my personal property and you don't have the right. Besides, why do you want to know?"

"Well, let's just say, there are some rumors going on about you."

"Really, what rumors?"

"Oh, that you have a liberal bent. Perhaps an allegiance to the Republican Party?"

"Well, you're welcome to listen to whomever you wish. I don't live my life by rumors and here say. Good evening." Lawrence brushed by W.E. and quickly hopped onto his horse. He began to gallop up Peach Street, occasionally looking behind him, expecting W.E.'s carriage to soon be heading in the same direction. He quickened his pace and was back at the Fuller house by 10:30 pm.

The following Sunday, Lawrence was to give the sermon. He typically alternated Sundays with his father for giving the sermon. Today, he was a little concerned about how his message might be received. While the two families had been ebullient with the news of Sarah's pregnancy, there was enmity starting to build between Lawrence and his father and W.E. Lawrence's father was a mild-mannered man. "The meek shall inherit the earth" was always his motto. He never liked controversy and typically stayed out of any fray. While he loved his father, this meekness was something that Lawrence sometimes disdained. It was his belief that his father's meekness was just a cover for being indecisive and not wanting to be responsible for taking a particular position on certain issues. At least for now the news about the pregnancy was making W.E. very happy. Maybe he wasn't too happy with his son-in-law, but the good news of a furthering of the Fuller family tree might distract him for the time being and keep him out of Lawrence's way. In any event, it took some of the tenseness off of recent interactions with W.E.

"Good morning everyone. The Lord has blessed us with another beautiful morning. We have much to be thankful for. We, as a town, are relatively healthy, in mind, body, and spirit. As I get to know each of you I find we have a vibrant town. A town that loves the Lord and wants to do the Lord's will. But what exactly is the Lord's will? How do we know if we are doing the Lord's will…the Lord's work?

"There may be a simple answer. What did Jesus say were the two most important commandments. Succinctly it was to love the Lord and to love our neighbor as ourselves. Sometimes though we have trouble remembering this simple rule. Sometimes we say, 'who is our neighbor?'

"Is our neighbor only those whom we like? Some would say that you can't expect us to consider a criminal to be our neighbor? Yet that is what Jesus did on the cross. What did He say to the thief on the cross who said, 'Lord remember me when you come into your kingdom.'

Does anyone remember?" Lawrence waited patiently for someone in the congregation to respond. Everyone looked around, not used to being called upon for answers during the sermon.

"Truly I say to you, today you shall be with Me in Paradise."

"Exactly Mrs. Philpot!" Mrs. Philpot smiled as her chest began to swell up with pride.

"How about prostitutes? Are prostitutes our neighbors? Mary Magdalene was considered a 'sinful woman,' and yet became one of the pillars of the early church.

"How 'bout adulterers? Are adulterers our neighbors? What did Jesus say to the woman caught in adultery?" Lawrence again looked around the congregation for participation.

"Go your way and from now on do not sin again."

"Very good Mrs. Philpot!" Given the delay in responding and Mrs. Philpot's continued looking down toward her lap, Lawrence surmised she was cheating.

"So we know that Jesus was a friend to sinners, basically calling them His neighbor. But who else is our neighbor? Are we only to call people our neighbor if they are of a certain background, a certain economic standing, a certain heritage?"

Lawrence looked over the congregants and again noted that it was a full house. Were these people really there to listen to his words? Sometimes that thought would overwhelm him and he often prayed that his words would have an impact. He looked toward the front row where Sarah was; she was her usual encouraging and smiling self. W.E. on the other hand, had an expression of little support, seeming to know where Lawrence was headed with his message.

"And how about all of God's people? Jesus himself was of Semitic origin...and before anyone else gets too excited, yes while Jewish he was also God and therefore not attached to any one particular race. But we know that there was various colored folk in the Bible; the Queen of Sheba being most likely from Arabia or Africa, the Ethiopian eunuch who was in search of Biblical truth. And of course who could forget Simon of Cyrene who helped take the Lord's cross for Him? We are all of God's people. We are all one people, one race. It doesn't matter about the color of one's skin..."

At that point, several people, including W.E. stood up and walked out of the church. Their intent was clear and Lawrence began to wonder if he would have a job or an education after his comments. The scene had been an awkward one with W.E. motioning to his wife and children to follow him. Luckily Sarah ignored his request and continued to look at her husband.

When the service ended there were very few people who greeted Lawrence and he could see that he had maybe overstepped his bounds. As for Sarah, she stood by her man, literally holding on to him. But she was one of the few who did. Even his own family was not supportive, his father giving him a cold scowl as he walked by and then quickly exiting to the parsonage.

"Maybe it's time we moved?" Lawrence said to Sarah.

"Yes, but where? You haven't finished your studies yet. Who would hire you as their preacher?"

"We might have an opportunity in Atlanta. Professor Thompson knows of a position that's coming open."

Sarah nodded as they then turned and headed back to the Fuller house. It was a walk with some trepidation.

Monday morning, Lawrence was summoned before a tribunal of sorts. A group led by W.E. included his father, three church deacons, and the church treasurer. Mark Fleming was also the city accountant and great with numbers but what theological perspectives he offered Lawrence wasn't sure.

"Lawrence, we called you here today to discuss a few things."

The scene was reminiscent of a courtroom. Thc five church elders were on one side of a table and Lawrence was on the opposite side.

"I think I can speak for all the church leadership and say that while we appreciate your convictions and the forceful way you convey your message, I think you do not appreciate the culture we have here in Irbyville. We are an older community and a lot of our members, who we depend upon for financial donations, will not understand these fancy words and concepts you're tryin' to preach to 'em.

"Now, as you go along your theological trainin' you'll learn how to better present your thoughts and ideas so we understand it may take a little time. So in the meantime, I would like your father to read and approve your sermons whenever you preach."

"And if I disagree?"

"Well, then we'll have to remove you from your role in the church."

Lawrence stopped and thought of the gravity of what it meant. He wanted to react with anger and outrage but did his best to control his emotions.

"So what precisely is the issue with my sermon yesterday?

W.E. in his usual walrus-like continence propped himself up in his chair and leaned back eyeing Lawrence up and down. He shook his head and then spoke, "I think you know what I'm talking about Lawrence. You don't have to play the innocent with us."

"No, I need clarification on what y'all have issues with."

"You know what the issues are. You fought for those issues didn't you?!!!"

"What if I don't agree with those issues anymore?"

"What are you sayin'?"

"I'm saying that God has revealed to me about the sin of slavery that it was wrong what we did, what the Confederacy was about!" W.E. rose out of his seat as if he was about to reach over the table and strangle Lawrence. Lawrence was not intimidated and stood up as well, ready to receive any blows his father-in-law would attempt to deliver.

"This meeting is adjourned. Gentlemen, you are dismissed!" W.E. thundered and then turned and walked out of the church. Lawrence sat back down and then just shook his head, wondering what the good Lord had gotten him into. He had survived a very bloody and violent war, and thus the Lord had already prepared him for this confrontation. He was more than capable of handling a frustrated racist father-in-law and his gang, or so he hoped. He began to pray in earnest for the Lord's discernment.

The following day Lawrence went into Atlanta and spoke to the head deacon at Peachtree Baptist Church.

"Mr. Ambrose, good to meet you," Ernest Gaines said as he extended his hand to Lawrence.

"Good to meet you deacon, you have a lovely church here," Lawrence said as he tried to convince himself. The church was in a state of disrepair but it was set on a nice piece of land just south of downtown, off of Peachtree Street. It was right next to the AMA building. The deacon smiled and tried to reassure him.

"Don't worry Mr. Ambrose, we are getting some much-needed funding from the AMA so we can do some repairs. As you are aware we just got the approval to build a school in the lot next store. Thc school plus morc funding will allow freedmen to get better educated and better job placement." Deacon Gaines motioned for Lawrence to walk inside of the church. The inside looked a little better, much smaller though than the church in Irbyville.

"Now the church was originally a mostly white congregation but it is quite mixed now." Lawrence nodded and smiled, he knew that was most likely the case.

"I think it's important that whoever we choose as pastor must be able to speak to different audiences. What are your feelings about that?"

"Well, absolutely. I've learned that God has created a great many different kinds of people; white, black, Latin, Asian, and not only many races but many kinds of individuals who have all different kinds of problems to deal with. I can't say that I fully understand per se what the average black man or freedman is going through but I will do my best to try. I have been working with the AMA at least one day a month and it has been an eye-opening experience. I feel the plight of the freedman. It's a whole new world where many of them have no clue what the next step is. Some are not educated and wouldn't know what questions to even ask. I think I can help. I can help these people with their physical needs and their spiritual needs. At least I'd like the opportunity to try."

"How would you say the average congregant views your current ministry up in Irbyville?"

"Some like me, others question me. You see I want to change hearts and minds. To live in the past and follow the ways of the past is not going to allow those folks to survive. If they do not change their hearts it will be a dark and difficult world for many of them. I try to expand their minds, tell them that Jesus Christ is the savior of all men, not a select group."

"Professor Thompson says you are one of his top students."

"Well, there's only ten of us so it wouldn't be difficult to stand out."

"And how 'bout your wife, would she be okay with this kind of move?"

"I have mentioned it to her. Sarah is very flexible, plus she is studying education and if you are building a school that would be perfect."

"Well, the job pays $15 a week. It includes room and board. The parsonage is down the street there on Douglass. Just down the block, about five houses down. If you and the misses want to take a look and then let me know if you would like the job, that would be great."

"Thank you deacon," Lawrence said as he grabbed his hand to shake. "Let me just run this all by Sarah and we'll make a decision.

"That's fine son, just fine."

Lawrence hopped onto his horse and headed back north to Irbyville. Sarah was eagerly awaiting his arrival. When Lawrence and Sarah married, W.E. gave them a small cottage on the edge of the property so they could be alone. While not the most elegant building it was still nice for a newlywed couple. It would be hard to leave. It would also be hard to pass up the pay, the tuition, and the good food. Lawrence assumed that if he took the position W.E. would no longer be willing to pay their expenses. He did not look forward to the confrontation that was coming.

The following day, everyone in Irbyville assembled at the town hall. It was a festive day with bunting and decorations all over the building. There was a cover over the normal sign that read *Irbyville Town Hall.* People were in much speculation as to what the event was all about. Behind a platform with a podium sat the mayor and W.E. as well as all of the council members. The mayor stepped up to the podium when the clock tower hit 1 p.m.

"Ladies and gentlemen, boys and girls, welcome to another happy event here in Irbyville. We have much to be thankful for here in Irbyville. A prosperous town with many thriving members. A lot of our gratitude has to be given to our main patron, W.E. Fuller..." There was applause throughout the crowd with a few shouts of praise.

"We've had difficult times as well here in Irbyville, but thanks to W.E. stepping in and giving the city loans at very reasonable rates, we have been able to pay our debts and again start building up the city, fixing buildings and streets, adding street lamps, and the great city park!" Again there was applause and various cheers and yelps of accord.

"And so because of W.E.'s great work in town, especially with everything he provides via the mill, it gives me great pleasure to announce that Irbyville is now Fullertown!!!" Some burst out into applause while others were a little confused. The city's name was changing? At that point, the mayor pulled on a cord that was attached to the cover on the building. When he pulled the cover off the building now read *Fullertown Town Hall.*

Even Sarah was surprised when she saw the name change. She had heard nothing of such a move. Lawrence smiled knowing that he had underestimated W.E.'s ego. He soon learned that there were no ends to what W.E. thought of himself. Rather than congratulating W.E., Lawrence grabbed Sarah by the hand and they headed back to the cottage. He had to get to class anyway and he didn't want to contribute to W.E.'s self-emplaced divine status further. He gave Sarah a kiss, hopped onto his horse, and was off for school. He wondered if he would be able to afford his schooling once they made the move to Atlanta.

Two weeks later the time came for Lawrence to give another sermon. The sermon he had given to his father, which his father approved, was not the one he delivered. The whole town was in a tizzy over what he might say not knowing the mandate that W.E. had instituted with regard as to what Lawrence could or couldn't say. The church was bursting from the ground floor to the balcony. It was standing room only and there were even people milling around outside who couldn't get in. W.E. always scoured the congregation for mill workers, making sure they were all in attendance. When Lawrence walked up to the pulpit and began to peer around the church, he could see many concerned faces in the crowd, mostly that of W.E. and his cronies. Sully and Sarah gave bright smiles which is what he focused on. After a word of prayer, he began his sermon...

"Ladies and gentlemen, thank you for coming out today despite this inclement weather. Looks like it will be raining much of the day today, at least according to the Farmer's Almanac. Any chance it's accurate Mr. Paul?" Lawrence joked with Samuel Paul, one of the local farmers who smiled and shook his head with embarrassment. Lawrence felt almost free now, now that he had made a decision as to his future.

"My dear brothers and sisters of Irbyville...excuse me Fullertown," he corrected himself looking at W.E. in the front pew. Lawrence had a broad smile on his face.

"We have such a loving and good God. I should know. I was in an awful war for four years. I saw death and destruction no one should ever have to see and yet the Lord saw fit to keep me alive. You see every man, and woman has a purpose in this life. I used to think I was like everyone else, and in many ways I am. I was created in the image of God like everyone else. I have a heart and a brain like everyone else, but I also have a unique purpose, which is different from everyone else. For some, their purpose is to build and make things out of wood. For others, like Farmer Paul, it's to tend to the land. For me, it's to preach.

"I remember during the war that Jefferson Davis made a speech at the Spotswood Hotel in Richmond back in 1861. He said, '*the cause in which we engaged is the cause of advocacy of rights to which we were born, those for which our fathers of the Revolution bled – the richest inheritance that ever fell to man, and which it is our sacred duty to transmit untarnished to our children. Upon us is devolved the high and holy responsibility of preserving the Constitutional liberty of a free government. Those with whom we have lately associated have shown themselves so incapable of appreciating the blessings of the glorious institutions they inherited, that they are today stripped of the liberty to which they were born. They have allowed an ignorant usurper to trample upon all the prerogatives of citizenship, and to exercise power never delegated to him; and it has been reserved for your own State, so lately one of the original thirteen, but now, thank God, fully separated from them, to become the theatre of a great central camp, from which will pour forth thousands of brave hearts to roll back the tide of this despotism.*'"

Lawrence stood silent after reading from his notes on Davis' speech. He then picked up his Bible and walked around to the other side of the pulpit. The congregation took note as typically all the preachers at the church had stayed right behind the pulpit.

"I was one of those 'brave hearts' that Davis was speaking of. I too held all of those beliefs. There was a time I completely agreed with his sentiments, that we as southern men and women were in the grip of tyranny and despotism. When we read these words we have to wonder what perspective he was speaking from? When he uses the word 'Constitutional' what did he mean? Of course, this was a time before the thirteenth amendment to the constitution. But as I've said in the past we need to forge ahead and we need to have the South rise again, but not in the old ways that we knew, but in the new way and new law. Just like we were not slaves to the Old Covenant in the Bible, the Lord set us free with the New Covenant. No longer were we subject to death which the law brought because we have Jesus as our advocate. We still obey the law but we have salvation if we fail to adhere to the law.

"So what am I saying? We are free to follow God if we choose to or not. We can obey His laws or he gives us free will not to follow those laws. We have a new law in the land which is the thirteenth amendment which says there is no longer slavery. Are we going to choose to be mired in the old ways, to be enslaved to the old southern way of life or are we going to move forward? Move forward to the New Covenant, the Covenant that brings freedom to everyone?"

Lawrence looked over at W.E. who was about to explode. He then made a shocking announcement.

"I know my words are not popular here in Fullertown and so as of today, I will resign as the associate pastor of First Baptist Church. It has been a genuine honor and privilege to serve the people of Irbyville," Lawrence purposely did not correct himself.

"And so my wife and I bid you adieu," Lawrence immediately walked down to the front pew, grabbed Sarah by the hand, and headed down the aisle toward the front exit. Everyone in the congregation looked around in puzzlement. What had just happened? Outside of the church waited Ernest Gains and a carriage. In it were several suitcases.

"Are we really doing this?" Sarah asked. Lawrence nodded and then helped her into the carriage.

"I can't stay here another day if they are going to muzzle me."

Sarah had agreed to the plan but the reality of separating from her family had not fully set in until that moment.

"Let's go, Ernie."

The deacon pulled the reigns on the horses and they were soon heading down the road. W.E. and family and the rest of the congregation were soon outside. W.E. was beside himself with anger and began to yell at the fleeing couple. Lawrence clutched onto Sarah who he could see was now reconsidering the move.

"C'mon my love, it will be okay. We can't stay in this town any longer. We have to follow the Lord's will and staying in that town will kill us spiritually."

Sarah had a faint smile but now being pregnant she couldn't imagine not being near her mother and siblings. Lawrence gave her a reassuring smile and a big hug. She would need all the encouragement she could get. She remembered that they were also going for the purpose of starting a church and a school in which she would have a large part to play. She was torn with mixed feelings, but she knew that she would eventually have to leave at some point. She loved Lawrence and with her faith in God, she knew it was the right choice.

CHAPTER 17
A Major Move

November 1st, 1866

The parsonage at Peachtree Baptist Church was small but with a little cleaning and fix up Lawrence made it his and Sarah's happy new home. W.E. had become aware of Lawrence's new employment and went to the house several times imploring Sarah to leave Lawrence and come home. At one point he threatened Lawrence with physical harm if he didn't allow Sarah to come back home with him. Lawrence was becoming concerned. Not only did W.E. send several men to hang a straw effigy of Lawrence, but it was now clear that W.E. was behind several incidents involving the terrorizing of negro homes and businesses. One business was even burnt to the ground. No one was able to pin it on W.E. but it was clear he was behind the events. It eventually took a fed-up Sarah, who on her own, borrowed the church carriage and went to the Fuller house where she gave her father a piece of her mind. The confrontation ended with her throwing a parcel of new clothes he had sent her, directly at his head. He pleaded for her to stay but it was to no avail. He would never threaten Lawrence again after that. He would however step up the activities of his chapter of the Ku Klux Klan.

One day a knock came on the couple's front door.
"Good afternoon, Mr. Ambrose?"
"Yes, how are you. You appear to be a captain?"

"Faulkner, Captain Clarence Faulkner at your service."

"How can I help you, captain?"

"Well, more importantly, how can I help you, Mr. Ambrose. You recently wrote a letter to General Tilson, about the need for more troops in Atlanta, and I was asked by the General to see how we can assist."

"Thank you, Captain. Please come in."

"This is my wife Sarah."

"Hello."

"Howdy, ma'am. Nice to make your acquaintance."

"Likewise Captain. Would you like to take a chair?"

"No ma'am. I don't want to trouble you and your husband. I just wanted to drop by and let you know that we are here in the neighborhood. We understand there was some trouble the other day and we have a strong presence here in the Five Points area and will be doing patrols. I know your husband mentioned something about a rise in people being harassed…you said it was the…"

"KKK, Ku Klux Klan."

"Ah, yes, well we will be keepin' an eye on that group and we will make sure to keep the city peaceful. General Tilson has made a commitment to the city to keep the peace and will do all possible to make sure nothing of a violent nature is tolerated."

"Well, thank you, Captain. That is most reassuring," Lawrence said offering his hand to shake.

"Mr. Ambrose. I hear you are a war veteran. What unit were you in if you mind me askin'?"

"Not at all. The 12th Battalion, Georgia Light Artillery."

The captain sized up Lawrence.

"Hmmm, leadin' a congregation like this I'm surprised they didn't promote you to lead a group of men into battle?"

Lawrence was a little puzzled as to where the captain was going with the line of inquiry. Lawrence shrugged his shoulders and shook his head.

"I think we had good leadership. Wasn't necessary. I had enough to do on my own without being responsible for others, plus I was pretty young."

"Well, rest assured we have good leadership here as well and we'll take care of y'all. See you have a little one on the way." Lawrence was surprised that the captain knew of the pregnancy as Sarah was only a couple of months along and barely showing. Sarah blushed and nodded her head.

"Well, I'm much obliged to you, Captain. Don't want to hold you. I'm sure you have more pressing matters. Thank you for your time."

"Not'dall. It's been a pleasure and I look forward to seeing you around the community. I've been looking for a church so maybe I'll stop by."

"You do that Captain. I think you'll be pleasantly surprised."

Lawrence closed the door behind the captain and looked through the window as he walked toward his horse. Sarah walked up behind him to watch as the captain rode out of sight.

"What do you think about that?" Sarah asked.

"I don't know. I have an odd feeling about him. Probably a spy for your father I'm guessin'."

"Do you think my father would be that devious?"

"I don't put anything past your father."

"Well, forget about him. I've made you lunch."

Lawrence smiled and drew Sarah toward him. He held her close and squeezed her tight. He kissed her and looked into her eyes.

"I really don't know what I'd do without you."

"You'd be completely lost I reckon." Lawrence broke out into laughter and nodded his head.

"God knew what he was doing when he created women that's for sure," Sarah smiled and they again embraced.

The following Sunday was the first appearance of the Ambrose's at Peachtree Baptist. While he had already met with the senior leadership of the church, it would be the first time that he would meet with its congregants. A "mixed" membership was exactly as Deacon Gaines had described it; black, white, young, old, professional, and poor, all were in attendance. They began the day by having the AMA come before the 8 o'clock service and serve porridge and baked goods to everyone that was there. Lawrence and Sarah stood at the end of the table, helping to give out food and to introduce themselves. After everyone was adequately fed, Lawrence invited the congregants to go inside the church. The church was still being fixed up and there were blankets, ladders, and buckets of paint in the rear of the building.

Like a pied piper, Lawrence beckoned everyone to follow him down the main aisle and motioned for them to sit in whichever pews they preferred. He then escorted Sarah to the front pew where there was a black family as well as an elderly black woman. Sarah introduced herself to the older lady and was soon being regaled about the woman's family and where she had been raised. Lawrence laughed as Sarah could barely get a word in edgewise.

"Good morning everyone and welcome to Peachtree Baptist. My name is Lawrence Ambrose and I will be serving as your lay pastor. I am currently training at Franklin College so I hope you will bear with me as we get settled. I'd like my wife Sarah in the front row there to stand." Sarah stood and the congregation gave her a round of applause.

"My wife and I are truly humbled to be serving you. I am not just a preacher or a theologian, though I would say those are my specialties, but I've learned there is much more to being a pastor than just speaking. There are more important things than words. There are actions. I want to be not only helping you spiritually, but if anyone needs help physically, emotionally…well I want to know about that too. We are here to help grow this neighborhood. We see today what the war has wrought. We see what devastation it has brought us and the city still is broken from what has happened. But we want to raise the soul of Atlanta. We want to make Atlanta a beacon of the South like it once was or was about to be. We want to see all of its communities prosper and grow. We want everyone to have a proper education and access to housing.

"My wife and I are pretty young still and we need to learn from each and every one of you. This is not just a situation where a pastor leads a flock. I will lead but I need your help. I need everyone's input. I need to know everyone's needs, otherwise, it's just me paying lip service and just moving my mouth every Sunday without people's lives being changed.

"Going forward, we will have a weekly Bible study on Wednesday nights that everyone is invited to. Every Saturday morning we will be working at the AMA to help with food distribution. You are all welcome to join us for that. Every Sunday we will have an 8 a.m. service, 9:30 a.m. Sunday School and an 11 a.m. service. After the 11 a.m. we will have a social gathering of some form; maybe a lunch or potluck but a time to be together and have fun.

"As we grow we will be adding a school. That school will start off with younger students but one day we hope it will be K through 12th grade. My beautiful wife will be leading that effort. So as we grow hopefully they'll be all kinds of opportunities for everyone.

"Anyway, welcome and let's close in prayer."

After prayer, Lawrence and Sarah went to the front of the church where they greeted and spoke to each congregant. They repeated the same format for the 11 a.m. service. After it was all done they sighed and looked over the church; wondering how they were going to fulfill the plans they had so boldly announced. At least one person who was confident was Deacon Gaines who gave Lawrence a vigorous handshake after the 11 a.m. service.

"Well, I am truly optimistic son. I think we will do great things together!" Lawrence thought he would lose his arm, the deacon was shaking it so hard.

"Me too deacon. I look forward to the future."

When everyone else had left, the couple held hands and walked home discussing all of their plans. While doing so, Lawrence noticed a few federal troops that were patrolling the streets or sitting at various points.

He didn't know if he should be reassured or to feel like the eyes of W.E. were following him.

CHAPTER 18
Advent Season

Christmas, 1866

The week before Christmas, the Ambrose's put the finishing touches on the church. Lawrence had fixed all of the loose siding, floorboards and added new shingles. The church board was able to provide new carpeting and with a coat of fresh paint throughout, the church looked brand-new. Sarah had put up Christmas decorations throughout the church and it was looking festive. The couple were finishing up decorating the altar one evening when a lone figure walked through the front door.

"Can we help you?" Lawrence yelled from near the church pulpit. The figure moved slowly down the aisle until illuminated.

"Father O'Reilly, is that you?"

"Yes, my boy. So very good to see you and welcome to the neighborhood!"

"Oh, it's very nice to see you as well. You remember Sarah, my wife?"

"Oh yes, she was a great help to me that night in Irbyville. So very good to see you, my dear. How has everything been coming along?"

"Very good. The Lord has blessed us immensely. We have a wonderful church and congregation, we have a great little parsonage, things have been relatively peaceful for a change on the family front."

"Excellent, excellent. That is so good to hear."

"And how about you Father, all well in your world?"

"Oh very well. We keep serving the faithful over at the Atlanta Catholic Church and look for lost souls as best as we can which of course there are plenty of those. We did have some vandalism a few weeks back but we seem to be fine now."

"Really, what kind of vandalism?"

"A few of our relics and shrines were tampered with. One statue of St. Joseph was toppled over and was smashed."

"Any idea who was behind it?"

"I don't know exactly. It all happened at night. Young hooligans, I imagine with nothing better to do. They probably need jobs. I hear you are working closely with the AMA? That will surely be helpful. Get a little federal funding and what not?"

"Yes, we are very tied to the AMA. We hope to build a school next year so we plan to grow."

"That is wonderful my boy. Well, maybe we can work together on some event, perhaps an ecumenical meeting of some sort."

"Yes, Father that would be great."

"Well, we'll talk later. Good night to both of you and Merry Christmas."

"Merry Christmas Father."

Lawrence and Sarah watched as the kindly old gentleman walked slowly out of sight. Lawrence became concerned for his safety and wondered if the KKK was behind the vandalism. The KKK was not pro-Catholic and lumped the Pope in with a number of their enemies.

As the couple were about to leave for the night another dark figure presented himself toward the front of the church. As he walked into the light he was easily recognizable.

"Sully, what are doing here?!!!" Lawrence yelled as he ran to greet him. Sully had been doing well, ever since he had moved with his mother to Fullertown. He got a job at the mill and had moved into one of the apartments. He worked hard and was being considered for a position as foreman. That was until something terrible happened. Lawrence had thought things were going well for his old friend but he could see that Sully was not somewhat distraught.

"What's the matter, Sully? You don't look well."

"Hey Lawrence, I'm so sorry to trouble you and Sarah but we've been kicked out of the mill."

Lawrence looked at Sully incredulously.

"Kicked out of the mill. What do you mean?"

"When W.E. found out who I was and that I was a friend of yours he fired me."

"What? You're kiddn'?!!!" Lawrence looked at Sarah and shook his head. Sarah immediately ran over to Sully and hugged him. She was beginning to learn who her father really was.

"Sully, I'm so sorry this happened. Is there anything we can do?"

"Can you tell us where we can go for the night? It's a bit cold and we have nowhere to go."

"Come back with us. It's small but we do have another bedroom."

"I'm with my mother. Are you sure that's alright?"

"Of course it is. C'mon, let's get you over to the parsonage."

Lawrence was starting to see and feel the reach of W.E. Sometimes he could be subtle but other times he was downright horrible. To put a man and his mother out on the streets near Christmas time - it was despicable, to say the least.

The following morning, Lawrence met up with Thaddeus to get Sully set up with a job at the AMA. Though the Ambrose's didn't mind the Sullivan's staying with them, there just wasn't that much room. If they were going to have a large family they were going to need to do some expansion. Before they spoke about Sully's needs, Thaddeus brought up some urgent matters.

"Tilson is in the back pocket of your father-in-law."

"What…really? How do you know?" Thaddeus rolled his eyes conveying that Lawrence knew how. Thaddeus was now the eyes and ears for Lawrence via McMillan's Grocers.

"So he's gonna be turnin' his back on any activities of your father-in-law."

This was deeply troubling to Lawrence as well as the rest of Atlanta. He soon realized that W.E. wanted to control not only Fullertown but the entire state. He already had some of the politicians in his back pockets, but now the military. Most of the federal forces in Atlanta were run by ex-Confederates. It was clear where their sympathies lay.

"By the way, I'd like to introduce you to Chester Magee. Chester, this is Pastor Ambrose and this is Billy Sullivan. We call him 'Sully.'"

Stepping out of the shadows of the building's entryway was a very tall young man. He looked to be 17 or 18 years old. He was very meek and humble and looked a little raggedy, but he had the brightest smile Lawrence had ever seen.

"Chester just came from a farm down in Macon. He is now happy to be a freedman and we are helping him get set up with housing and work."

"Please to meet'ya acquaintance Pastor Ambrose…Mista Sullivan sir."

"Just call me Sully," the young man shook Sully's hand.

"You can call me Lawrence, I'm not a full-fledged pastor as of yet. Still going to school."

"Still that'sa mighty fine callin' you have Pastor Ambrose," Chester continued to shake Lawrence's hand until it became comical.

"Ok Chester, you can give the man his hand back now," Thaddeus said with a big grin.

"Sully, I got you right next door to Chester at the AMA apartments just behind the church. Why don't I help you with your mother's things and we'll head over there now."

"I appreciate it, Thaddeus."

"You're welcome. Chester, help me get Sully and his mother's things from the parsonage."

"Yessir Mr. Thaddeus."

With that, the three men walked back to the parsonage with Chester in tow. After picking up the Sullivan's things and starting to head back to the AMA, Chester turned to Lawrence and said, "Pastor Ambrose. I would love to be a pastor one day. Maybe you could help me?" Lawrence was stunned to think anyone would ask him for such help. He was learning that the subject of God was in one sense an overwhelming pursuit given that God was omniscient and omnipresent. But God had revealed himself through his Son and Lawrence poured himself in growing in the knowledge of Jesus. But even though he had a good grasp of the Bible, still knowing the true nature of God seemed unattainable at times. Despite his struggles with faith, he knew that the pursuit of it meant everything.

"I will try Chester. Why don't you come to the Bible study on Wednesdays? That would be a good start." Chester smiled with a bright grin, turned, and headed off into the night with Thaddeus and the Sullivan's.

When Lawrence returned to the parsonage he found Sarah in their bedroom, sitting on the bed and crying.

"What is it, my love?" Lawrence said as he slowly approached her.

"Oh, it's just that I really miss my family."

"I'm sorry Sarah. I know leaving like that wasn't ideal but I just can't live with your father anymore."

"I know. It's just being pregnant and not having my family around is a bit trying."

"Well, are there things I can help with?"

"No, you've been more than helpful. And you built that crib and bought me that rocking chair."

Lawrence leaned in and gave her a forceful hug. She reciprocated but then began to weep, shaking as she did so. Lawrence began to think about how he could get Sarah and her mother and sisters together. With W.E.'s proclamation that the Fullers could not interact with the Ambrose's, it would be difficult.

"You must think we women are silly?"

"No, far from it. I think women are the greatest gift that God gave to man, materially speaking I mean."

Sarah began to study his face with a bright gleam in her eye.

"You don't find us burdensome?"

"No. I think about the Bible and I think about how God saw Adam being alone. I think about that passage and wonder if God was with Adam wouldn't that have been enough…to be with God? But I think it shows how much God loves us. God couldn't be intimate with us in that way and so he created a mate, a companion for us men. And he didn't just create a biological equivalent, he created a human who has arms and legs, a heart and mind just like us, but so different in all the right ways. Women are warm, gentle, loving, kind…"

"Funny, intelligent?" Sarah retorted.

"Yes, of course, you're the funniest character I know. You always make me laugh."

"Forgiving?"

"Yes, very forgiving. Are you talking about something in particular?"

"Well, you did separate me from my family."

"And?"

"And I think it would be in your best interest if you arranged a meeting with my father for a truce?"

At that Lawrence stood up and began to pace back and forth. Sarah stood up and rushed over to him, grabbing him and pulling him into her. She gave him a look of adoration with pouting lips that he knew was comically forced. It was a look that he could never refuse.

"Alright, I'll see what I can do. Now put away that face."

Sarah burst into laughter and Lawrence began to smile. Behind the smile, however, was him thinking about how in the world he could ever reconcile with W.E., the man he hated the most. But as a Christian could he hate anyone? Wasn't he supposed to pray even for his enemies?

When Christmas Eve arrived, the Ambrose's held two services; one at 7 pm and one at Midnight. Flyers had gone out several days before announcing the services and that food and coffee would be provided by the AMA. Lawrence had become very close with Owen Lovejoy who would visit Atlanta often. The AMA had started Clark Atlanta University with the aid of two very well-educated freedmen. They were now eyeing other locations to start schools and had been speaking with Lawrence about starting one in connection with his church. Sarah was excited and looked forward to the work ahead. One of the great benefits of working with the AMA was the federal and private funding it received. Not that Lawrence was wanting money for himself, but he soon realized that the resources of the AMA came in quite handy, even if it was for food and coffee at their Christmas services.

"Good evening everyone. Thank you for coming tonight. We have a good turnout despite the drop in temperature. I hear we might get some snow before the evening is done." Lawrence was happy to see a full house for the Midnight service.

"Today is the savior's birth. Advent in the Catholic faith. But what does it all mean? We work hard every day to put food on the table and we break our backs with work and feeding our families. We spend hour after hour toiling and sweating, but for what? What do we get out of it? When we get wrapped up in the details of life, it can take away from the grander things that we really need to be thinking about. Yes, it is important to have a job and feed our families, but we also need to make time for prayer, for

Bible study." Lawrence could see Chester's bright face looking up at him in the front pew as he sat next to Sarah.

"What are those grander things we need to think about? Well, that there is a God number one. God does exist. But we are separated from God...why? Because of sin. What is sin? Well, we see it every day." Lawrence began to walk from around the pulpit as was now his custom so he could get closer to the congregants.

"We see how people are treated. We see how a whole class of people were enslaved. Clearly, man is in need of help. I saw sin in the war. I was a soldier. I was near death many times and at times it was dark. It was dark my brothers and sisters!!! War is a result of man's sin...man's heart which is dark. And when we read the Old Testament we see how often man failed. How man failed to live up to God's standard. He would try...with animal sacrifices at the temple. He would try and clean himself, but in his heart, he was prone to sin, he was prone to doing what he wanted and not what God wanted. The sin of pride. It's the sin we all have inside of us; chiefly that we want to be in charge instead of God being in charge. We know what's best for us versus God knowing what's best for us. And we all know it. We all have to kill ourselves spiritually, we have to die to ourselves and then submit to God. Then we can see the grander things of life.

"Jesus Christ came to this earth almost 2,000 years ago. Has anything changed as far as human corruption? No. Wars continue. Disease continues. Theft, robbery, murder...all continue. And why? Because we human beings want to do things our way. We were given an example; Jesus on the cross and yet we still want to do things our way. These deeds, these sins will not stop until we die to self until we accept the Savior and keep his commandments.

"And so, after Adam and Eve's expulsion from the Garden of Eden, we see sin continue to happen in the Old Testament. And so God in his infinite mercy sent His Kings, His Judges, He then sent Prophets. Surely they would listen to these God-fearing men who had the power and might of God on their side? But as in the Lord's parable of the Vineyard Keeper, even the prophets were slain. And so, it came down to God himself. Who else would He send? More Judges, more Prophets? Surely they will listen to My Son? But no. We killed him too. We killed the living God. And so on the anniversary of His birth, let us remember God's humility. He humbled himself to become a baby...a little baby!!! Does this not mean anything to you?!!!" People could sense that Lawrence was a little angry and frustrated.

"We insane and corrupt humans, who kill each other, why can't we just humble ourselves? Why can't we humble ourselves like God? God. God the creator of the universe, the heavens, and the earth. He saw fit to lower Himself to our level. To become a tiny, helpless infant. There's a reason we have a manger scene here in the church. It's to look upon that baby. That baby, weak and vulnerable. Never doubt that God doesn't understand how we feel. Look at him!" Lawrence then walked directly to the nativity scene that had been set up in one of the corners near the sanctuary. He walked up and then bowed before the wooden image of Christ. Just then, Sarah's mother and three sisters walked into the church where they stood near the front entryway. It briefly caught Lawrence's attention but then he continued to focus on the manger.

"We need to humble ourselves like our God did," he said pointing to the manger.

"Look at these wise men. They knew what was happening. A King had been born. Look at them on their knees. I want everyone in this church to now get on their knees. I want you to humble yourselves. Everyone, c'mon, please get on your knees. Let us be humble before our God. Lord Jesus Christ, thank you, Lord, for loving us so much that You humbled yourself to become a child for us and Your ultimate act of humility of dying for us on the cross. Not just a quiet death on some comfortable deathbed, but a violent and horrible death. We ask that despite how sinful we are that You would still come and bless us. We ask that You bless Peachtree Baptist Church. We ask that You bless the American Missionary Association and everyone affiliated with the good work these people do. Bless all the churches in Atlanta and all pastors and congregations and parishes around the world. Please guide us Lord, please lead us. We ask these things in Jesus' name. Amen."

Lawrence stood for several minutes with his head bowed. He then looked up and began to walk out of the church. Sarah's heart was pounding; she had never heard her husband preach like that before. It was so passionate. Everyone slowly sat back in their pews and eventually got up and walked out of the church. But everyone had been impacted by the message. When everyone had gone to the front of the church, Lawrence and members of the AMA were there providing food and coffee. The congregants had a newfound appreciation for their young pastor. Even Sarah saw a change in him.

"Boy, what got into you? Those were some powerful words," she said as she nudged him while also helping to hand out food.

"Yeah, I don't know what got into me either. Hopefully the Holy Spirit," he said with a broad smile.

"Pastor Ambrose, that was the best speech…ah sermon I done heard in my whole life."

"Thank you, Chester. I hope it helped you in some small way."

"It did indeed. I now want to become a pastor even more than I did before," he said with such glee.

"Well, we'll work on it," Lawrence said as he handed him a plate of chicken, green beans, and potatoes. Chester looked like he had just arrived in heaven he was so happy. Lawrence and Sarah were both warming to the young man and saw a lot of potential in him. With everything that was on Lawrence's plate, he needed to make time to help the young man.

As they continued to hand out food, Sarah and Lawrence were greeted by Sarah's mother and sisters. Sarah practically dropped the plate she was about to hand out when she saw them. She gave the plate to an elderly woman and then ran as fast as she could to her mother, giving her a long hug. Lawrence too came over and expressed his joy over their arrival.

"We didn't see it all but that must have been one fine sermon, Lawrence," his mother-in-law chuckled. Sarah and her sisters concurred.

"Well, we'll see. I hope my words have an impact but only God knows what goes on in men's souls. Say, I think the AMA staff have everything in hand. Why don't we get your mother and sisters over to the parsonage?"

"Heaven sakes no," Sarah's mother said. "You've got four able-bodied women here who can help."

"Ah ok, there are some aprons right over there."

"Girls, let's get to work!" Sarah's mother commanded.

"Does W.E. know you're here?" Lawrence asked his mother-in-law.

"No, thank the Lord. One thing you can say about W.E. is he is a creature of habit. Every night he is in bed and fast asleep by 10 p.m. Nothing stirs the man. Now let's get these people fed!"

For the next hour, Lawrence, Sarah, her mother, and sisters helped dish out the food until everyone had received a plate. Once the hand-out had been completed, they moved all the tables, plates, and utensils back to the kitchen at the AMA. It was 2 in the morning before everyone was able to leave for the night.

Back at the parsonage, Sarah's mother and sisters exchanged gifts with the couple. All of the items were earmarked for the baby which was much appreciated by Sarah and Lawrence. Sarah served coffee and apple pie knowing the party was just getting started. She had not seen her mother or sisters in over a month and she was so happy to see them. As they continued into the early hours, a thunderous knock came on the front door. Lawrence opened the door to find W.E. standing there fuming.

"What is the meaning of this?!!! He said shouting as he entered the house. Apparently, W.E. had been stirred. Most likely by one of his men.

"Phyllis, you and the girls get going now. I have a carriage outside waiting for you."

"Daddy, please don't do this!" Sarah shouted at her father.

"And as for you. If you don't come with me now, you will never be allowed back at the Fuller house!"

"Daddy, you can't do that to Sarah, she is your daughter!" Elizabeth yelled.

"I can say whatever I want to! Now everyone else go to the carriage now!!!"

Some of W.E.'s men were standing at the doorway motioning for the ladies to follow them. Sarah's mother, never one to disagree with her husband, kissed her daughter on the cheek and then left quietly. As for Sarah's sisters, they all vocalized their outrage at not being able to spend time with their sister.

"I hope you're happy!!!" W.E. yclled as he put his index finger into Lawrence's chest. Lawrence had done everything he could to withhold his anger and hatred for the man but it was becoming more and more difficult. There were times he just wanted to haul off and punch him in the face. That fat, pink-stained, sweaty awful face. The face of a boar, he used to think. Somehow he managed to muster all the decorum he could and just stood silent as W.E. bellowed at him.

W.E. stormed out of the house and Lawrence began to wonder how long he could go without a physical confrontation with the man. It would take a lot of prayer and patience to keep from losing control and letting his anger get the best of him.

Lawrence immediately turned around and tried to console a crying Sarah. He hugged her and brushed away the tears from her eyes. She continued to sob as he helped her to bed. She was in a terrible state. She needed her mother and sisters more than ever at that time. She would need them over the coming months and when the baby was due. She knew she could count on help from the AMA and the church, but there was nothing like having the help and wisdom of your own mother to get through a pregnancy.

CHAPTER 19
The Calm Before the Storm

January 1867

By mid-January, Lawrence was back in school and now tutoring Chester on the Bible and church history. He also introduced Chester to Father O'Reilly who could teach him about the early Church Fathers and Saints like St. Augustine and St. Thomas Aquinas. Lawrence had been getting close to Father O'Reilly, often they debated theological issues like the need for confession to a priest and the transubstantiation of Holy Communion. While he didn't see it as a threat to his own faith, he wondered if it were a good idea for Chester to interact in such a close way with the Father.

One Saturday morning, during the third week of January, most everyone from the church gathered to help with the food distribution. All the usual characters like Callie, Thaddeus, and Chester met at the dock to help out. It was a gray, cool day. There had been a light dusting of snow and the streets were a little slippery. In the afternoon, after most of the food had been distributed, Callie loaded a small cart as she typically did to take to several elderly people. Thaddeus and Chester helped her load up the cart and she was soon on her way. Thaddeus and Chester then began to clean up and put items away. As Callie disappeared down one of the spars of Peachtree Street, Thaddeus could make out a couple of figures crossing the street and seeming to follow Callie. Thaddeus patted Chester on the shoulder and then pointed to the two men. He motioned to Chester to follow him so they could find out what the men's intentions were.

Thaddeus and Chester were soon in hot pursuit and when they turned down the side street to where Callie was, they could see the men had caught her and were throwing the contents of her cart on the street. Thaddeus and Chester soon swarmed on top of the men and a fight ensued. Chester, given his size, grabbed one of the men by the scruff of the neck and sent him sailing to the side of the road. Before the man offered any resistance, he was high-tailing it in the opposite direction. Thaddeus was engaged with a straight-out fistfight with the other man, but when Chester joined in he too soon turned and headed out of sight.

"Are you okay Miss Callie?"

Callie was somewhat stunned by what had happened. Once she gained her composure she nodded and thanked the men for helping her.

"Looks like they damaged all the food. I'll need to go back to the store to get more."

"We'll help you, Miss Callie," Chester offered. The two men helped roll the cart back to the store, loaded up more food, and then helped Callie deliver it to the people in need. When they got back to the AMA, Thaddeus reported to Lawrence what had happened.

"Did you get a good look at the men?" Lawrence asked.

"They looked familiar. I think they're KKK affiliated with your father-in-law."

"We'll have to keep an eye on it. I think the federal troops are not going to help us so we need to come up with our own ideas."

"Maybe we need guns?" Thaddeus asked with a desperate expression on his face. Lawrence began to mull the idea over in his head.

"I don't think we've gotten to that point yet but we may need to think about arming ourselves in the future. The problem is everyone will keep obtaining arms and make sure they have more than the other side; it will escalate quickly."

"Do we have a choice if the army won't help us?"

"Well, I always say go to the top."

"God?"

"Yes, definitely God. We need to pray but also I can write to whoever is Tilson's boss. Let's start there before we do anything rash."

"Just know, the KKK is stockpiling weapons over at the store down the street. I think it's gonna get ugly quick."

"I share your concerns. Will have to trust God."

Thaddeus nodded his head and then headed back home. Lawrence was getting very concerned with the growing powder keg that was Atlanta.

The following Monday morning, Lawrence walked over to the Atlanta Catholic Church to speak to Father O'Reilly about instructing Chester. When he walked in he saw Father O'Reilly at the front altar of the church. He had his robes on and had just finished Holy Communion. A deacon was kneeling nearby as the Father finished up with the Eucharistic rite. There were about twenty other people in the church, all were kneeling in their pews. Lawrence wondered how they could pay such great respects to what he referred to as a "cracker."

When Father O'Reilly finished the mass, he prayed a closing prayer and then knelt by the altar and then with the deacon in front of him holding a cross, they exited toward the front of the church. Lawrence left his pew and then greeted the Father.

"Good morning Father, it is good to see you again."

"Oh yes, Lawrence, so very good to see you again. I fear it has been too long."

"Agree. I would very much like to spend more time with you as well."

The Father finished greeting those who had attended the mass and then motioned for Lawrence to follow him to his office. Lawrence walked down the hallway impressed with the various paintings that were hung on the wall. There were various biblical scenes along with images of past priests that had worked in the church. As Lawrence entered the Father's office, he was awed by the number of books that were encased on all four walls. From floor to ceiling in all four directions were book after book. And on the father's desk were more books, somewhat hidden by a vast amount of paperwork that was also sprawled across his desk.

"Wow, looks like you've been busy."

"Well, as they say, no rest for the weary."

Lawrence smiled and nodded as he took a chair on the other side of the Father's desk.

"So my boy, you want me to do a little tutoring for you on the early Church?"

"Yes, Father, I thought that would be a good way to inform Chester."

"I'm very happy that you have come to me for this. And a little surprised."

"Surprised?"

"Well, normally pastors from the Baptist or Evangelical churches do not seek out Catholic priests…typically they flee from them," the Father said with a jovial smile.

"Well, as I go through my own education, one of my professors at Franklin said that I should try and get some different points of view. To not be afraid of other denominations."

"Hmmm, that seems contrary for people who are typically of a fundamental point of view."

"I think he makes a great point. I think God wants us not to have such a narrow view as is the case with many of my colleagues. For example, I noticed today when you were handling the communion wafers that you handle them with such care and reverence. I know you view it as more than just a symbol but did the Lord really mean for the 'eating of his body and drinking of his blood' to be literal?"

"Well, of course, we as Catholics treat the Host as something more than a symbol…something more than a 'communion wafer.' It's clear to me that the early church, the apostles, all treated the Eucharist as the real body of the Lord and within it held the full divinity of Jesus."

"But it's just a cracker."

"Oh, my boy you are wrong. Doesn't the Bible teach you that God is everywhere? He made all things and is in all things?"

"Yes but…"

"So if God can be everywhere at once, can't He be in the Holy Eucharist?"

As usual, Lawrence was given 'food for thought' by this holy man of God. He sometimes wondered if he were in the right denomination. There was much he was learning from the Catholic Church. He even began to think about converting but then thought that his whole career would be thrown out the window. As a married man, he would not be able to be a priest. For now, though he was just happy he had a friend like Father O'Reilly to help him on his spiritual journey.

Later that day, Lawrence met with Chester to go over their lesson. Lawrence had started with the book of Genesis and he quickly learned that Chester would be a good student.

"Pastor Ambrose…"

"Please call me Lawrence."

"I can't call you that, I'm sorry. I've got too much respect for you."

Lawrence smiled and nodded. He never wanted to have too much authority because he knew the life of a pastor was under constant scrutiny. Every word he spoke was starting to be held in too much regard for his liking. Was everything he said needed to be held as gospel truth? While studying for the pastorate, he was beginning to have more questions than he had answers. Only God Himself knew it all.

"Anyway, do you think God created the heavens and the earth in a literal six-day period?" Lawrence was impressed. Sometimes Chester gave the appearance of just being a bashful and somewhat uneducated ragamuffin from the country, but it was clear he was a thoughtful young man.

"Excellent question Chester and one that many people have pondered. You'll find many of us in the South will prefer to have a literal translation of the Bible. If God said it then it must have happened exactly as written."

"So you believe that all of the Bible should be taken literally?" Lawrence shook his head. "I know that some of the Bible isn't meant to be taken literally. I mean for example, at the end of the creation story it says God rested on the seventh day. Do we actually believe God was exhausted and had to take a nap? A lot of the Bible and especially the Old Testament was not written down. It was verbally communicated and passed down that way. It was meant to take God's word and put it in easily understood terms."

"So when do we decide to take the Bible literally and not figuratively?"

"You sure are a deeply thoughtful young man. Where did you get your education; learn to read and write?"

"Oh, there was an old butler in Macon who had learned to read and write. I worked at the same plantation. He would come out to the barn where I worked and he would teach me for about a half-hour each day. He understood that the only way freedmen were going to get anywhere was through education." Lawrence shook his head in amazement. Chester was a true diamond in the rough.

"Well, going back to your question, as you grow and learn you will understand what is figurative and what is literal. We also have to be aware of the great strides in science these days. It's not just all about trains and telegraphs and what not but there are other things we have to take note of. Charles Darwin has put forth a lot of theories about the age of the universe through his theory of evolution. Believe you me there are a lot of people, especially here in the South who are not too keen on these ideas, especially the clergy."

"What do you think?"

"I think it has some merit. If we go through the Bible, you get about 6,000 years for the age of the earth. But many scientists think the earth is hundreds of thousands of years old or even millions."

"Do you agree?"

"I don't know. St. Augustine didn't think it was necessarily 6,000 years old. He said as it does in the Bible, that a day is as a thousand years to the Lord. We don't fully understand what God did, but we have to have faith that one day He will let us know. For now, all we can say is He wants us to trust Him and focus on developing a closer relationship with Him. In due time we will understand everything about the universe."

"Wow, you think so?"

"Oh yes. You know in Galileo's time they didn't think it was a heliocentric solar system. But he proved that it was. Now we know the earth revolves around the sun and so what? Does that change the way we think and learn about God? No, it doesn't. We still have to strive after knowledge and we will not know it all here on earth, but one day I believe we will."

Chester sat in rapt attention, hanging on every word that Lawrence uttered.

"Things we do know and we take literally are of course the life of Jesus. We know Jesus was a real human being that existed almost 2,000 years ago. His miracles and works are literal."

"How do we know that?"

"We know because of how many lives He changed. We know because if it wasn't literal, the world would not have changed as it did during the rise of Christianity. And we know because there are outside sources like the historian Josephus who also wrote about these events. He was a historian, he wrote about literal history."

"Man alive, Pastor Ambrose, you sure know everything!"

"No, no, quite the opposite. What I know is all thanks to the Lord and what he has revealed to me. I can still be a better student. And one day you will surpass me. Now let's have some supper. Sarah's made a fine stew for us."

The pair joined Sarah in the kitchen where they continued their theological discussion over the "best beef stew south of the Mason/Dixon line." At least according to Sarah.

After his sermon, thc following Sunday, Lawrence as always greeted the congregants at the main entryway to the church. After finishing greeting Deacon Gaines, another man quickly offered his hand to Lawrence to shake. He looked quite familiar.

"That was an excellent message Pastor Ambrose," the man said shaking Lawrence's hand enthusiastically.

"Thank you very much. Do I know you? You look very familiar."

"Why yes, that is good of you to remember. My name is Lieutenant Augustus Greenleaf. My friends call me Auggie."

"Great to meet you…ah, Auggie."

"You and your friend were kind enough to let me sit with you that night just after the war. You both were heading back home to Atlanta and we met on the main road out of Appomattox."

"Yes, yes, now I remember! You are the gentlemen from the Army Corp of Engineers. You used to 'blow up stuff'!"

Seeing Lawrence so animated, Sarah had to meet whoever it was that had him in such rapt attention. She walked over to the two men.

"Ah Lieutenant Greenleaf, I mean Auggie, please meet my wife Sarah."

"Sarah, Auggie, and I met while Sully and I were on our way back home after the war. He shared a campfire with us."

"Very nice to meet you Auggie. Are you from around here?"

"No ma'am, I am from up north, Virginia mostly. After the war, I realized there wasn't much left of my town so I came down here. I just got a job as a machinist at the mill."

"What's become of your family?"

"Well, my brother died at Gettysburg and my parents…my mother died just before the war and my father was killed in a…well a cross-fire during a battle, right around the last day of the war. The Union was pushing us through near to Richmond and came across our town. Some of our unit made a stand and my father decided he would try and help…the old fool!" Lawrence and Sarah could see tears welling up in Auggie's eyes.

"Mr. Greenleaf, ah Auggie, it would be a great pleasure if you would join us for lunch," Sarah said grabbing him by the arm and escorting him toward the parsonage. Auggie couldn't refuse such hospitality, "That's mighty kinda ya ma'am."

When the three got back to the parsonage, Sarah made sandwiches from the leftover turkey they had the night before. She made coffee and also served the remains of an apple cobbler she had made.

"Since I've come to town which was about a month ago, maybe two, I had heard about your work at the AMA and at Peachtree Baptist. I think what you are doing is God's work and I would like to be a part of it."

"Well, that's a mighty fine offer Auggie. We could use a man with your skills with the many projects we have in mind."

"And also know, I have many ex-rebels interested in helping out. You might have seen some of them in church over the past several weeks."

"Yes, we noticed more and more young men coming to our services," Sarah said with a bright smile.

"Well, some of them were from my unit and some I have met while here in Atlanta. I know you are not getting much help from the federal troops stationed here but we will help with both construction and security."

"You've heard about our plight?"

"Yes, and you need to be careful. There are forces in town that mean to destroy your work. They do not want the freedmen to…well, to be free."

"Yes, we are finding out that many people in authority are involved with the KKK."

"Yes, they are hell-bent on taking apart all the freedoms that have been given to the negroes. You know, I once was on their side. I thought it was God's design to have the black man as slaves…provide the labor that fueled the Southern economy…"

"And now?"

"And now I know it's evil. I do not nor does anyone else have the right to enslave another human being. And now I am willing to fight for it. I was once fighting to preserve slavery and now I want to fight for freedom, freedom for all."

"That is most encouraging Auggie. I think I noticed good in you the night we met. There are things you can tell about a person without really knowing them. I could tell you had a good spirit."

"Well, that good spirit is ready to get to work. Are there any projects I can help you with?"

"Well, we are getting some leaks again with the roof. I did some work on it but I am not really a carpenter. Any help with that would be great. Also, we have been working with the AMA on building a school. I would really appreciate your input on that as well."

Auggie smiled and nodded his head as Sarah brought in a plate full of sandwiches.

The ride into Athens was now about an hour and a half since the Ambrose's moved to Atlanta. Lawrence didn't mind the length of the journey as it gave him a chance to enjoy the countryside and the pleasurable breezes that often came through the fields. He was beginning to get to know the farmers and the country folk on the road to Athens. He would often stop and shoot the breeze with many of the people he encountered on the way. It was becoming more and more of a favorite pastime of his.

What was even more of a favorite of his was to be on the Franklin College Campus, studying and discussing theology with his professors and fellow students. With the school now fully operational there was now a full faculty of 13 professors and 125 students. It was a true center for learning and unlike most schools where students just wanted to get through the course study and graduate, the Franklin College student body wanted to learn and grow as human beings, spiritual human beings.

The day began with chapel. Professor Thompson gave a brief sermon…

"Gentlemen, it is a new day for us here at Franklin. We are now fully staffed and have a full student body. We have received additional funding and the future looks bright. But despite these positive things we cannot get complacent. We need to push ourselves and grow as Christian young men. It's one thing to learn the Bible and the theological concepts we are teaching you, but it is another thing to make an impact on the lives of other people. Franklin College needs to change the world. We have just come off of one of the bloodiest conflicts in human history. The country is hurting and we have many people who are devasted and their lives ruined because of this war. It is up to us as Christian men to help change that.

"And now more than ever we need understanding. We are in a vastly changing world where things will not be the same…and for the better. We have new brothers and sisters joining us in a free society. We are to be kind and just to all men, to all people. We hope to soon be allowing people of different ethnic origins to join us here at Franklin and we need to be accommodating and welcoming.

"As the Declaration of Independence proclaimed; *We hold these truths to be self-evident, that all men are created equal, that they are endowed by their Creator with certain unalienable Rights, that among these are Life, Liberty and the pursuit of Happiness.* That is all men are created equal, not that some are more equal than others, but that all men are created equal. So as a society we must start living as such. And that's not because some authority in Washington has told us to, but we want to. We want to be true Christians, giving our lives if we have to, to keep these ideals."

As Lawrence heard these words he began to well up with pride, but he also knew that the sad reality was that many southern Christian men would probably have to give up their lives to preserve this freedom.

"And so, please dwell on these thoughts. Some of you are from out of state but save a few, you are all from the traditional South. You are mostly southern men. But today, I ask that you be Christian men first and southern men second. Defend your country, but defend your faith first. Let's go make a difference as the Lord has instructed us. Professor Baird, will you lead us in a closing prayer?"

As chapel came to an end, there was much commotion and murmuring as the students headed to their classes. Lawrence caught up with one of his closest friends at school, Frederick "Freddy" Mulheim.

"Hey Freddy, what do you think about that?"

Freddy shook his head, "Easier said than done I suppose."

"You don't believe in what he is saying?"

"I suppose on a grand view I do, but when we do the everyday work of helping people who have been devasted by this war, well, it's going to be tough to change hearts and minds. They see the Union as oppressors who have wrongly occupied their land. Most southerners are entrenched in the old way of thinking."

Lawrence stopped in his tracks and began to think about what Freddy was saying. He immediately became depressed and wondered if what he was doing was making any difference. As he watched Freddy run out of sight, he gathered his thoughts and headed toward his classroom almost in a trance. It was like a blow to the stomach. How many others of a charitable mind believed what they were doing was helping? He knew that he had to pray and pray unceasingly for guidance and for the "changing of hearts and minds."

Lawrence's first class for the day was Hermeneutics. Next to his second year Greek class this was his most difficult. Professor Thompson noticed Lawrence seemingly distracted as he entered the classroom and so decided to call on him first to see if he could rouse him from his funk.

"Mr. Ambrose. I assume you read the assignment last night on Schleiermacher?" Lawrence nodded still walking to his desk. "What did you think when he says the goal of Hermeneutics is 'understanding in the highest sense?'"

Lawrence still quietly walking to his desk began mumbling to himself. He placed his bag on his desk and began to search it for the book in question. He finally found it, opened it, and went to the bookmark he had placed inside the correct page. He began to look at the bookmark. It was a bookmark that was given to him by his grandfather Walter. Walter Ambrose was the first person to teach Lawrence to love reading. From an early age, his grandfather would read him children's books like the Brothers Grimm fairy tales. He later would read to him from the classics and Lawrence would forever have a passion for the written word. That passion was soon starting to wear on his eyes and more and more the pages were becoming blurry. He knew he needed glasses but kept putting them off.

"I think it is an interesting proposition. Can we really know the mind of the author of the work we are reading?" The professor began to pace back and forth and then motioned for him to continue.

"I don't think we can. The author is like an artist. An artist looks at a sunset and then selects different shades of red, orange, etc. But when he looks at a sunset, is it exactly as I see that sunset?" Most of the class began to look back at Lawrence, somewhat impressed with his theory.

"Like the artist, we do not know exactly what's going on in the head of the author. Are they choosing the correct words like the artist is choosing the right colors? What environmental impact is on the author? Are they in prison so experiencing extreme stress and depression? If they write something in prison would they use different adjectives and thoughts if they were out of prison?"

"But would the word choice really change when the scene is different?" fellow student Max Boswell asked.

"Well, ask yourself. If you were in prison and you were mistreated, you might have a particular opinion about the nature of man. But if during that exact period you had not been in prison and mistreated, would your opinion of the nature of man be more positive?"

"So Mr. Ambrose, are you saying people like St. Paul might have written different things depending on the situation?" Professor Thompson asked.

"I don't know, I'm just questioning it. We sometimes make the Bible black and white. We know for a fact that we can't take everything literally in the Bible. The Psalms are poetry and are there for people to visualize beautiful scenes or horrible scenes. There are also passages in the New Testament that would lead one to believe that Jesus' return would have been soon after His resurrection. And with the book of Revelation do we believe there will be a literal beast or is it more of a literary device used by John to refer to a government entity like Rome? What stresses was John under when he was on Patmos? Do were really understand what he was trying to convey with these visions?"

"I think Mr. Ambrose brings up some excellent points. We need to understand all scripture in the proper context that it was given. We need to understand who the author was, what their origin was, education was, and what was the environment and situation they were writing under. Schleiermacher then goes on to discuss 'the art of avoiding misunderstanding.' He identifies two forms of misunderstanding, Qualitative Misunderstanding, and…"

Lawrence's mind began to drift as the professor continued with his talk. While Lawrence always liked to expand his mind, he wondered if some of his classes would really help in the real world. Was Hermeneutics going to help solve poverty? Would it help with racial issues? He supposed it would help him to be a better well-rounded individual, but at times he had his doubts.

After finishing his second year Church History class, he decided to eat in the school's cafeteria at Professor Thompson's invite.

"How are things going in Atlanta these days?"

"Oh, still cleaning up all the ruble. The streets are pretty clean but some buildings need to be knocked down or refurbished. It'll probably be ten years before it's back to normal."

"And your new church? How is that working out?"

"Really well. Sarah and I have really become a part of the community. We work closely with the AMA and hopefully, in a year we'll have the new school built."

"Education, that will be fundamental for the freedmen."

"Yes, there are plans to build several colleges in the city and there will be plenty of ways the freedmen can earn a living and get further education."

"Has there been turmoil with the white neighbors?"

"Here and there. There are a lot of ex-slaves in the city now, all looking for work. The important thing will also be to start negro businesses so they can be self-sufficient."

"How's that going?"

"Good, there have been several grants given and in the Five Point section there is a negro owned grocer, general store, blacksmith, and launderer."

"Will they be able to keep the peace?"

"I'm not sure. The Ku Klux Klan is definitely a presence. My father-in-law of all people is involved with them. There are the federal troops in town but my understanding is the leadership has been bought off by my father-in-law."

"Well, if it's any help, I'd like to try and get some freedmen here at Franklin College. If you have some candidates that have some basic education I'd like them to enroll here."

"I do have one in mind. Very young but very bright. Chester Magee. He has so much potential."

"Excellent, well bring him up here for a tour of the college."

"I'll do that."

While Lawrence finished that thought he waved to his old friend Dr. Sydney Rhodes who was just entering the cafeteria.

"Sydney, I think you know Professor Thompson?" Both men nodded at each other.

"Good afternoon professor."

"Good afternoon doctor."

"If you don't mind Sydney, I'd like to have a word with you out in the hall." Both men bid the professor a good day and headed to the hallway.

"Sydney, I have a proposition for you."

"Yes?"

"We have an opening at the AMA for a doctor. It pays $30 a week. What'dya say?" The good doctor thought for a moment and then smiled.

"I'll take it! I would need to finish out the term but I can be there in June."

"Excellent, I'll let the AMA know," Lawrence grabbed Dr. Rhodes on either shoulder and shook him with joy. He would now have another professional colleague that he could confide in.

For the next several months things were relatively quiet in Atlanta. There were minor skirmishes but overall there was peace. But many were unaware that there was a storm gathering.

CHAPTER 20
A New Arrival

June 1867

As Sam's education continued, Lawrence decided to take him to Atlanta one day to see the construction of the new school. He hoped that seeing it would bring a renewed effort to his studies. When they arrived they walked around the wooden frame of the school. Lawrence introduced Sam to Lieutenant Greenleaf who had been working on fixing some leaks in the roof of the church next door.

"Lieutenant Greenleaf, I'd like you to meet Sam. Sam this is Lieutenant Greenleaf."

"A pleasure to meet you, Sam. Please call me 'Auggie'," the Lieutenant reached out his hand to shake. Sam returned a very soft hand.

"Ah, good to meet you," Sam could barely be heard.

"I am working with Sam on his studies. We hope we can have him go to our very own school once it is completed."

"Why that sounds great. I wish you all the best Sam." Lawrence gave Lt. Greenleaf a look that it would be an uphill climb with Sam. Lawrence asked Auggie for a quick word in private and walked with him toward the AMA building.

"You've got a lot of work in front of you with Sam it looks like," Auggie stated.

"I know. There's Sam, but I'm also concerned about the school. It seems like it's taking forever to get past the foundation and framing. Being an engineer can you talk with the contractor? See if we can get some traction on things?"

Auggie smiled. "I'll see what I can do."

With that, Lawrence simultaneously patted Auggie on the back and waved over to Sam to follow him to the AMA building.

"Sam, there is also one other thing I'd like you to do this morning. I'd like you to visit with our Dr. Rhodes so that he can give you a look over."

"What?"

"You know. A physical. Make sure you are in good health. We want all our prospective students to be fit for school."

"Ah, no, I don't want anyone looking at me."

"Why, what's the matter?"

"Nothing. I just don't want anyone looking at me."

"Look, Dr. Rhodes is a good Christian man. You do not have anything to fear from him."

Sam started to look toward the horizon, weighing Lawrence's words.

"Look, Sam, if we are going to make this work, you have to trust me. I know you haven't had many people you can trust in your life but at some point, you will need to let go of that fear and let us help you."

Again Sam was deep in thought. He eventually looked at Lawrence and nodded his head. Lawrence smiled, patted him on the shoulder, and then walked him over to the doctor's office at the AMA building.

"Dr. Rhodes, this is Sam. Can you meet with him and give him a check-up?" The question didn't need to be asked as Lawrence had earlier arranged the appointment with Sydney.

"Why of course. Please come in young man. I hear you want to be a student at the new school?"

Sam nodded his head and slowly walked into the office. He had been standing at the doorway looking the office over.

"Well, I'll leave you to it," Lawrence said as he turned and walked back to the building site.

Later, after consulting with Lt. Greenleaf on the construction timelines, Lawrence walked back to the doctor's office to get Sam.

"Sam, can you wait outside while I talk to Pastor Ambrose?"

Sam nodded and walked outside. Lawrence turned to Sydney with a look of concern.

"Well, I gave Sam a thorough look over. His general health is good but his stomach and arms are covered in bruises. Any ideas on that?"

"Well, I think he is seeing someone at the mill who is mistreating him."

"Does Sam work at the mill?"

"No, but as I mentioned to you he is I guess you'd say…like a prostitute I guess would be the term. I think someone there is abusing him."

"And he won't tell you who it is?"

"No. I guess if I knew he thinks I would go have it out with whoever it is and then he would get in worse trouble."

"Any ideas of who it is?"

"I have ideas, but I need to confirm."

"How will you do that?"

"Well, I think I have most everyone in Irbyville's confidence, well at least I used to. I will check around."

"Well, good luck. He needs to get out of the hold of whomever it is. There is not only the physical abuse but as a male prostitute he is also subject to disease like anyone else."

Lawrence nodded and headed out of the office.

One day during the food distribution, Lawrence noticed that Thaddeus was getting friendly with one of the white female "customers." The AMA wanted those who were receiving the handouts to be referred to as "customers" rather than "poor people," or other synonyms for those without. When Lawrence questioned Callie about the interaction, she mentioned that the woman was Dorothy Bell. She was the daughter of Millicent Bell the older woman who Callie would take food to down the street. When Dorothy moved back home with her mother, Callie no longer had to take her cart to the house. Now, typically, Thaddeus would help Dorothy take the food to their home. The way Thaddeus and Miss Bell were speaking to each other, Lawrence sensed there was more to it than just pleasantries.

When Lawrence was heading back to the parsonage, he spotted Thaddeus working on the school with Lt. Greenleaf. He motioned for Thaddeus to walk with him.

"I saw you the other day with Dorothy Bell."

"Oh."

"You look pretty close."

"Yes, I guess so."

"Look it's none of my business but people will not be happy if they find out a black man and white woman are together."

"Would one of those people be you?"

Lawrence stopped and thought about it. He had come to grips with slavery and that all people were equal but equal enough to have intimate relationships? He was trying to deal with it but wasn't sure if he could get over that obstacle like he eventually did with slavery.

"You may be right but even though I have issues I won't do anything about it. Others might though."

"It was an accident really. I wasn't looking for a relationship. She's almost ten years older than I am."

"How did you meet?"

"She was in New York during the war. She had moved there years ago to go to school. Her husband was in the Union Army…was killed two years ago. Anyway, she wanted to come back to Atlanta to help her mother. We met about a month ago when she needed help taking food back to her mother's house. We just struck up a friendship and we would talk for hours over at her house."

"Has anyone questioned it? I mean there are laws about it…you know."

"I know. Again, I didn't mean for it to happen. I think, being from the North she has an open mind to things. She talked a lot about having fears coming back down here because of the narrow-mindedness of folk here."

"Thaddeus, just be careful. Yes, maybe I don't think that races should mix that way…but hopefully like with slavery I will grow to be more understanding, but my biggest concern is that if people like W.E. find out there will be trouble. Just be careful."

Thaddeus nodded and told Lawrence he would heed his warning. The truth was that both Thaddeus and Dorothy were becoming quite close and intimate and from

Thaddeus's point of view, he was willing to take the risk for someone he loved.

Along with education, the right to vote and to elect officials that would represent the negro community was a big priority for the AMA and the Peachtree Baptist Church. The landmark case of Ezekiel Gillespie in Wisconsin was an encouragement to the black citizens and the same enthusiasm for the vote was now gaining ground in Georgia.

Lawrence, with the aid of the AMA, helped identify and train freedmen for the purpose of being registrars. There were many volunteers and he used the church to set up training for the new "official registrars." Dr. Rhodes had finished his commitment to Franklin College and was soon down in Atlanta helping Lawrence with the training of the registrars.

The monumental task now was for Lawrence and the registrars to go throughout the city and find the voters and get them registered. Luckily for Lawrence, he had a new horse. His original horse had been retrieved by W.E.'s men. With the horse he recently purchased, he was able to go to the outskirts of town to the tent cities and shantytowns to meet with everyone he could. Many of them could not read or write so it was difficult to get them to sign their "X" on the signature line, but he was slowly making progress. Although due in a month, Sarah was able to help with the local canvassing of voters to get them to sign-up. Lawrence was unhappy with this activity and encouraged her to rest. She said she could not rest knowing that there were people needing to have their rights affirmed. Lawrence admired Sarah and knew that in many ways she was stronger than he. He was eventually able to convince her to work at the AMA main office and do more administrative duties.

The following day, Lawrence was greeted by Auggie and a group of men.

"Auggie, good to see you. Looks like you have quite the force there?" Lawrence said as the two men began to shake hands.

"Yes, these are a few of my friends from the Army Corp of Engineers. Also, a couple of friends of mine are carpenters. We'd like to help out with your building project."

"Wow, that's great. What about the contractor?"

"I think he's in cahoots with your father-in-law. Very evasive. Can't give me timelines or dates. I think that me and my boys though can get things going. By the way, our labor is free."

"Oh, we should pay you something."

"No, we decided that since we have jobs now and that the Lord has blessed us, we need to help y'all out."

Lawrence was speechless. He patted Auggie on the shoulder and motioned for him and his men to follow him to the AMA. As they were walking, one of Auggie's men approached Lawrence.

"Hello, Pastor Ambrose…"

"Please call me Lawrence."

"Okay, Lawrence. My name is Stephen Alexander."

"Good to meet Stephen."

"I just wanted to say how proud I am to be involved in this project. You have no idea how much your words helped me the other day."

"Words?"

"Your sermon. The sermon you gave on the 'Jewish Jesus.'"

"Oh yes."

"My parents hated Jews and unfortunately that had been fed to me for so long that I hated them too. You've really helped me to see now that people are people regardless of race, creed, etc. I've come to see that hate has held me down. It was like a sickness. Can I confess something to you?"

"Well, if you want to confess you might want to do that directly to God, not me."

"I feel like I need to get something off my chest."

Lawrence looked around and could see Auggie and the rest of the men waiting for him at the doorway to the AMA. They were puzzled as to what the two men were discussing.

"Or maybe you want to speak to Father O'Reilly down the road? He hears confessions."

"I'm not Catholic."

"Look, why don't you come over to the parsonage tonight and we can talk then?"

Stephen smiled and nodded. He looked like he was relieved.

Later at the parsonage, Stephen Alexander knocked on the door.

"Hello, Stephen. Come on in."

Stephen brushed the soles of his shoes on a doormat and then removed his hat and walked in.

"Sarah, this is Stephen Alexander, one of Auggie's men."

"Please to meet you, Mr. Alexander."

"Ma'am."

"Stephen, I thought we could talk on the back porch if that was alright?"

"Yes sir, that would be fine."

Sarah curtsied as the two men adjourned to the backdoor. As they walked outside they noted the full moon which illuminated the backyard of the parsonage. The parsonage sat on a small hill that overlooked the Five Points section of Atlanta. The entire town was visible with the full moon. Normally the buildings of the town were just silhouettes, but that night they could see everything in detail including the individual bricks. Lawrence motioned to Stephen to take a seat on one of the two rocking chairs that were on the porch.

"This is a mighty fine home you have here pastor."

"It's small but it serves us just fine for now. I think Sarah wants to have a large family so we'll eventually have to add on or find another home. Now, what did you want to talk to me about?"

Stephen began to stare off into space. He appeared to be analyzing the bricks in a nearby building. He then began to shake his head and then turned to look at Lawrence.

"You know how I was talkin' about the Jews?"

"Yes."

"And my hatred of them?"

"Yes."

"Well, one night I went to the Atlanta Temple you know the synagogue?"

Lawrence nodded his head. Lawrence was familiar with the synagogue and had met Rabbi Solomon on several occasions.

"Well, my uncle Jeb was swindled by one of the people at The Atlanta Temple. And well, I went over there one night. This was about five years ago, just before the war. Anyway, I was angry and I went over there at about 3 in the mornin'," Stephen paused and took a deep breath. "I set fire to the synagogue."

"Hmmm, I seem to remember that incident. Was anyone harmed?"

"No, thank the Lord but it has been weighing on me. To burn someone's place of worship. It wasn't right."

"Did you speak to anyone else about this?"

"No."

"Well, you'll need to tell the police."

"The police?"

"Well, the federal authorities. And I would say you would want to speak with Rabbi Solomon. I won't force you to do it but at some point, I may need to tell the truth of it."

Stephen turned away from Lawrence and began to stare again at the downtown. There were flickers of light from various houses and buildings. There were also a few street lamps that were aglow. It was a beautiful night. A horrible deed had been confessed on a night that should have been made for something more sacred. And as Lawrence dwelled on that fact he began to think about the Catholic faith and how confession was one of the seven sacraments. He had learned a lot from Father O'Reilly during their many conversations.

At that point, Stephen bid Lawrence a good evening. He hadn't committed to making his crimes known to the authorities but Lawrence prayed that he would.

The next day, Lawrence decided to visit Sam. When Lawrence got down to the river, he saw someone emerge from Sam's tent. It was dark but he could make out the figure of Bobby Noble. Bobby was a foreman at the mill and held a lot of sway, not only with the workers but with W.E. He was well-educated, graduating from UGA with a degree in chemistry, and had somehow managed to avoid the war altogether. It was said he came from a wealthy family in South Carolina, but that could never be verified. He was arrogant and pompous and most everyone feared him. He was very tall with sandy blonde hair and deep blue eyes which caused most of the ladies in town to have a keen interest in him, but he was seldom in the company of women, or anyone else for that matter. The main thing for W.E. was that Bobby kept a tight ship and as long as the mill ran efficiently, he didn't care who was in charge. His presence at Sam's tent, however, cleared up a lot of things in Lawrence's mind. He knew Bobby Noble was the type who would get anything he wanted, even if he had to employ threats of violence or actual violence.

When the day came to celebrate a new wing being added to the mill, W.E. had various dignitaries attend a ribbon-cutting ceremony. Among the key employees, there was Bobby Noble. Bobby even gave a little speech…

"Today marks another important date in the history of the Fullertown Mill. With this new looming machine, we will be able to increase production by another 40%. This is all thanks to our founder Wilberforce Edward Fuller. Mr. Fuller provides over seventy percent of the employment in the county and with this new wing, we will be hiring twenty new employees. This is again a testament to Mr. Fuller and what he means to this city and county. Thank you Mr. Fuller for all you do!!!" Bobby then raised his hands in an attempt to get more enthusiastic applause from the crowd. His display and antics, smacked of one being W.E.'s lackey and it was believed that Bobby would grovel at the snap of W.E.'s finger.

After the ceremony, with the crowd beginning to dissipate, Lawrence walked over to Bobby.

"Nice speech there Bobby," Lawrence said as he offered his hand to shake.

"Oh, uh, Pastor Ambrose. Thank you," Bobby said as he weekly offered his hand in response.

"Say, this may be none of my business but I am working with Sam Cullington over by the river."

"Who, I'm not familiar with that name."

"Sam, he lives over there by the prostitutes."

Bobby shook his head conveying he had no idea what Lawrence was talking about.

"Anyway, I am trying to get Sam out of there and having him educated in Atlanta."

"And how is that my concern?"

"Well, I know it is you who is using the boy. Hurting the boy."

"Is that what he told you?"

"It's what I've seen. Anyway, I am warning you to stay away from him."

"Or what?"

"Or I'll expose your deeds. I don't think folks 'round here would look too kindly on this behavior."

Bobby's facial expression went from concern to practically convulsing with anger.

"Here I thought you were a man of God. Seems you are just as corrupt as any of us."

"I am trying to prevent corruption, the corruption of Sam's soul by someone who wants to take advantage of him."

Bobby had no response. He continued to seethe with hatred for the young pastor. He then turned and stormed off. Lawrence decided that it was a good time to move Sam down to Atlanta before he was subject to any more of Mr. Noble's aggression.

It was a hot day on June 7th when Sarah's water broke. Dr. Rhodes was there for the delivery. She had been up since 4 a.m. and Lawrence helped her with wet towels for keeping her cool and getting her to walk around the house to get labor moving along. As was the custom, Lawrence eventually retreated to the living room, or what was called the living room while Dr. Rhodes worked with Sarah to help push the baby. And so at 7 o'clock that evening, Abigail Marie Ambrose came into the world. Mother was fine and father was ready to pass out. Dr. Rhodes revived him however and he was soon able to cradle his child, his adorable "Abby."

For several hours Lawrence laid in bed with Sarah as she recuperated. He made sure she had plenty of water to drink. She had been through a lot and Dr. Rhodes stayed over to make sure there were no complications. While initially having problems feeding the baby, Sarah was eventually able to get Abby to nurse. Apart from the baby waking up a couple of times, everyone was able to go to sleep for the rest of the night.

The following morning, Lawrence had to go to school, having just registered for summer classes, but before he did so he made sure Sarah had something to eat and was given a pitcher of water. Dr. Rhodes planned on staying with her the rest of the day to make sure that everything was going well for mother and baby. Lawrence brushed the hair from Sarah's eyes and gave her a proud smile.

"You're doing great mama. You rest and just focus on the baby." Sarah smiled and nodded her head. She looked dazed after the previous day's delivery. Perhaps she hadn't received the necessary rest to recover properly? Lawrence was no expert but he hoped that she would continue to convalesce for the rest of the day.

As Lawrence left the house, he was greeted by his mother-in-law and three sisters.

"Congratulations Lawrence! I hear everything went well with the delivery?"

"Yes. labor was a little long but both mother and baby look great."

Lawrence's mother-in-law smiled and quickly entered the house with daughters in tow. As he got on his horse he could hear squeals of joy coming from inside the house. He had timed his departure perfectly, he chuckled to himself as he saddled up and was soon galloping down the street. Before heading to school he went over to the AMA to see how voter registration was doing. He found Thaddeus and got a quick update.

"Things are going well but there is a report that someone was killed last night down in Sharpsburg."

"Killed, how? Like an accident?"

"We're not sure. The authorities are silent and not giving us any information."

"But it involved a registrar?"

Thaddeus nodded his head. He looked toward the ceiling as if to gain divine inspiration or message. He then shook his head and sighed.

"I have a feeling we've got a long row to hoe. The KKK is going to start coming out of the woodwork as we give people more and more rights." Lawrence nodded his head, grabbed Thaddeus by both arms, and smiled, "Freedom will continue to come at a price, but we can't look back now. We have to move forward no matter the consequences. And remember what I told you?"

"Pray, pray, pray," Thaddeus said as he mustered a forced grin.

"Where's Chester?"

"He's up north working on registration. He should be back tonight."

As Lawrence headed northeast to school, he had an ominous feeling come over him. He felt as though he was being watched. After several miles, he confirmed his suspicions. He could see several men on horseback hiding out in between trees watching him. On one occasion he stopped his horse, got off, and walked over to hide behind a tree. One of the men who had been following him came into sight. The man began to pick up speed when he could no longer locate Lawrence. As the man came closer, Lawrence sprung out from behind the tree and tried to lasso the man. The rope however missed the man and then slapped the horse on the head, causing it to buck. The man was thrown from his saddle and landed hard on the road. He laid on the ground groaning in pain, holding his shoulder. Lawrence ran over to him and assessed his injuries. He seemed to be alright but Lawrence fashioned a sling so he could put his arm into it.

"So why were you following me?" Lawrence said as he continued to work on the man's shoulder. The man would not speak.

"If you like, I can break your other arm if you don't start tellin' me what you're up to!"

"Okay, okay. Just let my arm alone. I work for your father-in-law. He wanted me to tail you to see what you've been up to."

"And?"

"Well, I plan on telling him everything I know."

"Like what?"

"Like how you're helping the freedmen register to vote."

"Well, I suppose you have to tell 'im the truth."

"Well, that's what I'm paid to do."

"Well, why did he pay someone to follow me? With every contact he had in Atlanta, he would find out eventually."

"Don't know. My orders were to just follow you around."

"By the way, you make a lousy spy. I could tell you were following me a mile outside of town."

"Well, there's not much to hide behind." Lawrence nodded and then helped the man get back onto his horse.

"If you wouldn't mind also telling my father-in-law something?"

"Yeah, what's that?"

"Everyone including God is watching him. We will all be watching his actions in the coming days." The man nodded his head and then headed down the road, eventually taking a spur that led to Fullertown. Lawrence rode next to him to make sure he was okay and that he was able to navigate down the road by himself to Fullertown.

"God is watching all of us!" Lawrence yelled to the man, watching him ride out of sight. The man just kept his head down and didn't respond. Lawrence began to think about the reach of W.E. and how far it really extended.

When Lawrence arrived at Franklin College for his first class, Professor Simmons gave him a note that he needed to go to the president's office. Lawrence implored Professor Simmons to let him go after the class, but was rebuffed and told he had to go immediately. Lawrence ran as fast as he could across campus to the administration building, ran through the hall and up the stairs to the president's office. Mrs. McCready was at the front desk and told Lawrence to go into the president's office without delay. Lawrence had had little interaction with President Samuel T. Higginbotham or "Higgi" as his friends frequently called him. He had been a pastor of a large church in Boston before deciding he wanted a post that was more quiet, taking the pastorate of a small church in South Carolina before coming to Franklin. He studied theology at Harvard and so everyone held him in high esteem. He had the more liberal bent of someone from the Northeast and so Lawrence hoped he would be of a similar ilk as himself.

"Mr. Ambrose, so good of you to see me on such short notice."

"No problem President Higginbotham. How can I help you?"

"Well, it's more about how I can help you. You see, I know you are close friends with Professor Thompson who has a good heart and a kindly nature."

"And?"

"And while I support those things he can also be a little liberal with his theology."

"Are you removing him from his post?"

"Heavens no. He is a good scholar and a passionate Christian, but he does have a reputation. Your father-in-law was here to see me the other day."

"What...why?"

"He wanted to see how you were doing. I told him you were doing very well."

"Well, I'm not exactly seeing eye-to-eye with my father-in-law these days."

"Yes, that is what he told me. He also told me he wants to be on the board of directors of the school."

"What? No!!!"

"Well, he has said that he will make a generous endowment to the school and I don't think we can refuse such a gift."

"You'd refuse it if you knew you were taking it from Satan."

"Now, I don't think that was called for."

"Look, President Higginbotham, my father-in-law is involved in some serious business, terrible business, the Ku Klux Klan."

"How do you know?"

"A good friend of mine listens in on their meetings...I tell you the man is no good."

"Yes, well, that just sounds like here say to me."

"No, I've listened in once to one of their meetings to confirm it. I can tell you that he's up to terrible things."

"So at this meeting, they said they were a part of the Ku Klux Klan?" Lawrence stopped to think about the meeting he had listened to. The words 'Ku Klux Klan' had not specifically been used.

"Well, they referred to themselves as the 'Sons of the South.'"

"And what did they say they were going to do?"

"They were going to harass people and get weapons."

"Is that all they said?"

"Well more or less but these people want to prevent giving rights and education to the freedmen."

"Well, until you have more proof I will say we will be going forward with his election to the board."

Lawrence stopped and thought about what that meant. Would he kick professors out who didn't agree with his ideas? Would he kick students out, specifically his son-in-law? There was clearly something dubious at work.

"So, is this what you wanted to talk to me about President Higginbotham?"

"Yes. I understand you do not live with the Fullers anymore and so just wanted to give you the news. I also hear congratulations are due to you and your lovely wife. We at Franklin are happy to welcome another future scholar. Congratulations my boy," the president said, standing and offering his hand to shake. Lawrence stood up and nodded accepting his felicitations. He felt stunned by the news and quietly walked out of the president's office, completely ignoring Mrs. McCreedy's salutation and congratulations. He only smiled and nodded his head as he walked out of the administrative office. The news was bad and he knew that W.E. would kick him out of school. While he no longer needed W.E.'s money and support, the man still had power and a long reach. He knew W.E. to be vengeful and spiteful and he could influence what would happen to Lawrence directly or was often the case indirectly.

After classes, Lawrence headed home, still in a daze from the news. He hoped that maybe a grandchild might mollify W.E., but he still had the dark feeling that his dismissal from Franklin was the true intention. To say Lawrence was concerned was an understatement.

When he arrived home, W.E. became the least of his concerns. Sarah had seemed to be battling a fever and Dr. Rhodes was keeping a close eye on her. A woman from the AMA had come over to help watch the baby while Dr. Rhodes tried to nurse Sarah back to health.

"What's happened?"

"Sarah has developed a high fever and am giving her liquids and cold compresses."

"Is this typical?"

"No, but it can happen. There is endometritis, an infection in the uterus. When she overworked herself at the AMA we had to give her bed rest for a couple of weeks and she might have picked up a bacterial infection if she wasn't bathing sufficiently."

"Yes, I brought the tub into the bedroom so I could make baths for her."

The doctor stood up and put a towel over his shoulder and then shook his head.

"We just need to watch her closely. In this heat, I would have thought it difficult to pick up an infection but you never know."

"You go rest Sydney. I appreciate everything you have done for us."

"My pleasure. I'll go lay down in the living room and take a nap. I'll make us something to eat later."

"No, no. You just watch Sarah. I'll put something together. How's the baby?"

"A nurse from the AMA is watching her now."

"Shouldn't we keep her here, close to Sarah?"

"Well, she was a little fussy and I wanted Sarah to rest."

"Doesn't she need to feed?"

"Ah, she's a wet nurse so she will be able to feed Abby."

Lawrence wasn't too keen on someone else feeding Abby but given the circumstances, it would have to suffice. Lawrence again urged Sydney to get some rest. He then sat at Sarah's bedside, praying that the Lord would revive her.

Lord Jesus, I don't know what I would do without my wife. You gave me the most beautiful gift a man can have; a loving wife. I won't be able to go on my Lord if you take her away from me. Please, please don't let anything happen to my Sarah. Tears began to roll down Lawrence's cheeks. He began to think about Sarah and everything that she meant to him. Growing up he thought he knew love. He loved his mother and father and sister, but he realized it was a different kind of love. As he was learning from his Greek classes he definitely had experienced Eros, but now he was experiencing something different. Was it Philia? Philia was going beyond just the physical lust for someone, it was the feeling one had for their soul mate. Sarah was definitely his soul mate.

As the night went on, Dr. Rhodes eventually came back and helped with the care of Sarah. Her temperature had gone down but the doctor was still concerned for her health.

"Any ideas what caused this?" Lawrence asked as he wiped the sweat off Sarah's forehead.

"There's a lot of different ways someone can get an infection. It probably didn't help that she's been lying in bed for a couple of weeks. Have you been able to change the sheets?"

"Yes, every day. Mrs. Fuller, thank the Lord, has been sneaking down with fresh linens every day."

"Hmmm, that is a mystery. Let me take her temperature."

The doctor took a reading of 104.5; the fever had returned.

"This is troubling," Dr. Rhodes said as he showed Lawrence the thermometer. Lawrence looked like he had seen a ghost. He became very concerned for his wife's life.

"I think we will need to do some bloodletting."

"Bloodletting?"

"It's a way for the body to produce more iron and help fight the infection. I make a small incision in one of your wife's veins and it allows some of the blood to seep out."

Lawrence had a look of pained confusion. It sounded barbaric. He wasn't sure how to respond and returned to the work of helping his wife revive. He tried to get her to sit up and take water but she was unable to. He eventually had to lift her head to a cup that contained cool water. He could feel how hot she was. Dr. Rhodes left and quickly returned from the kitchen with a bowl and a jug of water. He took his medical bag out and opened a smaller bag that contained a scalpel. He motioned for Lawrence to move away from Sarah and then moved a chair next to her. He wiped down her arm with water and then taking some alcohol applied it to the area where he intended to make the incision. Lawrence looked on in horror as the doctor cut into Sarah's skin. Blood began to squirt out along her arm. He moved the bowl onto the bed and dangled her arm over it so the blood would drip into it.

"Isn't that a lot of blood?" Lawrence questioned. The doctor didn't respond but continued to let the blood flow into the bowl. He eventually wrapped her arm with gauze and the blood flow stopped.

"How long does it take?"

"It's different for every patient but I would think in a half-hour we should know if it helped or not."

"There's no medicine we can give her?"

"I do have some herbal remedies but let's give this a try first. It has worked for me in the past."

For the rest of the evening, the two men hovered over Sarah. It wasn't until 2 a.m. that the fever broke. By 3 a.m. she was awake and taking water. Lawrence went outside into the cool air and thanked the Lord for sparing Sarah. He could never have imagined life without her. They had been together less than two years but his life had changed forever. She was a part of him now and he realized how alone he had been before she came into his life.

Once out of the woods, Dr. Rhodes went back to his apartment with the eternal gratitude of Lawrence. Whether it was the bloodletting that had cured her or not, Lawrence was comfortable with the idea that it indeed had done the trick. He slept with Sarah for the next several hours.

At nine o'clock, Lawrence arose, keeping quiet in order to not wake Sarah. He took some water from a large jug in the kitchen and gave himself a quick sponge bath to revive himself. He grabbed some bread, butter, and jam from the kitchen and had a quick breakfast. He hadn't eaten since the morning before. He then found a clean shirt and pants, changed, and then headed over to the AMA.

Inside the AMA he found Abby in a makeshift nursery that had several other newborns in it. They were making plans to build a larger nursery as there was now a big need to fill. With the war over, the population needed repopulating. Lawrence spoke to the nurse on duty and he was able to retrieve Abby. She had been sound asleep and while the nurse put up a slight protest, he managed to convince her to let Abby be with her mother.

When Lawrence arrived with the baby, Sarah was still asleep. He sat in a rocking chair near the bed and took a quick nap himself. The baby was also tired from the whole ordeal. At noon, everyone awoke and Lawrence proudly presented Abby to Sarah.

"Dear, is there any way I can get more rest?" Sarah asked. Lawrence nodded his head, a little disappointed that Sarah would not take their daughter to feed. He complied and took Abby back across the street to the AMA. He looked back at the baby in the crib and thought that maybe it was a good idea after all, given what Sarah had been through.

For the next couple of days, Sarah showed little interest in Abby and Lawrence became extremely concerned. She would continue to say that she had to recuperate and needed to sleep. Lawrence explained this to Dr. Rhodes.

"I wouldn't be concerned. Some women have a type of depression, after all, they've been through. Just give her some time."

Lawrence heeded the doctor's words and just continued to work with the nursing staff over at the AMA. Lawrence was concerned for Abby's well-being as she had not spent a lot of time with her parents. While the AMA had been graceful in helping out with Abby, he began to feel depressed that her parents were unable to provide her with the nurturing she needed.

Four days after the delivery, Sarah perked up and asked to see Abby. Lawrence was over the moon, happy that it looked like his Sarah was returning to her old self. While she held the baby for an hour or so, she eventually tired again and asked that Abby be taken back.

"What's the matter, darling? How can you be so cold toward Abby?" Sarah was at a loss for words and just shook her head, not knowing herself why she felt so distant.

"Look, I know you have been through a lot, but the baby needs her mother. Can't we keep her here today?" Sarah thought and then reluctantly nodded.

While trying to bond with the baby, Lawrence had Sarah get up and move to the rocking chair while he changed the linens. He then put the baby in the crib and gave Sarah a sponge bath to cool her off. While in many other scenarios the scene would have been erotic, the two were so tired that they just went through the motions with a mechanical precision. Luckily Sarah's mother and sisters arrived and it seemed to put vim and vigor into her. Her sisters argued over who should hold the baby while her mother made sure there was plenty of food and drink in the kitchen. While in the kitchen, Lawrence pulled his mother-in-law aside and told her about what was going on.

"Don't worry my boy. It's natural. What you don't understand is all the things that a woman goes through to have a baby. It isn't easy. It's like going to war labor is and sometimes you come out of it in a bit of a funk. You are kind of out of it for a few days. I'm sure she'll come 'round." Similar advice as from Dr. Rhodes, yet somehow it was not reassuring. He knew Sarah and the woman that had been lying in bed the past four days was not the woman he knew. The Sarah he knew was strong and full of life. Yes, maybe for a day she would be in recovery but four days later? It didn't seem right. But was forcing the issue the answer? He had no other choice but to go with the advice he had been given.

CHAPTER 21
Battling for a New South

July 4th, 1867

With the arrival of his granddaughter, W.E. had seemed to quiet down with concern to his Klan activities. While Sarah had taken Abby several times to the Fuller house, Lawrence avoided any contact with his father-in-law.

With an invitation for fireworks at the Fuller house that 4th of July, Lawrence could not refuse his mother-in-law. He decided he would stay clear of the house however and just hang out in a nearby field, taking plates of food from various servants throughout the day.

For Sarah, having previously been banished from the house forever, it was a tense but welcomed reunion. She would never want to deprive her father of seeing his granddaughter. W.E. quickly took to Abby and there was new hope that there might be an overall reconciliation. For Lawrence however, he knew too much. He knew the real W.E. and what his plans were so he continued to be invisible to his father-in-law.

As for Sarah's melancholy, it had subsided, but she seemed different to Lawrence. Dr. Rhodes had explained that Sarah could have lost her life. The battle to live had taken its toll and the doctor felt that was a big reason for the new Sarah. Lawrence, having heard the stories of many women having trouble in childbirth wondered why Sarah felt the way she did. He eventually came to terms with it and began to think that having a large family might not be in the Ambrose's best interests. At least they had Abby and that thought made him happy. To sacrifice having a large family was something he could deal with knowing it would keep Sarah from future suffering. Abby was happy and healthy and that was all he needed. He was content again.

Lawrence took a large blanket and with several pillows made a large backrest from which he and Sarah could watch the fireworks. A large basket that worked as a crib was settled in one corner with Abby sound asleep. His trusty steed stood close by tied to a nearby tree. The scene was idyllic and Sarah seemed in a good mood.

"I'm sorry my sweet for pressuring you the past few weeks."

"No, it's okay. I know you want Abby and I to bond."

"Hey look, you're mom gave us some cold cider to enjoy. I think it's been fermenting a bit." Sarah smiled and nodded. She looked intently at Lawrence as he pried the bottle open and pour themselves a couple of cups of the brown ale. She reached over and kissed him on the cheek.

"I know it hasn't been easy for you but things will get better. I just had a really bad time of it after Abby came."

"I know. I see it now and I apologize for being so inept."

"You were not inept. You are a first-time father and it's all new to you. It's new to me. I didn't realize what the delivery would take out of me."

"But you are okay now?" Sarah nodded but with a look of concern. "I came close to dying. I thought I saw a light and then the Lord coming toward me at one point. He said I had much more to do and that it wasn't my time yet."

Lawrence was stunned at Sarah's revelation. Had she really encountered the Lord? Of course, it could be hallucinations considering the high fever she had. But maybe her vision was real? In any event, she had survived and she and Abby were alive and healthy. At that point, the fireworks began and with the cider in hand the happy couple settled in with Sarah resting back on her husband as they looked up into the sky.

If there was one thing that Lawrence could count on in this world it was that Chester would be at their Wednesday night tutoring session right on time at 7 pm. Lawrence would have a Bible Study with the rest of the congregation from 6 pm to 7 pm on Wednesdays and then right after was his time with Chester. It was an hour or so that he always looked forward to. Chester, although intimidating from the standpoint of physical stature, was the most kind and gentle soul Lawrence had ever met. His smile was infectious and if he started laughing the whole building seemed to shake. He was a gentle giant.

"How did registrations go today Chester?" Lawrence asked as Chester ran into the sanctuary out of breath.

"Excellent Pastor Ambrose. I made it all the way to Buck Head!"

"You must be exhausted?"

"Yeah, I would have made it down here sooner but I ran into a bit of trouble."

"What happened?"

"There were some white men who hassled me a bit. I was trying to get a couple of older people registered and they came up to me and yelled that I had to leave. I told them I had a duty to fulfill. They said they had a duty to kill uppity niggers." Chester took a deep breath and continued the story. "They then grabbed me and roughed me up a bit. Luckily I punched one guy right in the face and knocked him flat. There were some of the kin of the older couple arrived and they helped me chase the white men away."

"I'm sorry about that Chester. That is not right what they did to you."

"Why is there so much hatred Pastor Ambrose? Can I hep it if I'm a different color?"

Lawrence nodded and put his hand on Chester's shoulder to help console him.

"Ignorance plain and simple. And I used to be that ignorant."

"You Pastor Ambrose?"

"Oh yeah. Remember about Saul, before he was Paul? Well, I was that fanatical about slavery at one time."

"I can't believe it! You?"

"I'm not proud of it but it is the truth. When we don't understand things we can be averse to the truth. We don't want to know. I am sad to say that at one point I didn't believe my negro brothers were equal to me, that they, you, were inferior."

Chester sat back in his chair with a look of complete disbelief, shaking his head.

"When you look at white people who are ignorant, you need to feel sorry for them. There are people out there that we not only have to evangelize to the Christian faith but evangelize to be better human beings. I thought that if I didn't get to know a negro man I could continue to dehumanize him. But when I got to know one, I got to see that they had a heart, a mind, and feelings just like mine.

It took some time but thanks to Miss Callie I finally understood. And it's not just white people. There are people all around the world that live in ignorance of other people, live in fear of other people. It's the reason we have wars. The only way to stop hatred is with education. And you with your education, you'll be able to help ignorant white people like me."

Chester seemed to finally come out of his trance. He appeared to have slipped into a different state not able to comprehend the story he was being told.

"Are you okay?"

"Yes. Perspective is sometimes a smack on the cheek."

"How so?"

"It's just that I had always had this view of you as someone who was always good and kind and educated."

"I think my story is an important one. It reminds us that we have so much work to do. We have to pray for those in ignorance. The Lord spoke to me through Callie and Thaddeus. Some do not have those kinds of people to help them see the light. It's important that with love and patience and a whole lot of prayer that you help people. Help those ignorant white men that you met earlier. Pray for them. The Lord says we need to pray for our enemies. Take each person you meet without prejudice. You don't know what their story is until you meet them and talk to them."

"Okay, Pastor Ambrose. I think you've opened my eyes today. I will always love my fellow man regardless of color."

"I think you always have Chester, it's just that you have to be patient."

Chester nodded his head and then pulled his books out of his backpack.

"Now where were we? I think we were starting the book of Isaiah."

The rest of the evening, while a little more subdued than most, Chester began to cheer up and interact with the lesson. Lawrence smiled and continued to be impressed with Chester's intellectual growth. It reminded him of another young man that he needed to work with as well – Sam.

Meanwhile across town, Thaddeus deftly made his way into Dorothy's apartment building and up the stairs to her apartment. He cautiously looked around as he knocked on Dorothy's door. The door quickly opened and she ushered Thaddeus inside.

"You're here late Thaddeus."

"I know, sorry. It's just that I needed to see you."

"Oh, why is that?"

"You've been on my mind a lot. I like spending time with you, talking with you."

"And I you."

"Anyway, I just wanted to spend some time with you."

"I wonder if it is a good idea you coming here? There are people who don't like this kind of thing."

"I understand. I know a whole lot of people who wouldn't be happy about it. But, for me, I think it worth the risk."

Thaddeus walked over to Dorothy and sat next to her on the sofa. He put his arm around her and drew her close to him. She smiled and put her head on his chest as he sat back on the sofa.

"I never would have imagined spending time with a white woman."

"Nor I spending time with a black man. I never knew we would have so much in common and so much to talk about."

Thaddeus, apart from being a jack of all trades when it came to maintenance work, his skills were coming in handy with the new school, was also quite the artisan. He could whittle the most beautiful and detailed wooden sculptures. Dorothy was now the recipient of many of his "little projects" and she loved the stories he would create for each piece.

"I brought you another little project," he said with glee as he pulled it out of his backpack.

"Wow, this is wonderful Thad."

Thaddeus had whittled and chiseled a very detailed image of an owl sitting on a gate post. He recalled the story of how his mother had an injured owl land in her backyard. They spent weeks nursing it back to health. Thaddeus made detailed sketches of the owl and would later use them to make his final product.

"I feel like he's just gazing at me. How do you get such great detail?"

"I don't know. I just study how my characters look. Like with the owl, I watched him for hours. How his head would turn, how he would move his wings. How his feathers would move around. Another one of God's beautiful creations," he said with a bright smile. Dorothy nodded. She looked around for an appropriate place to put it and settled on the mantle above the fireplace.

"Perfect!" she exclaimed as she moved backward getting the full effect of the piece. The two stood side-by-side inspecting the image. Thaddeus took advantage of her proximity by putting his arm around her. She then turned and smiled. He reached in and kissed her. As they pulled back from the kiss, Dorothy began to blush. As she was in her late-thirties and really hadn't been with a man, this was all new to her. She had been courted several times before but the men had seemed uninteresting to her. Thaddeus was more than interesting. He was good and kind, strong, and had a creative side. And a very humorous side; after all, "you sometimes just have to laugh," he would often say. It was something that he would express as a juxtaposition to what slavery had wrought on the black community. Whatever comical situation occurred or whatever joke was made, it was all against the backdrop of subjugation and bigotry. A backdrop that was continually projected in the lives of all negroes, especially those who had grown up in the South. But now things were changing and there was a bright future for all, at least they both hoped so. Thaddeus kissed her again and then excused himself for the evening. She wanted him to stay but she knew that it would not look good.

Thaddeus finally pulled himself away from Dorothy and quickly exited the tenement building. He walked down a dark secluded Peachtree Street and headed for his apartment at the AMA. As he walked down the street he turned to see that he was being followed by two white men. He turned back to confront them.

"Can I help you, gentlemen?"

"No, but we can help you."

"How so?"

"Just a nice, friendly warning to stay with your kind."

"My kind?"

"You know, niggers."

As Thaddeus studied the men he could tell they were the two that he and Chester had chased away from Callie during the food distribution. But now it was two against one and he didn't like the odds.

"I'll take your suggestion under advisement," Thaddeus said as he began to estimate the distance to his tenement. But before another thought reached his head, one of the men punched him in the side of his face. Before he could respond, the other man grabbed him from behind and held his arms behind his back. Somewhat dazed from the earlier punch, he wasn't able to respond as he was repeatedly punched in the stomach. He then fell to the ground where they kicked him several times. He held his arms up around his head as they continued to kick as hard as they could. He slowly lost consciousness and the life force was beginning to retreat.

Later that day, Thaddeus woke up in the AMA hospital with Dr. Rhodes at his side.

"Thaddeus, can you hear me?" The doctor asked as there was a flicker in Thaddeus's eyes. As he slowly responded, he could see Lawrence rushing to his side.

"What happened Thaddeus?" Lawrence asked in a horrified voice. It was clear that Thaddeus was groggy and began speaking in a slurred speech. Part of the reason he was difficult to understand was that he had three teeth knocked out of his mouth. He finally managed to regain some strength and relayed what had happened to him.

"It was the same two we had encountered when we were helping Miss Callie with the food distribution."

"So they're W.E.'s men?"

Thaddeus nodded and then seemed to pass out. He had lost blood and his face was swollen and bruised. Lawrence got up and motioned to Dr. Rhodes to walk with him toward the exit of the hospital floor.

"Is he going to be okay Sydney?"

"He's lost some blood and took quite a severe beating but I am hopeful he'll recover."

Lawrence turned to look at Thaddeus. He began to burn with anger at what was done to his good friend. He really understood now that what had been going on for so long was truly evil. To act this way toward another fellow human being was despicable. How was he going to help change hearts and minds when so many hearts and minds were ruled by evil?

A week later, Lawrence and the rest of the Freedman Bureau staff went to work making sure everyone was registered for the upcoming elections. As Lawrence walked up Peachtree Street he walked past the Sons of the South store. When he walked by, he could hear the gruff voice of W.E.

"Where d'ya think you're going?" W.E. asked. Lawrence handed him one of the voter registration flyers. W.E., with a cigar in his mouth, began to peruse the document up and down.

"What is it about you boy that you don't learn?"

"How do you mean?"

"This is nonsense. The negroes can't read anyhow."

"Many can, and those who can will help those who cannot."

"You know, after meeting my granddaughter the other day I was about ready to forgive you."

"Forgive me for what?" W.E. walked over to a nearby stairwell where he put his right foot upon the first step and then leaned back against the railing. He looked like a walrus contorting his body into an awkward position.

"For your lack of allegiance."

"Allegiance to whom?"

"To your own people."

"And who might they be?"

"The men of the South, men like me. Men of rich European stock."

"White?"

"Precisely," he said through gritted teeth as they held the cigar tightly.

"My allegiance is to God and to all the people he created."

W.E. took his hat off and began to sun himself. He continued to puff hard on the cigar and started to shake his head.

"One day you'll have to make a choice and I won't be able to help you if you don't make the right one."

"Likewise. One day you'll stand before God and if you didn't make the right choice, I won't be able to help you either. Good day to you W.E.." Lawrence felt almost dirty being in W.E.'s presence. He oozed darkness and hatred and he could no longer stand being anywhere near him.

As Lawrence continued to walk, W.E.'s cronies began to follow him. Lawrence turned to W.E., "You'd better get these men away from me or they may pay the consequences." Lawrence had no idea what he meant or how far he would go. He was sworn to keeping the Lord's commandments and raising a hand to someone was off-limits. He just hoped the verbal threat was enough. Unfortunately, it wasn't as the two men continued to follow him. He continued down the street until he was near North Atlanta. He would continually look over his shoulder and each time he would find W.E.'s goons right behind. He went west down 10th street and began to put up the flyers at various spots. Each flyer was subsequently torn down by the men following him. Lawrence turned to confront the men.

"Hey, what are you doing?!!!"

One of the men, a larger hefty, and a menacing creature with scars and red blemishes on his face met his gaze and then walked right up to him.

"Followin' orders."

"Well stop it."

"What are you going to do about it?"

Lawrence did all possible to hold his temper in check. He was seldom angry but this type of blatant attack on freedom was about all he could bear. Rather than fight, he decided on a more unusual approach. He began to do a jig around the men. The men were stunned at this display and began to shake their heads and laugh.

"What the hell are you doing?"

"If you won't leave me alone then I'll embarrass you."

"You're crazy!"

"That's right!!!" Lawrence yelled in the man's face while making an expression of a village idiot on his. He then began to recite poetry and sing shanty songs. The men were perplexed and didn't quite know what to do. Lawrence's performance was drawing the attention of half the block as well as some of the officers of the federal troops. The men decided they had better leave and quickly exited down the street. Everyone applauded Lawrence when he had finished and he made a grand bow, lifting his hat and waving his hand in gratitude. He began to chuckle and was soon on his way. He started to distribute flyers and made sure they got into the right people's hands.

When Lawrence got home that night, Sarah was waiting for him with dinner ready on the kitchen table. Lawrence was surprised, to say the least. Sarah had the baby in a crib nearby and it was clear that she had freshened herself up, looking quite lovely.

"Wow, this is an unexpected surprise."

"Well you know I've been in the doldrums a bit, but now I'm feeling much better."

Sarah then wrap her arms around Lawrence's neck and began to kiss him rather passionately.

"I'm sorry I haven't been myself, I think the Lord has helped me and now I am feeling much better." Lawrence pulled back to look into her eyes.

"You know it is fine by me however long it takes you to get right. I'm just an ignorant man and was never really taught the ways of a woman so forgive me for not understanding."

"You don't need forgiving. It's just that bearing a child is not easy. Some women have it really rough, not only the delivery but feeling the blues afterward."

"And now I know. Say, I was thinking that maybe we shouldn't have a big family anyway."

"Why not?"

"Well...I couldn't bear it if anything happened to you. One good thing that came from it is I realize that I could never go on without you by my side." Sarah laughed and shrugged her shoulders.

"Oh Mr. Ambrose, I know you'd find a way. But I am better now and I want to have more children."

"Well, why don't we take our time?"

"Well how about we have dinner and then make love?"

"What, already? Aren't you a little sore?"

"Nah, I have some stretch marks but I am fine down there."

Lawrence was a little concerned that they might be getting back to amorous activity a little too soon, but if she was fine with it who was he to argue?

Before they could talk further, a knock came on the door.

"Thaddeus, how are you? You look a lot better." Lawrence said noting that he seemed to be limping and somewhat bent over. He could still see some bruises and scratches on his face from the fight he had been in. Thaddeus nodded and slowly shuffled his way into the house.

"When did you get released from the hospital?" Lawrence asked, smiling to see his old friend once again. The grin on his face quickly turned to concern however when he saw the expression on Thaddeus's face.

"Thaddeus, what it is?"

Thaddeus stood there with tears in his eyes, trembling and shaking his head.

"Chester…"

"…Chester what?"

Thaddeus could not make the words come out. He continued to cry.

"Thaddeus, what's happened?"

"Chester's dead," he managed to get out and then collapsed into Lawrence's arms. Lawrence helped him onto a nearby sofa and Sarah rushed to get him a glass of water.

"How?"

Thaddeus continued to shake his head. "I just got out of the hospital yesterday. I wanted to help out with the registrations and so I headed over to the AMA building. They told me to go up north and help Chester. I was heading out toward Fullertown, walking up near the Hooch…up the main road…" Thaddeus seemed to be in a trance as he recounted what he had found.

"I got as far as Miles Creek when I saw something in a tree. At first, I thought someone was hangin' a bag or maybe some food, like a side of beef or something, but then when I got closer…" Sarah made Thaddeus take some swigs of water. "…when I got closer I could see. I could see…it was Chester!!!" he practically screamed out.

"Alla 'is flyers and registrations forms…all scattered everywhere," Thaddeus said as he was about to vomit, almost heaving with sorrow and pain. Lawrence grabbed on to him and held him tight. Sarah began to sob as well and put her hand on Thaddeus's shoulder. Lawrence too began to sob. He and Sarah had gotten very close to Chester and saw the young man as having so much potential. Someone who would really have an impact in his community. And now all of it was gone. As they continued to cry and console each other, the next emotion Lawrence felt was anger. It seemed to well up inside of him like hot steel. He eventually had Thaddeus lay on the sofa. He then grabbed a pistol from his top desk drawer and headed outside.

Once Lawrence was outside, he saddled up his horse and then rode away from his house up Peachtree Street. He headed over to the Sons of the South store but found it locked up and dark. He then went into a full gallop up the street with the intention of getting to Fullertown as soon as possible. The entire ride up to Fullertown was a blur to him as most things were at that point. He could not think straight and had no idea of what his next actions were to be other than getting justice for Chester.

When Lawrence arrived at the Fuller house, he was greeted by one of the servants on the front porch who told him that he wasn't welcome. He brushed the servant aside and then pushed through the front door. Inside was his mother-in-law and sisters-in-law who all had a surprised look on their faces. They immediately welcomed him but he wasn't interested in pleasantries.

"Where is he?" Lawrence said with gritted teeth.

"Why, he's on the back porch. Is everything okay?..." his mother-in-law asked but with no reply as he began to run through the house toward the back porch. As he came bursting through the backdoor, he turned to find his father-in-law perched on the porch swing.

"I thought I told..." Before W.E. could say another word, Lawrence, with all the strength he could muster, grabbed W.E. by the lapels of his jacket and pulled him up.

"You bastard!!!" Before Lawrence could try to speak, he realized that he was punching W.E. in the face and stomach. He was now in some sort of hysterical frenzy as he continued to punch W.E. incessantly. W.E. was a large man but not in very good shape and didn't take the blows too well. It didn't matter to Lawrence what his state was and soon he had him by the stairway where he exacted a final blow on his face sending W.E. careening to the bottom of the stairs in a crumpled heap.

His mother-in-law and sisters-in-law came out onto the porch and when they found W.E. at the bottom of the stairs began to scream. Lawrence, still in a hate-fueled haze, began to yell at the barely conscious W.E.

"If you come near me, my wife, my daughter, and any member of the AMA again, I will kill you!!!" Lawrence then ran back through the house and front entrance found his horse and galloped back home as fast as he could. Once at home he ran inside. Thaddeus was asleep on the sofa and Sarah was in the bedroom holding the baby, rocking her to sleep. Lawrence ran into the bedroom.

"What is it? Where did you go? You look like you've seen a ghost."

Lawrence shook his head and then ran over and clutched both Sarah and Abby.

"I've done a terrible thing. I just beat the hell out of your father."

"What!!! Why did you do that?!!!"

"Because it was him that killed Chester, or had him killed."

"How do you know?"

"Because...he is the leader of the Ku Klux Klan in Atlanta."

"But how do you know they killed Chester?"

"C'mon, who else would it be?" Lawrence said as he began to pace back and forth. He had acted on pure emotion. He hadn't stopped to think what would be the repercussions of his actions. Maybe now he was a murderer? Who knows what had happened to W.E.? With a sense of impending doom, Lawrence ran over to the AMA and sought counsel from Dr. Rhodes and Thomas Whitman the new leader of the AMA. There had been many in the community hovering around the AMA after the announcement of Chester's death. Some were also in front of the church, hoping that Lawrence would open it so they could seek solace and comfort.

"Lawrence, you look horrible. What's wrong?" Sydney Rhodes asked.

"I've just skinned my father-in-law within an inch of his life. He might be dead."

"Why did you do that?" Thomas Whitman asked.

"Because he killed Chester…or had Chester killed."

Like Sarah, Dr. Rhodes and Thomas Whitman were unsure how Lawrence could make the connection between Chester's death and his father-in-law. But it was something that was now deep within his psyche and he was certain that W.E. was responsible.

"The main thing now is W.E. will seek revenge. We need to get everyone prepared."

"Prepared for what?"

"I'm sure he will be coming here with his thugs to destroy us."

"Are you sure about that?"

"As God is my witness. This man is willing to destroy Atlanta if it means clearing us out."

The men were unsure of Lawrence's view but decided that preparing a defense was not a bad idea. Lawrence quickly enlisted Auggie and his men to help save the AMA. Being engineers they were able to help with constructing a quick barricade around the perimeter of the church and AMA. There was surplus furniture in the basement and along with other lumber that was being used for the construction of the school they would be able to build two walls that would stretch between the church to the AMA. They then could bunker down in the annex building that sat between the church and the AMA. Using labor from the men of the congregation, the engineers instructed them on where to place the various pieces of furniture. There were multiple bunk beds that could be used as frames. From the lumber supply, larger particleboard panels could then be fastened in front of the beds. It was an engineering feat of the first of its kind. Lawrence was amazed at Auggie's inventiveness. He certainly had been an asset to the Confederate Army. And now like himself was a convert to a new cause.

Lawrence then took Thaddeus, Dr. Rhodes, and Thomas Whitman to the church cellar. He opened it and it revealed a trove of arms and ammunition.

"Where did you get all of this?" Thomas Whitman asked.

"I've been slowly stockpiling it. I've gone around to various vets we know, like Sully and his friends, and asked if we could borrow a few of their guns."

It wasn't a lot but it might help deter anyone who tried to take vengeance with their own arms.

By 10:30 a.m., Lawrence had set up the "fort" with men stationed at various places around its perimeter. They all had guns, but it was only ten men who would have to fend off whatever W.E. was bringing which probably included federal men. Lawrence went around and made sure all of the women and children, including Sarah and Abby, were safe inside the AMA.

At 11:15 a.m., the streets cleared and there was a rumbling coming through the city. Leading a large group of men on horseback was W.E. And as Lawrence surmised, there were some federal men with him. As he came into view, he had a bandage over one eye and around the top of his head. He had bruises all over his face.

"Ambrose, you need to come out and surrender yourself!" W.E. yelled from just outside the barricade.

"It is futile to attempt resistance. You will all get hurt so it's best that you just surrender yourself. If you surrender I will let everyone else leave in peace."

Lawrence began to consider the offer, but would he really let everyone else off? W.E. had recently vowed to destroy the AMA, at least according to Thaddeus. Thaddeus himself was shaking his head profusely to not surrender. The thought though of putting innocent women and children at risk was starting to weigh on him heavily.

"The Captain here has told me that you will be treated fairly, you will be given a fair trial."

"And was Chester Magee given a fair trial?!!! Lawrence screamed from the top of the barricade.

"I don't know who that is but again if you come out not bearing arms and surrender yourself, I will see to it that everyone else goes free. Otherwise, you could be not only facing your death in a gunfight but death by hanging. If you surrender now I am sure you will just get a couple of years in prison. What do you say?"

"How about you guarantee my friends the freedmen the right to vote and I'll be happy to give up."

W.E., with a cigar in his mouth, began to chomp down hard. A crowd had gathered in the streets and it was now becoming a little more difficult to avoid a showdown. Some of the freedmen and their families began to shout for support of the people inside the barricade.

"I wouldn't listen to these people out here Ambrose. They don't represent the law or have your best interests at heart..."

"Oh, and you do?!!!"

Behind the barricade, in the main AMA building, Sarah had emerged from the back hallway to see what was happening. She looked through the front window and could see her husband shouting at the top of the barricade to her father. She wondered how things could have gotten so out of hand. Was her father really the monster that her husband said he was? She knew he could be stern but to actually kill people?

"I want all of you people here to disperse...I don't have a quarrel with any of you."

"Yeah, but we have a quarrel with you!" yelled a young black man who was one of the registrars.

"You killed Chester Magee!"

"Quiet down, quiet down all of you. I don't know who this Chester Magee fella is so stop blaming me for his death." W.E. began to get nervous as the people milling around were starting to disturb the horses.

"Stay back!" yelled the Captain who then pulled out his service revolver. Things were starting to get tense but the people who had gathered would not be deterred from helping Lawrence and everyone behind the barricade. It was turning into a pleasant surprise for Lawrence as he thought anyone not near the church or the AMA would have headed for the security of their homes. But he was also very concerned for the safety of these innocent bystanders and supporters.

As the Captain removed his service revolver, several people panicked which caused the horse to rear up on its hind legs, this in turn caused the Captain to fire his revolver into the air. One of the men on the barricade, thinking they were being fired upon shot his rifle into the crowd, hitting one of the men on horseback in the arm. W.E. had his men disperse to a side street where they dismounted and then began to fire upon the barricade. The two sides exchanged fire for several minutes until it became apparent that the people behind the barricade were out of ammunition. W.E. and the Captain had their men hold their fire. With the scene now quiet and still, W.E. slowly emerged from behind a small brick wall that he and his men had taken cover behind. The captain motioned for several men to follow after them and they headed slowly toward the barricade.

W.E. and the Captain quickly ascertained that the most vulnerable part of the barricade was on the western side. At that point, there was just a pile of boards that were stacked up against a sofa. The men could easily move the boards out of the way and then move the sofa. They were able to quickly penetrate the bulwark and found no one in the makeshift compound. The Captain silently motioned for twelve of the men to follow him. W.E. stayed behind and told the remaining men to keep back.

The Captain walked slowly into the front door of the AMA, waving for the men to follow him. Shots rang out from behind a wall which caused the Captain and his men to quickly retreat outside. As the men retreated, two freedmen who were on a balcony on the building's front façade, pushed a large container of water over the railing that landed on top of the group. The water had been mixed with grease and tar and coated the men completely, leaving the men on the balcony laughing uncontrollably.

The men were basically covered in goo and could barely move.

The sight of the Captain and his men covered in grease angered W.E. to no end. He immediately ran into the front doorway of the AMA and demanded to see Lawrence.

"Ambrose, you'd better come out here now!!!" shouted an utterly annoyed W.E.

From the back of the main entryway, Lawrence emerged. It was dim but W.E. could make out his silhouette.

"Why don't you put down that rifle and we'll have a little talk," W.E. said as he pointed his rifle at Lawrence.

"Maybe you should put your gun down first."

"I thought you were a man of peace Ambrose, bein' a preacher an all?"

"And I thought you were a human being. But it is clear you have no soul."

W.E. began to tremble with anger and shot at Lawrence. Lawrence ducked behind a large desk. A loud scream was let out from behind where Lawrence had positioned himself. Then the cries of a baby could be heard. Lawrence looked behind him.

"My God, Sarah!!!"

When W.E. heard Lawrence scream out Sarah's name he began to shake. He threw down his gun and began to run toward the main office where he had fired upon it.

"Lord, no, no, no, no!!!" Lawrence continued to scream. W.E. ran to where Lawrence was and became horrified by what he saw. There lying on the floor was Sarah, covered in blood. W.E. knelt to see what was happening. Hearing the commotion, Dr. Rhodes ran to the scene. Thaddeus quickly grabbed the baby and tried to console her. Sarah had been holding Abby when she was shot and both hit the floor hard. Callie, who had been hiding with the other women and children in the basement came running up to get Abby from Thaddeus.

"What happened?!!! Callie yelled.

"Sarah came up from the basement to see if she could talk some sense into her father!!!" Thaddeus yelled back.

"Quick, let's get her over to my apartment!" the doctor urged Lawrence. Lawrence quickly picked up Sarah and followed the doctor out of the AMA building and over to his apartment.

"Everyone hold your fire!" yelled W.E. to the rest of his men. Lawrence, finding the same open area in the barricade that W.E. and the Captain had breached earlier, used it to run over to the doctor's apartment. W.E. and several of his men were in hot pursuit. Dr. Rhodes had Lawrence lay Sarah down on a bed in his very small bedroom. He instructed Lawrence to run and get a bowl of water. Before bringing Sarah over to his apartment, the doctor had wrapped a piece of cloth over the wound. As he took the wrapping off he could see how extensive the damage was. The bullet had penetrated her shoulder. It looked like it had not hit any major arteries like the brachial but most likely had shattered one of the shoulder bones or possibly the clavicle. He took out a scalpel from his bag and began to make an incision around the wound in order to get at the bullet. There was a lot of blood but it appeared to not have damaged any artery so he was able to quickly find the bullet and was able to pull it out with a large pair of medical tweezers. Lawrence held his breath, in complete agony over a second time where he might lose his beloved Sarah.

Outside of the doctor's apartment, people from all over the community assembled along with W.E.'s men. Sarah had become a well-respected member of the town and she was held in high esteem by everyone who knew her. W.E. continued to keep vigil at the front door, being able from that vantage point to see into the doctor's bedroom. The only thing he could do was hope, pray and pace, he was unable to control his nervousness.

As the doctor finished removing the bullet and what fragments he could find, he dressed the wound and prepared Sarah for the hospital.

"Lawrence, I think Sarah will be fine but we need to get her to the hospital immediately. I got all the fragments I could but if there is any remaining it could cause infection. Best to have the surgeons look at her." Lawrence nodded and quickly picked up Sarah.

"You can take my wagon," Thaddeus urged Lawrence as he quickly walked down the stairs of the doctor's apartment. Like a somber holiday parade, everyone began to follow Lawrence as he took Sarah in Thaddeus's wagon to the hospital. It was like the procession of some state dignitary there were so many people on hand.

Later at Grady Hospital, a surgeon was able to look at Sarah's wound. They determined that Dr. Rhodes had done a good job of removing any fragments and redressed the wound. They would need to keep a close eye on her however for any signs of fever. The surgeon spoke to Lawrence about Sarah's condition.

"Mr. Ambrose, your wife is in stable condition. The bleeding has stopped but she has lost some blood so she will be in a weakened state for a while. She is conscious now if you would like to go in. The surgeon motioned for him to go onto the hospital floor. There were numerous beds and a nurse had to help Lawrence find Sarah. When he saw her his heart lept for joy seeing her awake and taking water.

"My love, I thought I lost you again!" Lawrence exclaimed as he sat in a chair next to her bed.

"I thought I was lost as well. How's Abby?"

"She's fine. She's with a nurse at the AMA. How are you feeling?"

"They gave me some laudanum to help with the pain but I think I'll be alright. They want me here overnight…what is it darling?" Sarah asked Lawrence as tears began to well up in his eyes. He began to shake his head.

"As I said, I thought I lost you again. I think everything was drained out of me when you had that postpartum fever and I didn't think I would ever be able to get through something like that again, but knowing you are going to be fine…that makes me so happy," Lawrence said as he clutched her hands in his. Sarah gave him a reassuring smile as Lawrence reached in to kiss her. He began to silently thank the Lord for once again bringing them through another difficult ordeal. As Lawrence pulled back from kissing Sarah, he noted an expression of concern on her face.

"Now, I want you to forgive my father. Nothing will come of this if we do not forgive and move forward." Lawrence stopped to think of what that meant and the ramifications. He began to shake his head.

"I don't know if I can ever forgive him for this and for Chester."

"You have to forgive. The Lord commands us to forgive all of those who have done us harm. You not only have to do it for Abby and me and the family but for yourself. You can't go through your life with hatred...it will eat you up."

"So you have forgiven your father for this?" Sarah thought for a moment and then nodded her head. "We need to move forward. If we continue to fight we will not get anywhere, especially in light of the freedmen. We have to forgive and move on."

"Well, there's some good news on that front."

"What do you mean?"

"Well, remember that letter I wrote to President Johnson."

"Yeah."

"Well, he must've read it, or at least someone from the president's office did. Anyway, right after I got you to the hospital a battalion of federal troops arrived in the city. They relieved General Tilson of his duties and sent his men packing."

"Really? That is great news! That should help with the elections."

"Yes, we can only hope."

As Lawrence said this, Sarah's eyes began to focus on something behind him.

"My dearest, I'm so sorry I did this," W.E. said. Lawrence looked at W.E. with horror and disdain and immediately got up to walk away.

"Lawrence, please don't go. I want to apologize that things got so out of hand."

"I don't care for any apologies from you..."

"Lawrence, please listen to what he has to say," Sarah implored.

"Look, I spoke to my people and there is someone in our ranks who might have done what is said to have been done to Mr. Magee, but I tell you on the soul of my granddaughter I knew nothing about it. I did not order that anyone to be killed. Yes, we wanted to harass people but that was as far as I wanted to go with it."

Lawrence looked at him unconvinced. The truth was that W.E. would have killed if necessary but now with the near-death of his beloved daughter and a new generation of Fullers having been born, he was having a revelation himself.

"So, will you disavow the Sons of the South?" W.E. began to think about it. He sighed and nodded.

"Good, then I'll expect you to help us out at the AMA?"

"I wouldn't go that far. We'll just have to wait and see what happens."

"Thank you, daddy…it means a lot to me." W.E. embraced his daughter and then set off for home.

Things were different from that day forward. W.E., while not admitting what his full intentions were with the Sons of the South, did eventually leave the group. Some however felt he had an outside influence and was a contributor to the organization. As for future elections; they were held in Georgia and freedmen were able to vote en masse. Jefferson F Long became the first negro congressman to serve the state of Georgia in 1870.

For Lawrence, he would continue to serve as the pastor of Peachtree Baptist. He eventually graduated from Franklin College with honors. With Sarah finally getting her teaching degree and with Auggie and his men's help, the school finally opened. Sam graduated from the school two years later and went on to get an engineering degree from Georgia Tech. Much of the credit for Sam's success had to be given to Auggie for helping him with his studies. Tutoring him whenever he got the chance. Sam's life changed profoundly and he eventually married and had five children. Thanks to Lawrence and Auggie, and God, he was a new man. And thanks to hard work and prayer, the Ambrose family saw Atlanta rise again.

Made in the USA
Columbia, SC
27 March 2022

58035575R00176